BAD
CHEMISTRY

by the same author

IN THE SHADOW OF KING'S
MY SISTER'S KEEPER

NORA KELLY

BAD CHEMISTRY

HarperCollins*Publishers*Ltd

http://www.harpercollins.com/canada

First published in Great Britain by HarperCollins Publishers: 1993
First Canadian hardcover edition published by HarperCollins Publishers Ltd: 1994
First Canadian mass market edition published by HarperCollins Publishers Ltd: 1996

Canadian Cataloguing in Publication Data

Kelly, Nora, 1945-
  Bad chemistry

ISBN 0-00-647964-2

I. Title.

PS8571.E4478B33 1994   C813'.54   C94-930688-8
PR9199.3.K35B33 1994

---

96 97 98 99 ❖ OPM 10 9 8 7 6 5 4 3 2 1

Printed and bound in the United States

There is a Department of Chemistry at the University of Cambridge, and the chemistry laboratories are located in Lensfield Road, but this is a work of fiction, and the characters and events described are entirely imaginary.

ONE

It was May in Cambridge, and hot.

"When I was a student," Gillian said, "the cold almost killed me. Everything's different now, even the weather."

"The summers are hotter," Bee said. "The winters haven't changed."

They were walking through Christ's Pieces, breasting a stream of shoppers moving towards the market square. A ragged man shambled over the neat green lawns, threatening the empty air. The flow of shoppers on the pavement halted to let him pass through and then swept on. Gillian glanced about, at the women with their arms full of parcels, the babies, the bare-legged students striding energetically, the spreading trees, the bright, precise flowerbeds.

"It's lovely to be back."

They crossed Emmanuel Road at the pedestrian signal and walked down Orchard Street. The houses were small, the street narrow. An astonishing variety of flowers was squeezed into the minuscule gardens. A man sat in a window reading the paper, hardly three feet from Gillian. He looked the wrong scale, as if he might have to put his foot up the chimney like Alice in the White Rabbit's house.

Bee looked at her watch. "Are you in a hurry? I want to stop at Grafton Street to pick up a testing kit before we go to the pub. It's not far."

"Is someone you know worried?"

"Yes, a friend's daughter. She's two weeks late, and she's supposed to go to Greece on Saturday."

It was just past noon, and a pleasant meaty fragrance wafted from the Free Press as they passed by.

"I'm hungry," Gillian said. "I hope we get back before whatever smells so good is all gone."

The Cambridge Counselling Centre, where the Pregnancy Information Service usually met its customers, was in a two-storey row house in Grafton Street. The door, in brilliant contrast to the muddy brick façade, was painted in a neo-Klimt swirl of colour and symbols. Inside, the walls were scuffed and papered with notices. A smell of coffee and a murmur of voices drifted down the narrow hallway from somewhere in the back, but no one appeared.

"The space the PIS uses is upstairs," Bee said, and

trotted up the carpeted steps. Gillian followed. At the top there were several small rooms opening off the hallway. Bee went directly to the middle one. Gillian, at her heels, saw a pile of huge square cushions embroidered in sunset hues, a sprawling potted plant, a couple of metal chairs covered in orange canvas, and a sink. Bee opened the door of a little refrigerator under the counter.

"This is where we keep the kits." She peered into the stark white interior. "They're not here," she said, puzzled.

Gillian looked. The fridge was empty. "How many do you have? Could someone else in the group have borrowed them?"

"Two. I can't think why anyone would want two. Besides, we're not supposed to make off with the last kit on the premises without letting people know. Maybe they're in our cupboard." Bee shoved one of the orange chairs away from the counter and flung open the door under the sink. "We keep the book and the rest of the supplies in here."

Gillian looked over her shoulder. There wasn't much on the shelf: pipettes, empty specimen jars, and a timer like a large alarm clock with a sweep second hand and a stop button on top.

"The money's gone!" Bee said, bewildered. "And the book."

"You had cash in there?"

"Very little. Not more than seven or eight pounds.

I'm going to see if anyone downstairs knows about this."

Gillian ambled to the back and looked out of the window at an unkempt yard and then glanced curiously into the front room. There were two desks mounded with papers, a telephone, an electric heater and more orange chairs. Either orange fabric had been a bargain, or the counselling centre thought orange was good for the psyche. She went downstairs, following the sound of Bee's voice.

In the kitchen at the back, Bee was talking to two men in their late twenties and a slightly older woman wearing a T-shirt emblazoned with the yin-yang symbol.

"I'll check with everyone in the PIS," Bee was saying, "but I don't think any of us has been here since last Saturday's testing session."

"We've used the room, of course," said the woman. "Everyone's in and out. But I never noticed the kits were gone." She folded her arms and leaned broad hips against the kitchen table. "Are you sure they haven't been mislaid?"

One of the young men noticed Gillian hovering in the doorway.

"May I help you?" He was tall and thin, with a cleft chin and bovine brown eyes fringed with thick dark lashes. "I'm Peter."

"I'm Gillian Adams. It's all right. I'm just tagging along." Gillian nodded at Bee.

"Oh. Well, would you like some coffee?" He was

already picking a mug out of the dishrack. Gillian glanced at Bee, who nodded.

"We might as well. We're not leaving just yet."

"This is Josie," Peter said, "and that's Ben. We're all counsellors here. Milk?"

"Who could have stolen your kits?" Ben asked.

He looked like Friar Tuck, Gillian thought: short and chubby, with a good-natured face and a round bald spot above a fringe of brown hair.

"The money, that's one thing," Josie said. "Somebody wanting a pint or a packet of fags might have whipped it, especially if the cupboard was open. We've got all sorts of people coming in and out every day, you know that. We can't keep an eye on all of them."

"But why take the kits?" Bee frowned. "For one thing, you have to know how to use them."

"Is anything else missing?" Gillian asked. "Anything that belongs to the counselling centre?"

"There's really nothing worth taking," Josie answered drily, with a sweep of her hand at the shabby kitchen.

"It's very odd," said Bee, "but there must be some explanation. Perhaps someone took the kits and the book and just forgot to bring them back. I'm going upstairs to telephone the rest of the group. Is that all right?" she asked Josie.

"Go ahead. We won't need that room for a while."

Bee and Gillian went back upstairs, this time to the front room, where there was a telephone. Bee sat

down at one of the two desks after removing a stack
of envelopes from the seat of the chair. Paper was
everywhere: the floor, the counters, the tops of the
cupboards. An enormous notice board bristled with
pins; the announcements, letters, lists and greeting
cards were several layers deep and had spread beyond
its borders to the walls. The wastebasket was full. On
the nearest desk was a pile of letters, unopened,
addressed to several different names. Gillian wondered how many people shared this office and its two
desks. She wouldn't—couldn't—share a desk. The
mere thought of it made her feel fierce and territorial,
like fish that swelled and turned bright colours at the
sight of an intruder.

While Bee dialled and talked, Gillian roamed
about the room sipping her cooling coffee and watching her friend. Bee had gained weight this year. It
suited her. She had a big body, broad-shouldered and
narrow-hipped, and a bony face that was all hollows
when she was unhappy. Now she had a round-
cheeked look, like a Brueghel peasant at a feast. Her
coarse dark hair was cut shorter than ever, but she
was wearing eye make-up, Gillian noticed, something
she wouldn't have countenanced some years earlier,
and she had on a beautiful pair of big enamelled ear-
rings. They hadn't yet had a chance to exchange
news, but Gillian guessed that Bee was thriving.

Whenever Gillian took the train from Liverpool
Street to Cambridge she remembered the occasion,

now almost ten years in the past, when she had come up from London to give a lecture and had landed on Bee's doorstep to find Bee and Toby preparing to divorce. It had been such an uncomfortable visit that Gillian hadn't been sure the friendship would survive. That had been the year of her first sabbatical in London. Since then she'd been back many times, most often in the summers, which she glimpsed on her way to and from the reading rooms of various libraries. Today, Thursday, she was still jet-lagged from her ten-hour flight to London. She had been in England for only three days. It was a stretch, holding the two halves of her life together, and she felt less elastic than she used to. But Edward was in London, and her job was in Vancouver.

There it was, for now.

Bee was dialling again. Gillian inspected the children's drawings tacked to the wall. She'd hardly seen Edward since she'd arrived in England; he'd been working almost round the clock on a child-killer case in Lambeth, and had come back to the flat only to snatch a few hours of sleep. Now he was going to have five days off. Gillian amended her thought: now he said he would have five days off. Edward was a Detective Chief Inspector at Scotland Yard, and she had learned not to put much faith in his holiday forecasts.

Bee swung round in her chair. "That's the lot. Except Wendy, who doesn't answer. I've asked Caroline, Pat, Irene and Vicky, and none of them has been in this week or borrowed the kits. I don't expect Wendy has either. I should call the police, I suppose, though I don't think they'll be awfully excited. A few items of small value stolen from a place where anybody might walk in—there's not much for them to work with. I wish the thief had just taken the money." She turned back to the telephone.

Gillian sat down in an orange chair. She needed something to read.

"I want to report a theft. My name is Bee Hamilton."

A stack of pamphlets filled a box on the floor beside her. Whirling eyeballs between pouchy lids stared up from a pamphlet labelled INSOMNIA in thick black letters. Insomnia was an old acquaintance of hers, but perhaps there were new cures nowadays. She picked up the pamphlet and scanned it idly. "*Curing insomnia can be a simple matter of avoiding caffeine, alcohol, heavy meals and smoking*," one paragraph began, optimistically. Right, she thought, returning it to the box. And if you're dead, you have no trouble sleeping.

"I've got to get my hands on a testing kit," Bee said. "We can't just shut up shop on Saturday. I'd better tell Joan—the one who's going to Greece—that I can't help her. And I'd better try Wendy again, just in case. She's testing with me this week." She rang Wendy's office number and waited. "She must be having lunch."

"Speaking of which—"

"Oh God, our lunch." Bee looked at her watch.

"It's getting on for one o'clock. There won't be anything but crumbs in another half-hour. We'd better go. We'll be fighting our way through the hordes."

The Free Press was hot and crowded, but they arrived before the food ran out. They ate lunch perched on the end of a hard little bench in a corner.

"Another half-pint?" Gillian asked Bee.

"Why not? My meeting's not until three, and I can stop at the police station on the way."

Bee was a NUTO—"a Non-University Teaching Officer," she'd explained to Gillian when she got the job. "Sounds horrid, doesn't it? Like 'neuter.'" It meant that she taught for one of the colleges but was not hired by the university. "I'm better off than I was when I only had supervisions," she said. "I've got an office, and a bit more money and a bit more respect. And that will have to do me, because I'll never have a position in the Department of Modern and Mediæval Languages. Not in this incarnation. It's a bleeding miracle I've got this job—most of the women I know who hung about Cambridge for years doing scut work finally gave up." She laughed. "They're all therapists now."

Her position had improved her outlook, Gillian thought. And no wonder. She'd earned a pittance before, supervising "silly little girls," as she'd sourly called them.

"What a bore this is," she said now. "I'll be very distressed if we've lost our book. Not that we need it to go on testing, but it's the only record of what the group has been doing for the past eighteen years. Never mind. Tell me about your life."

"The main thing about my life right now is, I'm *here*. I've seen enough of the University of the Pacific North-West for a while."

"Are you in England for the whole summer?"

"Yes, except for a trip to Italy."

"Is Edward going with you?"

"Oh, I doubt it. He's busy. He's been on that grisly child-murder case, you must have seen it in the papers, so I practically had the flat to myself for two days. And then I had to rush off to Cambridge or miss the Guinness lectures. Basil—my old supervisor—is giving them this year. But Edward's writing up his report now, and then he's coming up tomorrow for a few days."

"I suppose it's just as well you're staying with Murray, then. I couldn't invite you because we're renovating, which is really a pity. I know I won't see so much of you this way. But if Edward's coming it wouldn't have worked anyhow. You know Pamela," Bee added awkwardly.

"Yes," said Gillian. Pamela didn't think much of men in general or the police in particular. "The last time we argued she called the police 'establishment muscle.' So what's she if not the establishment they're supposedly protecting? She's loaded—and what about the Stubbs she inherited, for God's sake? She's hardly Emma Goldman."

Bee shrugged. "Yes, well . . . She sold the Stubbs, did I tell you?"

"Good Lord! She must have gotten a whopping price."

"I'll say. The Getty bought it."

Gillian whistled. "But how could she part with it?"

"She cares more about her elephants. She's putting a lot of the money into a preservation scheme in Tsavo. And there's the orphanage for elephant babies. She was in Kenya for four months this year; she just got back in March." Bee looked round the little room, less crowded now, but still occupied by several talkative clusters of undergraduates. "The world's such a mess. The elephants don't stand much of a chance. And even these students—" she nodded at a jolly group—"what are their prospects?"

"Better than most people's."

"You said you'd seen enough of your campus for a while. Are you still head of department, or was this your final year?"

"My term's up next year. So I have to decide whether I want to do it again."

"Don't I remember you swearing that you wouldn't?"

"I'm sure you do. But the man who would probably replace me is a dinosaur. I don't know whether I could stand by and let it happen. On the other hand, I'll never finish my book if I don't get out of administration soon."

"Don't worry. Historians improve as they get older,

like wine. They don't peter out like mathematicians. What's your book about? Which aspect of our departed glory?"

"Women and political patronage. Or matronage. The influence of the great political hostesses. I've drafted a couple of chapters, but I'm still collecting material for others—hunting through diaries and collections of letters, and so on." Gillian paused. "You know, I'm thinking about quitting my job at UPNW."

"What? Not just department head, but the whole thing?"

"That's right."

"Why?"

"I'm tired, Bee. And discouraged. You have no idea how awful this past year has been."

"But it wasn't a normal year."

"That's true. Murder isn't a regular feature of campus life. But I've been through a wringer. I've had to rethink a lot of my assumptions. Politics never lets up, either. Once you start, there's always more to do. More issues, more meetings: the problem you started with becomes a smaller and smaller piece of an endlessly unwinding string. There just aren't enough women around; the ones who have any sort of clout end up doing too much. It's exhausting. Besides, the department hasn't recovered; we're all rubbed raw."

"You sound burnt out."

"Maybe. I think I'm entitled to be tired. But even normal years are starting to get me down. I want to settle down and stop moving back and forth so much."

"But what will you do if you quit?"

"I don't know. I have to think about it."

"Would you look for a job here?"

"Maybe in London, but there aren't many openings."

"Don't I know it. Could you survive without one?"

"Not for long. Like a lot of academics, I groan about the obligations, but I need the university structure. It's great to have a year off now and then for research and writing, but an endless vista of solitary study would turn me into a quiet dipsomaniac. I'd twiddle with my file cards forever, hiding the empties under the sofa and fooling myself that I was getting on with it."

"And there's the money."

"There is. I certainly couldn't face not having any."

"Would you live with Edward in London?"

"Not in that shoe box in Pimlico. I'm used to more space. Anyhow, I'm not really sure about London. Or any particular choice. The truth is, I'm a victim of modern mobility. Sometimes I envy the people who grow up in one place and stay there. They know where they are."

TWO

The pudding at lunch was one that Oliver Paine Scudder particularly liked. He had two helpings, and then, full of crème brûlée and goodwill towards men, he walked down Trumpington Street to the chemistry laboratories. Tennis Court Road was a slightly shorter route but provided nothing interesting to look at, and it was a lovely afternoon for a walk. His long legs took him rapidly past Little St Mary and Peterhouse and the gigantic portico of the Fitzwilliam Museum gleaming white in the spring sunshine. He had a busy afternoon ahead, as usual. There was always more to do than time to do it in. He had half-a-dozen substantial papers to write and new results piling up all the time, his research group to look after, and there were always ideas waiting to be tried out . . . It seemed to him that the world of chemistry grew more interesting and complicated every day. The satisfaction of a nice result, the fizz of excitement, there was nothing like it. He wanted his work to go on and on, until he was dead or gaga. But the fact was that he would have to retire in little more than a dozen years. The thought of it nearly made him break into a run.

The labs, designed in the 1950s, occupied a large site on Lensfield Road, a few minutes' walk from the cluster of ancient colleges that drew crowds of tourists to Cambridge. There was nothing about the labs to attract the attention of sightseers or anyone else. The building was huge and dreary, dwarfing the domestic terraces opposite. It was approximately U-shaped. "U for Utilitarian," as someone had remarked at a committee meeting about the cost of the new addition. The U, built of dull brown brick, lay along the south side of the road. The bottom of the U faced a car park to the west. Its two long, uneven arms enclosed an enormous lecture room which filled and emptied like a tide pool in the mornings when more than four hundred first-year students attended their courses. Two smaller but still capacious lecture rooms were tucked in behind it. Although it was one of the largest of the university buildings, it was no longer large enough, and new offices were under construction, connecting the two arms of the U at the eastern end.

The construction was a nuisance, but the noise and

dust were not as irritating as all the meetings he'd had to attend. There had been a tiresome amount of squawking about who would move and the size of the new offices. Oliver's mood dipped a little with this thought but rose again as he crossed the car park. The traffic signal at the gateway turned from red to green as a colleague drove in and parked in an empty slot. At least there would be no more meetings about the parking problem. They had finally beaten the shoppers.

He hauled on one of the heavy glass doors at the main entrance and went in through the lobby, stopping to check his postbox. That had been another improvement: when he and the rest of the faculty got their own boxes. In the old days, he'd often wasted precious minutes pawing through the "S" box, only to find that none of the letters was for him. His box was empty. Good. He loped up the stairs to his office, opened the door and stepped into a puddle.

He looked up. The ceiling was dripping. Then he rushed to his computer, ready to snatch it out of harm's way. It was dry. The big desk was dry, too. He was about to heave a sigh of relief and go in search of the mop, when he noticed that the puddle extended all the way to the wall where floor-to-ceiling shelves housed most of his journals. He let out a cry of dismay. An entire section of shelving—hundreds of pounds' worth of journals—had been drenched. The pages, unless they were carefully separated and individually dried, would adhere, the volumes stiffening into solid blocks, as if the pressed sheets of pulp and bleach were turning into wood again—a nasty, trashy wood with brittle edges. There were thousands of pages. Salvage would require an army.

He raced out of the office and up the nearest flight of stairs. He knew where the water was coming from: Wendy Fowler's lab bench. It was right above his office. The last time had been bad enough, but this was intolerable. He hurtled down the corridor above his own and nearly collided with Roger Hill, who came steaming out of Wendy's lab just as he reached it.

"Another flood!" Roger snarled. "My computer was sitting in a bloody pond."

"Where's the water coming from? The tap?"

"Not this time. There's a damned great bag lying on the floor. There *used* to be water in it."

He followed Oliver into the lab and pointed to Wendy's bench. A large, clear plastic bag lay on the wet floor, empty and flaccid.

"Ten gallons of distilled water. How in the name of God does she do these things?"

Oliver bent down and twitched at the bag. There was a six-inch gap along one side.

"A split seam," he said, incredulous.

"The girl's a menace. The last time she didn't seal her apparatus properly. If I hadn't come back to my office when I did, my desk would have been floating. I lost all my print-out, remember? And I had to have my keyboard repaired. Twice. Where is she, anyhow?"

"Lunch, probably." Oliver sighed. "There's nothing to do here. I'd better go and mop up."

"What could have possessed Bailey to leave her in charge of his group? She's shifting over to organic chemistry now, isn't she? Let's move her down a floor, make her share a bench with some students. That'll teach her to be careless." Roger glared at the empty water bag. "I don't see why we have to put up with this sort of thing. We could just as well do without these research fellows who cost us money every time we breathe. Tiresome bloody bitch. I could strangle her." He marched out of the office, muttering and fuming all the way down the stairs. Oliver followed close behind. At the bottom, they saw Wendy.

She was coming along the corridor, unaware of them, her carrot-orange hair unmistakable even at a distance. At twenty-seven, she was half their age, with narrow features and large white teeth. When she smiled her upper lip revealed most of her gum. Her short, wiry body was restless with nervous energy. "Horse-faced and flat-chested," Roger had said in his crude way when he first noticed her. She wasn't his type; he favoured large bosoms, a fact which Oliver had received as a free if unwanted gift on several occasions. Oliver, had he thought it fitting to comment, would have said that Wendy was quite an attractive person; her colouring, especially, was striking: that brilliant hair framing a pale face with black eyebrows. Pre-Raphaelite, one might say. Besides, he thought, did Roger ever look in the mirror? A man with that red face and those enormous, bristly ears wouldn't win any beauty contests—not unless some unknown tribe far away believed big hairy ears were a sign of sexual prowess. The point was, Wendy was very talented and she worked like a demon. Her ambition was naked; that bothered some people. Oliver didn't quite like it; something fastidious in him, something English, preferred not to see ambition unclothed. But he knew that without that aggressive self-confidence she would have little chance of distinguishing herself. Her work was good, but lots of people did good work. You had to have drive, even a kind of ferocity, to rise to the top.

Roger bellowed down the hall at her. "You've gone and flooded my office again!"

Wendy stopped short, astonished. "I can't have done. I haven't even used the apparatus today."

"No, you just opened a bag of water and poured the whole lot through the floor," Roger said with heavy sarcasm.

She frowned. "What are you talking about?"

"Look!" Roger, his face mottling as the blood rose, gripped her upper arm and bustled her down the hall to the door of his office. Water still dripped from the edge of the desktop. He had moved his computer to a dry shelf. "My computer was half drowned. I may have lost *all my data*."

"There's a bit of a disaster in my office too—a whole shelf of journals gone," Oliver put in.

Wendy pulled her arm from Roger's grasp and stared at the mess. "I don't get it. There was a bag of distilled water near my bench when I left for lunch, but it hadn't been opened. There must be some mistake."

"That might have done if it was the first time, but this is the *third* flood. You're making a damned habit of it." Roger's voice rose. "I'm going to see that you're moved out of that lab. We'll put you in the basement where you can't do any more damage." He shouldered past them into his office and banged the door, leaving them standing in the hall.

How very like Roger, Oliver thought. He himself was an equally injured party, but Roger's boorishness made it impossible to complain. His journals were ruined, yet here he was on the verge of apologizing. He hadn't wanted to move into one of the new smaller offices, but when he did, Roger would no longer be his immediate neighbour. That was something to look forward to. None of his other colleagues was afflicted with as short a fuse or as foul a tongue. And, Oliver reflected, there would be nothing above him but a roof. Unless that leaked, he would never be flooded again. But the new offices wouldn't be finished until next year. In the meantime, something had to be done about Wendy's penchant for pouring water through the floor.

Roger's behaviour had had the predictable effect. Wendy was more offended than mortified.

"That's unfair," she said indignantly. "The first

flood never came from my lab, and he knows it." She peered into Oliver's office and her face fell. "I swear to God there was nothing wrong with that bag when I left. I'm dreadfully sorry about your journals. Let me help you clean up."

"Never mind that now," Oliver said testily. "Go and mop your own floor. Mine won't take a minute." Then he relented. "I could use some help trying to dry out a few journals—ones I need and can't replace. But I can't start now, I'm demonstrating in ten minutes."

"I'll come back later then. I want to have a look at that bag." Wendy hurried away and Oliver went to get the mop. Glancing back as he opened the cupboard, he saw Wendy stick her tongue out at Roger's closed door. A head poked out of the lab opposite.

"Trouble?" Ron Bottomley asked, blinking froggy eyes, as Oliver returned, bearing the mop.

Bottomley took an almost prurient interest in departmental squabbles. "A flood in my office," Oliver replied briefly. "Roger's too."

Bottomley looked at Wendy's retreating back. He smirked. "The Sorcerer's Apprentice again?"

Wendy went quickly up the stairs to her lab. No one else was in the room. There was the bag on the floor. She squatted down to examine it and found the split along the seam. It was about six inches long. She held the bag up to the light and then let it drop. The floor was sopping wet. She picked up a sponge from the counter by the sink and began wiping with short, angry strokes. These accidents were like a curse, like something in Greek drama. She worked, she planned ahead, she drove herself single-mindedly. But these absurd disasters threatened to undo it all. They made her look like some kind of clown: Wendy the Wacky Chemist, who is always flooding the laboratory. She felt hot tears behind her eyelids and squeezed them shut.

The first flood had had nothing to do with her, no matter what Roger Hill chose to think; it had come through her ceiling like a waterfall and soaked her own bench and had only then continued through the floor to bespatter everything in Hill's office below. No one had ever found out where the water had come from. Oliver Scudder had explained something of the building's structure to her that time. There was a three-foot gap between her floor and his ceiling— between each floor and ceiling in the building—to allow room for the many huge pipes that ran between the floors. He'd shown her the little metal stairs that gave access to the crawl space.

"That's how they get up inside to fix the pipes," he'd told her. "But water can travel for ages along a pipe before it runs down again, and then it's terribly hard to find precisely where it's coming from."

He was a funny bird, Scudder, she thought, squatting on her haunches, always on about keeping the doors of your fume cupboard properly aligned. It was an old system, he'd told her several times, as if she couldn't see that for herself. It wasn't good enough, not really, especially now. New cupboards had been added, and the weakest ones in the system barely functioned. The fumes just hung about, waiting for people to breathe them. Scudder had fussed for ages one day when he'd come in and smelt sulphur dioxide in her room. Told her she'd poison herself if she wasn't more careful. But he was nice, really. Sweet. Just a bit daft, like a lot of men who had no life outside the lab, who'd been bachelors for too long. At least she supposed he was a bachelor. The presence of wives was not felt in the chemistry labs. Occasionally, there was a department party, and then some came out briefly, like seasonal decorations. She'd never seen Scudder's wife, if he had one. Not that she'd remember. The wives, while apparently well-disposed towards her existence, had little to say to her. And she hadn't worked out how to talk to them. Consequently, they ran together in her mind, imperfectly remembered from one occasion to the next. Except Alan Kennedy's wife, of course. No one would forget her. Anyhow, Oliver Scudder had always treated her decently, and he was a topnotch chemist. Not like Roger Hill, who was a pompous bully, or that twit Bottomley. Ron Bottomley, in his pinching little way, had been unpleasant ever since she'd returned from her post-doc in Canada, behaving as though her area of research were his personal property and she had no business trespassing. It was lucky that his standing in the department wasn't high, or he might have given her real trouble. Still, a woman in the sciences had to have a thick skin, Wendy had concluded early in her career, and her experiences with Hill and Bottomley simply confirmed it. But she hoped Scudder wasn't too angry with her.

In moments of adversity, she fixed her thoughts on her grandfather. At ninety, he ploughed the same Norfolk fields he had worked as a lad living in the house his father built. He had held on through the century's great cataclysms, only to watch with bewildered fury as the labourers left the land for the towns and the old rural fabric crumbled away. "There's nobody left who cares to do an honest day's work," he would grumble, sitting by the Aga in the kitchen, cleaning his boots at the end of the day. Yet he had still held on. Her mother would sell the farm when he died, Wendy supposed, though her parents also talked of moving their antiques business there and living in semi-retirement. She didn't mind, really. She didn't want the farm. But she liked to think of her grandfather's strength as her own. His heroic character and fate were a heritage from which she drew lessons and comfort, no less because she was perfectly conscious of doing so. She would work hard, and she would prevail. This she believed, and it kept her going.

Finished with the floor, she mechanically rinsed out the sponge, her gaze fixed on the bag again, on the mysterious tear. She thought back to the second flood. That one had come from her bench, no question. She'd left her rotavap turning like a little merry-go-round and gone off to one of the labs to see about another experiment. She was sure she'd wired the rubber tube to the condenser properly, but it had come off while she was out, and water had poured over the edge of her bench into both offices below hers. Luckily it hadn't run for hours before one of the students discovered it. That one accident had been bad enough, but now they would start to think she was accident-prone. And that could affect her future.

She picked up the bag and studied it more closely. Could someone have slit it open deliberately? She shook her head, dismissing the thought. "Don't be ridiculous," she muttered. There were people in the department who would prefer the lab to remain a men's club, but none of them was sneaking in and slicing up her sacks of water. Unless it's Hill they're after, she thought, momentarily struck. That was possible. He wouldn't win any popularity contests in the lab. She sat down in the chair at the desk in the corner. The oak seat creaked on its swivel. If it was bad luck, she thought, with a rueful smile, at least Hill was having his share of it. Whatever, she had better take extra precautions. She would rather not give bad luck any further opportunities. No more water sacks would be stored near her bench. She couldn't afford another leak. Or any sort of accident. Not if she wanted a good job when her fellowship was over.

It was time to check her results downstairs. She was damned if she would be pushed out of this lab, she thought, getting up. If she moved from the third floor, she'd probably end up sharing a bench, which wouldn't suit her at all. The whole department was terribly squeezed for space. She was shifting into organic chemistry now, and the organic chemists were the group most severely affected. But of course none of the other divisions would cede a square inch. She didn't even know where her office would be, come September. She wouldn't be able to use Bailey's any more. It would be great to have him back, though. She admired him. And even if he was in the field she was moving away from, he was in her corner.

From the top of the steps she could see right down to the bottom of the open stairwell. Students in baseball caps, knapsacks dumped beside their chairs, were clustered at several tables. It was symptomatic of the state of things that supervisions sometimes had to be held in the stairwell—the so-called Palm Court. A noisy place to work, what with people belting up and down the stairs all day long. The labs were noisy too, but one learned to shut out the din. She reminded herself to check on Simon later in the afternoon. He hadn't been in for a couple of days. Bailey's students were doing all right, but Simon needed a lot of encouraging. He might start to drift if she neglected him.

She descended and walked along the corridor to her office, passing a tall blue cylinder of argon gas and stacks of cardboard boxes and endless glass-fronted cupboards jammed with even more boxes. Most of the corridors were full of things that couldn't be stuffed into any of the rooms. Hill's door was still shut. Bottomley's lab was empty. He was probably off spreading the story, she thought morosely.

She picked up a notebook from her office at the front of the building and set off to find out whether her newest spectrum was ready. Halfway down the hall she stopped, extracted her keys from the bottom of a pocket and went back to lock her office door. An unnecessary precaution, she believed, but it made her feel better.

She was anxious to see what she'd got from the NMR machine. It ought to be a nice result this time. She was getting ready to write up the work she had been doing for two terms, and she wanted to publish in the autumn. She might just make it, if she could finish her paper by the end of May.

As usual, there were five or six people clustered about the behemoths. These machines were so expensive—six of them at half a million pounds each—that they were in use twenty-four hours a day. A small but devoted crew of gnomes hung about them even in the pre-dawn hours. The machines, which could process several dozens of samples overnight, saved thousands of tedious hours of waiting for results. Hers were ready. She took them away and stared at the spectrum. It looked good. The biphenyl had formed, just as she had hoped. The flood was forgotten as exultation shot through her. It had come right this time. Associated Chemicals would be glad they'd funded her—she'd returned their money's worth and more.

When she returned to her bench, the lab was no longer empty. Simon and several other students were at work, and the Beach Boys were singing. "Help, help me, Rhonda," they chorused over a rattling vacuum pump and the steady roar of extractor fans. Bright fluorescent light glared from the ceiling. There were nine benches in this lab, some communal, some individual. She crossed the stained wooden floor and waved to two students who had their heads together over a bench at the other end of the room. She chatted briefly with Simon and then went to her own bench. The empty water bag was still lying there. She picked it up, intending to throw it in the rubbish bin, but changed her mind and tucked it into a box under her bench. Then she pulled up a stool and began to assemble the apparatus for the next set of reactions.

THREE

On Friday afternoon at tea-time, Gillian lay propped on her elbow in the back bedroom of Murray's house on Earl Street. Edward lay on his back, his hands clasped behind his head.

"I suppose we ought to get up," he said without moving.

"Murray won't be back for another hour at least." She pulled the rumpled sheet over her bare legs; it was never hot enough here to lie about naked.

The house wasn't Murray's, actually; as she'd explained to Edward, it belonged to Jesus College, and Murray was renting it for eight months. Like the others in the row, the house was tiny, with two rooms downstairs and two bedrooms plus a bathroom upstairs. The bathroom and the cupboard for the hot water tank had been afterthoughts; their walls pushed awkwardly into the bedrooms. Murray had given her the room at the back.

"It's quieter," he'd said, "though you'll still hear the students rolling home from the pubs, especially on Friday night."

Right now she could hear the traffic on Emmanuel Road and the pedestrian signal bleeping. The curtains bellied gently inward and then hung still. A narrow stripe of sun lay diagonally over the bed, banding her hip and Edward's chest. He uncoiled an arm and traced the golden track across her skin with his finger.

"You look exotic," he said. "Is it because I haven't seen you for days, or it is the sheer romance of Cambridge?" He looked at her bare white shoulders and aureole of dark curls, backlit by the glow from the window. "All that's missing is a gardenia behind your ear."

"It's travel," said Gillian. "If an hour on the train to Cambridge makes me exotic, just think how I'd look in the golden light of Italy. Here, let me read you something." She turned and reached for a book on the table at the side of the bed, and leafed through it. "Listen to this," she said as she found her place. She looked up. He was asleep.

His hand lay curled, palm upward, by her thigh. It was broader and blunter than her own, but neat, like the rest of him: a smooth economy of flexibility and strength that was repeated in the flat, hard muscles of chest and shoulder, the heavy curve from hip to knee, the broad base of the throat. His hair was dark against the white pillow, dense and shining like a mink coat. There were few grey hairs, fewer than she had, though they had both turned forty-seven in the spring. Asleep in the half-light of the curtained afternoon, he looked younger, the wariness of the brown eyes hidden, the firm mouth relaxed. It was hard to believe that he was Detective Chief Inspector Gisborne of Scotland Yard, a man with more than twenty years' experience of police work under his belt, when he wore it. Did other men seem so different when they were asleep, she wondered; was their vulnerability a recurring surprise? It had been so many years since she had slept with anyone else that she had no comparisons to make.

The sun's gold spinneret had drifted across his shoulder. Time was passing; Murray would be back soon. Reluctantly, she sat up.

At the same hour, Wendy Fowler sat at tea with a journal propped open in front of her, ignoring the hubbub of voices and the jostle of elbows and cups at the table. She sat with her back to the tea-lady at the counter, who had sniffed on seeing the journal under her arm when she'd collected her tea. The tea-ladies disapproved of books and papers in the tea-room. At the moment, Wendy didn't care. Neither Bottomley nor Hill was present, to her relief, but she wasn't feeling very sociable. She had endured enough curiosity and teasing about the flood already. Moreover, she had spent hours the previous day and again this morning wrestling with a hair dryer and the pages of selected items from Oliver Scudder's library, and she was behind in her work according to the schedule she had set for herself. But she needed a hit of sugar.

The tea-room was packed. Each afternoon between three and half past four tea and biscuits were dispensed from a central counter, where hundreds of students and faculty gathered like pigeons in a city square, landing in large flocks from their various labs, which were left temporarily deserted. The tea-room was on the top floor of the building and looked out over a broad view of Cambridge, but the sight was too familiar to hold anyone's attention. Even on a pretty May afternoon the crowd turned its back to the windows and crammed in along the rows of tables.

Alan Kennedy had already finished his tea. As he passed Wendy's table on his way out, she looked up, her bright hair fiery in the sunlight.

"Hullo, Alan."

He smiled his perfect smile. It had cost his parents $5000, he'd told her once. "At the time, I wanted flying lessons instead. I was going to be an astronaut when I grew up." She'd wanted to fly, too, when she was that age. In fact, she still thought she'd like to learn, if she ever had the time. "Wendy! How's it going, kid?" His voice was soft, his accent American, unmodified by five years in Cambridge. He was a big blond, an Aryan dream of marble muscle, even white teeth and ice-blue eyes. His features were small, the scant eyebrows and pale lashes almost invisible, the nose and ears delicately decorative on the big skull with its close-cropped hair, the rosy mouth primly curled, like a doll's.

"My work's going beautifully. I got a splendid result yesterday afternoon. Everything I've done in the past six months is finally coming together. I have one last set of reactions to finish and I'll be ready to write it all up."

"Hey, that's great." He began to move away. "Come and tell me more about it later, OK? I'm on a schedule right now."

Wendy raised her voice slightly. "Actually, there's something I need to discuss with you. When will you be in your office?"

He looked at his watch, calculating. "Um, let's see. How about six?"

"Six? Fine."

He ambled away. Wendy sat and finished her tea. By the time she left, the room was quietening down. She went straight to her lab, to check the condenser on the rotavap. Oddly, there was rather a lot of fluid in the flask. It should have been down to a couple of millilitres by now but looked more like twenty. That was too much. Way too much. She peered closely at the flask. Something was definitely wrong.

"What the hell?" she muttered. She swung round suspiciously as Simon sauntered in from tea.

"What's wrong?" he said, seeing her frown.

"This is really weird," she replied, still staring at the flask. "My experiment's gone totally off the rails."

Gillian and Edward were downstairs when Murray got home. He came in laden with groceries: chicken, onions, asparagus, bread, cheese, two bottles of wine, and fresh pasta from Pasta Galore.

Murray Kopf was an old and dear friend of Gillian's. A chemist at the University of the Pacific North-West in Vancouver, where Gillian was head of the history department, he had taken a leave of absence for the coming fall term and was spending the months from May to December in Cambridge. Murray had been married once, but it hadn't worked out, and during the Christmas holidays he'd broken off his long-standing affair with a sociologist who had a husband and children and no intention of leaving them. "In the old days, I didn't care," he'd said then. "I didn't take holidays, especially at Christmas. Christmas has always made me nervous, so I'd get a lot of work done at the lab. But now I *want* holidays; I want to go places, enjoy something different. Widen my horizons. And I want someone to do it with. Marilyn can't go anywhere with me, not even to the movies." He'd been planning his stay in Cambridge for over a year, and after the break-up with Marilyn it had suddenly seemed important to get out of Vancouver as soon as possible. He had settled into the house on Earl Street in early April.

He insisted on cooking dinner the night Edward arrived.

"We could take you out," Gillian had protested.

"No, I'm determined to show off. We'll go out another night."

Gillian let it go. She knew Murray liked to cook for people.

Now he bustled about the kitchen, setting out pâté and bread, browning the chicken and chopping onions, assigning minor tasks to his two guests.

"So you caught that creep," he said to Edward. "The guy who killed the little girl."

"Yes. We pulled out all the stops. Frankly, it was sheer good luck we caught him so soon. Bad luck for him: he was seen picking her up in a street near her school. The sort of thing we pray for, especially after three days of door-to-door inquiries and nothing to show for it but worn shoe leather. This witness popped up on her own. We'd have found her eventually, of course, but it might have taken weeks. She's a nurse and had been on shift when we were knocking on doors."

"What made her realize she'd seen him?" Gillian asked.

"The girl's picture and the time of day. Thank God for the gutter press—she was reading about the case and bells started ringing. She says her mind replayed the scene as if it was in front of her eyes. Witnesses often say that; I'd think they got it from books, except I'm told nobody reads any more." He paused. "She remembered the car. She didn't know anything was wrong at the time, but something caught her attention. Something in his manner, maybe. And she knew the child by sight and remembered that she usually walked home." He shook his head. "Poor little thing. She was only six." Murray had given him the asparagus to prepare for cooking, and he was breaking off the tough ends. The thick green necks snapped neatly between his fingers; "I hate those cases. They bring out the hangman in me."

"In everybody," Murray said. "When were public hangings abolished, Gillian?"

"Here? In 1868." She took the corkscrew Murray handed to her and peeled the lead foil from one of the bottles of wine. "In New York, 1835. Much later in some southern states. After World War I."

"Now we have television instead," Edward said. He had finished with the asparagus and stuck his hands in the pockets of the old pair of flannel trousers that along with a soft white shirt served him for holiday clothes. "You're here for the summer?" he asked Murray.

"Until December. There's a chemist here I've worked with before, and he's got some fancy new equipment I want to use."

"What sort of chemistry do you do?" Edward said.

"Don't ask." Gillian grinned. "He'll just tell you he can't explain." She yanked hard on the corkscrew, and the cork slid out with a soft little pop.

"It's true," Murray said, mildly apologetic. "I don't know how. The vocabulary doesn't make sense if you don't know a lot of chemistry already."

Gillian was opening cupboards, looking for wine glasses. She smiled to herself, having been through this with Murray in the past.

Edward was trying. "It's organic chemistry?"

"That's right."

"And that's the chemistry of carbon compounds?"

Murray nodded. "That's more than some people remember from their high school science. In the left-hand cupboard, Gillian, if it's glasses you want."

"I know a bit about forensic science," Edward said, "but I've forgotten most of the general chemistry and physics I knew."

"Forensic science is more interesting to talk about," Murray said, chopping away at the onions. "So tell me, the picture of modern crime-busting we get, that you guys are always solving cases by finding microscopic fibres that identify the murderer's over-coat or by analysing the unique muck on his shoes— is that true?"

It was Edward's turn to smile. "I wish it was. But trace evidence isn't usually the key. I don't mean it isn't important. It can make the difference between getting a conviction and watching a murderer go scot-free. But if a killer is determined to cover his tracks, how often do you think he leaves a set of bloodstained fingerprints behind?" He held his palm out, and then dropped it to his side. "The truth is, most murderers are caught because somebody saw them or knows what they did. The forensic evidence nails down the case for a jury, but it isn't usually what catches the killer."

He accepted a glass of wine from Gillian and propped himself comfortably against the fridge. "There are spectacular exceptions, of course. And I believe that forensics will become more and more important. For one thing, people expect forensic evidence. The chap's mother can get up on the stand and swear she saw him do it, and the jury still wants to see fingerprints. Science."

"Surely it helps you," Murray said.

"Up to a point. Ideally, what you want is your murderer up to his knees in blood, holding the knife and screaming 'I done it' at five eyewitnesses. And sometimes that's what we get. Oftener than you'd think. But if he's chucked the knife in the river and run away, and the witnesses at the pub were half cut, then the forensic evidence is going to give us enough to put him on the sheet. And the lab can work miracles these days. Give them a paint chip and a few little pieces of glass, and they'll tell you within a day that you're looking for a pale green Fiat Uno registered later than 1983. But it's easy to be seduced into thinking you've got what you need when you haven't. If we find fibres or stains, the lab can't always be exact. That is, precise enough for our purposes. They'll say the twine used to bind the victim's hands is the same type as the twine found in the kitchen of the accused, and the defence will say that it's also the same kind of twine that's sold in shops all over the country."

Gillian handed Murray a glass of wine. Tears were running down his cheeks. She opened her mouth to ask him what was wrong, her mind scampering backwards over the conversation.

He chuckled. "Don't look so worried, dear. It's only the onions." He went to the sink to rinse his hands.

Gillian poured wine for herself. They were getting on fine so far, she thought. She was pleased. Only her small group of London friends ever had a chance to spend time with Edward. He occupied an almost watertight compartment in her life. And his friends were mostly members of the force. She didn't know them intimately or feel relaxed in their company. The force was a club, and she didn't belong. It was lucky he'd just come off an important case that had gone well. At such moments he was more outgoing, ready to laugh, to tell stories, to take an interest in people who were unconnected to his work. Had she planned this meeting for months, she couldn't have improved the arrangements. Now they were talking about the

Yard's forensic science lab, about their new £70,000 Zeiss micro-spectrophotometer, which, she gathered, compared colour samples.

Murray was only a year older than Edward, but he looked more, she thought, seeing them together. His hair was nearly gone on top, and he had just confided to her that his new trousers measured forty inches round the waist. A few years ago, after he'd tried running and twisted his knee, he'd dismissed exercise as a masochistic ritual performed by youth cults. Edward seemed younger because he had a flat belly and his hair had stayed put. But their faces were the same age. Edward was no boyish cop any more. He looked permanently tired now; his eyes were more deeply set in their sockets, the eyebrows were bushier, the lines on his forehead heavily scored. He muttered of aching and stiffness in the joints, of a back that objected to hours of desk work.

"You're in much better shape than most old coppers," Gillian had said the last time. "They're usually a yard wide across the bottom from all that sitting. You're not. And your thigh muscles feel like iron."

Edward had looked more cheerful, but all he'd said was, "And my knees feel like glass."

FOUR

On Friday evening, the chemistry building was largely empty. The secretaries and the technicians had left; most of the faculty had gone home to their spouses or were preparing to dine in college. And youth had better things to do on a Friday night in May than hang about the lab. Here and there in the cavernous reaches a lone student pressed on, finishing some task that could not be left, or struggling with an incomprehensible set of figures. Oliver Scudder sat at his computer until half past seven and then collected his briefcase, locked his door and went home. A few dedicated souls clustered about the NMR machines, running spectra and drinking bad coffee from the machine in the basement. Here and there the warm glow of a desk lamp or the cold shine of a computer screen indicated some human presence. But the long corridors, lit by naked fluorescent tubes, were empty; in the labs the bottles and flasks stood unattended on their benches; the big refrigerators hummed to themselves; the new ultra-high vacuum chamber stood alone like an abandoned space ship. The roar and grumble of the ventilators had shut down for the night.

Wendy returned to her lab after dinner. The meeting with Alan had gone more or less as she had anticipated. At least she hadn't been under any illusions about it, and she was glad to have the discussion out of the way, although she might well have done better to eat a sandwich in the lab and get on with re-doing her experiment. Water over the dam now, anyhow; time to finish this piece of work and get on with her life. She had a lot to do and to think about in the next few weeks. The delay this afternoon had made her want to tear her hair. She couldn't really think straight about anything else until she finished this. Resolutely, she picked up a piece of clear, flexible tubing, but instead of beginning to reconstruct her apparatus, she sat on her stool, twisting the tubing through her hands. Her mind was racing in circles. She went over and over each detail of her experiment, trying to think of a plausible reason for its failure. Each time, she came up against the suspicion that it had been tampered with, and each time, that idea seemed absurd. The moment couldn't be worse, she thought again. She was so close to the end of this long project, and she had promised to give a paper at the Oxford meeting; the series of experiments had been going so well that she hadn't been worried about completing it in time. But without this final result, she had no proper conclusion to offer. It required patience and accuracy to set up the experiment properly, and this was the second time things had gone wrong, though they had gone wrong in a different way. The first time, she'd thought perhaps her chemistry had been contaminated by dirty glass, or that she'd made a mistake: picked up the wrong bottle, or used one that was mislabelled. It could happen to anyone now and then. But two failures? In a row?

Propping her elbows on the bench, she rested her chin in her hands and looked at the remains. What had she done? She could think of no plausible reason for finding ether peroxide in the flask. Except the one she didn't want to believe. Someone else had added it, possibly while she was at tea. A practical joke? Simon and the rest of the boys in the lab had laughed rather a lot when she had been so puzzled. But they'd stopped laughing when she'd showed them the NMR spectrum she'd taken from the crude residue. She'd distilled the ether just before she'd used it, but where she was looking for a few milligrams of her bisalkaloid, her flask was awash with something that gave distinct ether peroxide signals. She looked at the spectrum again. How else could she have that quartet? They'd had to admit it was awfully strange. She'd probably said more than she should have about her suspicions. Pranks of this sort weren't unknown, of course. But everyone in the lab knew how important this stage of her work was, how tight a timetable she'd set for herself. She'd made no secret of it. If it was a prank, it wasn't student high jinks, it was real malice. She sat up straight. What if she hadn't noticed the liquid level and had tried to distil the residue? At the higher temperature, the peroxide might well have exploded. Another accident, she thought. Maybe an injury. A serious one. She smiled grimly to herself. She had had the right instinct when she hid the flask away. When she had the time, she would think about what to do.

Slowly and painstakingly she began to set up her apparatus again. She would repeat her experiment. And she would sit by it this time if it took all weekend. Fleetingly, she thought of confiding her suspicions to Murray Kopf. He wasn't part of the department, and she trusted him. He'd been an ally in Vancouver during the kerfuffle over the centrefolds pinned up in the lab, and he had treated her with equal friendliness before and after she had refused to go out with him. A shame he was so doughy round the middle. Whippet-thin herself, she was sexually repelled by flab. But Murray was a nicer man than the ones she seemed to fancy. Where did sexual preferences come from? If she was looking for her father, she thought wryly, she wanted him well disguised. But what could Murray do? She couldn't think of anything. It would just be nice to talk to someone. Someone who knew enough chemistry to understand, and who wouldn't think she was losing her sanity. She couldn't talk to Scudder, not after the disaster with the water bag. Bailey was in Australia. If the students' reaction was anything to go by, people would have a hard time believing she hadn't botched things herself. In which case, any suggestions she made to the contrary would further undermine her credibility. A wave of tiredness swept over her, and she considered going home. Then she straightened her back. There was nothing for it except to do the damned thing over again.

Much later, sitting on her tall wooden stool, she put her head down on her arms and closed her eyes. She dozed. Then something roused her: a sound, perhaps, or a smell. There was a strong smell of ether nearby.

Gillian, Edward and Murray were clearing up after a late breakfast on Saturday when there was a knock at the door.

"That's Bee," Gillian said. "I'll get it." She felt a tiny flutter of nerves followed by a spasm of irritation. It had been arranged that Bee would stop in for coffee on her way from the PIS office to the market. Bee's private life since she had left her husband had for the most part excluded men, which made it hard for Gillian to invite her to Murray's house without feeling self-conscious. She thought it was only natural to introduce him to Bee, since she would certainly be

telephoning and dropping in while Gillian was staying with him, but she was aware that Bee—or more
likely Pamela—might think she was playing mission-
ary. She had no desire to evangelize. On the other
hand, avoiding the encounter would be ridiculous.
She would hope for the best. "Here is a friend," she
would say, in effect, and screw the politics.

Bee and Edward shook hands. They already knew
each other slightly and shared an unstated intention
to avoid more intimate acquaintance. Their differ-
ences, both thought, would lead them to dislike each
other, which would matter little to them but would
cause Gillian distress. Gillian, conversely, thought
their mutual mistrust would subside when they knew
each other better. However, she could do nothing to
force the pace.

"I'll make coffee," Murray said.

"No you won't, you cooked breakfast." Gillian
went to the kitchen to put the kettle on. When she
came back, Murray was chirping about the delights of
Cambridge, and Edward had become the silent
observer. Bee was looking distracted.

"I don't mean to be rude," she said as soon as
Gillian returned, "but could we dispense with the
phatic prerequisites? I'm in a temper."

"What's wrong?" Gillian asked, sitting down beside
her on the sofa.

"Wendy never turned up this morning."

"At the testing session?"

"Exactly. There I was at the office, and I had no kit. I talked to her yesterday afternoon, and it turned out that she had borrowed one of the missing kits. The other's still AWOL, but she said it was there on Monday when she stopped in for hers. The point is, she said she'd bring hers this morning. Then she never came—never came at all. And I had to ask a fearfully upset student to come back next week. I felt really awful about it. I couldn't even offer to test the poor lamb at home, because both kits are gone, and I couldn't reach Wendy. I don't understand it. I've rung her five or six times at home and at her office, but there's no reply."

"What kits?" asked Edward.

"Who's Wendy?" Murray said simultaneously.

"Oh, sorry." Bee, who had been speaking to Gillian, seemed to focus on the two men for the first time. "I've just come from the PIS office—the Pregnancy Information Service. We're open Saturday mornings. Anyone can come in and have a pregnancy test on the spot. It's the same type of test that the hospitals use: it tests urine for human chorionic gonadotrophin. That's a hormone you secrete when you're pregnant and don't when you're not."

"Who's Wendy?" Murray said again.

"Wendy Fowler. She's a research fellow at the chemistry lab. She just did a post-doc in Vancouver." A thought occurred to her, and she added, sounding surprised, "You might know her."

"I do, actually," Murray answered, equally nonplussed.

The kettle was shrieking. Gillian went to make the coffee. She could hear Murray's voice murmuring in the other room; once she'd poured the boiling water into the coffee pot she could hear what he was saying. "She's pretty wrapped up in her work right now; maybe she just forgot about you this morning."

"It wouldn't be like her. Wendy is extremely well organized." Bee's tone became crisp. "I'm sure there's a good reason why she didn't come. I wouldn't have been in a bother about it, except that the damned burglary has left us without any kits at all."

Gillian noted the tonal shift and knew what prompted it. Bee was thinking that Murray might have an influence on Wendy's career. Annoyed as she was, she wouldn't do unnecessary damage.

"You've had a burglary?" Edward said, speaking for the first time. "When?"

"Thursday. We've already reported it to the police, but there's nothing they can do, really."

Gillian replayed the sentence. Was that gratuitous rudeness? No, she decided. Bee was simply being matter-of-fact. She hoped Edward thought so too. She did wish they'd take to each other, but her hypersensitive scrutiny of their every remark wasn't much use.

"What was taken?" he asked.

"A few quid. The kit that was there, our book. Nothing that was important to anyone but us."

Gillian came in with four steaming mugs on a scratched metal tray, hot milk, which Bee liked, sugar, butter, jam and a dozen croissants from a new bakery Murray had discovered in Burleigh Street. Bee, who hadn't eaten since the early morning, gave a little cry of pleasure and devoured three croissants while Gillian, still full of bacon and eggs, nibbled slowly at one. She watched Murray, who liked his food, put away as many as Bee. And that was on top of—what had it been? Two eggs, toast and four rashers of bacon. Perhaps he and Bee would find common ground at the patisserie. Edward, characteristically, plied Bee with questions about the burglary, forgetting the croissants until they were cold.

"Do you have any idea who the thief was?"

"Not really. There's a constant stream of people flowing in and out of the counselling centre. Most are young people in crisis over love or sex or their exams, but they're often short of money, and some of them are, umm, a bit off."

"In what way?"

"Young drug addicts, raging alcoholics who chuck things about, people whose stability is barely maintained with psychiatric drugs . . . now and then we hear one of them ranting on when we're upstairs testing."

"Do you think the thief might be one of those?"

Bee shrugged. "It doesn't make much sense, does it? But I can't think of an explanation that would. An ordinary thief would only have taken the money. So maybe it was somebody who was stoned. Stoned and skint. Thought they could sell the kit for a couple of quid. Or it could have been a student prank, or a dare."

"What's the book you mentioned?"

"Just our notes. They wouldn't interest anyone but ourselves. Or feminist historians," she amended. "It's a weekly record of who came and whether they were pregnant and what contraceptive method they were using if any, and whether they wanted to go on with the pregnancy, that sort of thing."

"Are their names in it then?" Edward asked in the same casual tone, but Gillian knew him well enough to sense a difference. If lie-detectors were attached to the questioners, she thought, the needle would have jumped at that question.

"Never," Bee said. "No surnames. Sometimes a first name is, but usually there's just an initial. Their names are none of our business, and we don't want the people who come to us to think they have to forfeit their privacy for a test."

"I see."

Bee looked sceptical. Gillian could read her mind. What does a police detective know or care about privacy, she was thinking. She shrugged. "Whoever took it probably threw the book in the nearest dustbin after they looked at it. It's such a pity, it would make interesting material for research some day, but apart from that, it doesn't matter."

"Maybe someone thought there were names in it," Edward suggested.

"That's possible," Bee admitted. "I hadn't thought of that. But the whole business doesn't add up, however one looks at it. That's why I thought perhaps it was a prank."

"A queer prank. Your office—not an ideal situation for you, is it?"

"It's paradise compared with where we used to be."

"Well then, I hope your book turns up," Edward said. He picked up a croissant and asked no more questions.

"What will you do about Wendy?" Gillian said.

"Ring her again tonight, I suppose." A flaky corner of pastry disappeared into Bee's mouth, and she licked her lips furtively, a neat, feline gesture at odds with her baggy trousers and angular pose, ankle crossed over knee, elbows out. "Where did you find these? I must take some home to Pamela."

"T'rific, aren't they?" Murray said, lavishly buttering his third. "Not just bread cut in crescents, like the usual so-called croissant these days. I was overjoyed to find them. Now if you could just do something about the potatoes . . ."

Bee looked blank. "Potatoes?"

"Those awful dirt-balls in the market. They're called potatoes, but I can hardly believe they're genetically qualified. Francis Drake would never have bothered to bring them back to England, and the

Incas would have sneered. You must have tried cooking them. It's impossible. Stones or mush, that's it. Nothing between."

"There's an easy solution," Bee said drily. "M and S. They have nice, clean potatoes in several varieties."

"But it seems immoral to walk past the old market stalls in order to shop in a chain store," Murray objected, only half joking.

"Then you'll have to live on potato mush and virtue," Bee said, laughing a little. "A diet even odder than Byron's."

In the afternoon, Gillian and Edward threaded their way through the crowded centre, visited the bookshops, bought some wine from a shop off Bridge Street, stopped in at the Pepys Library and slowly drifted back along Sidney Street towards the market.

"This college looks a bit silly," Edward said, flattening himself against the Sidney Sussex battlements and narrowly avoiding crucifixion by an aggressive cyclist.

"I know," Gillian said, following his glance upward to the crow-stepped gables. "Disney Tudor. It would be right at home in Fantasyland. Including Cromwell's head."

"Cromwell's head?"

"Oliver Cromwell attended Sidney Sussex for a year. So someone who'd got hold of his head donated it."

"Only the head?"

"If it is his head. According to one story, it hung about the Master's Lodge for ages, and then the Master buried it and died without telling anyone where. But there are other versions. I've also heard that it's buried in the chapel."

"There are computer programs now that can measure the facial bones and recreate the shape of the flesh—make a portrait from a skull. They could dig it up and have a go."

"If they can find it. Maybe that's what we should do with our holiday. Look for Cromwell's head."

"Funny sort of present to be lumbered with. I'd like to have been there when they opened the parcel."

"Do you remember writing thank you letters when you were a child? 'Dear Aunt Margaret: Thank you for the lovely pincushion.' Sheer torture. There was nothing else to say, but one sentence wasn't a proper letter. My mind used to turn to concrete."

"Are pincushions a Christmas custom in America, like turkeys? Did you have one every year?"

"Only once. It was a bright red one, an imitation tomato."

Edward grinned. "You haven't suffered. I had an aunt who always gave me socks. Imagine writing variations on the theme of 'thank you for the socks' for years on end."

"Did you?"

"I suppose I did. Now and then my mother would have a spasm of conscience about my upbringing; it

seems to me they usually happened at Christmas."
He laughed. "Maybe it was something in the plum
pudding."

"I could eat some plum pudding right now. I can
hardly believe it after Murray's breakfast, but I'm
hungry."

"Let's find that street vendor with the striped
awning. He was near the bus station. I'll buy you
some explosive Mongolian chicken strips or whatever
they're called. They smelled terrific."

"They did, didn't they? It's amazing. I used to have
to hold my breath whenever I got anywhere near the
carts."

FIVE

The timing of experiments is indifferent to weekends and holidays, and the chemistry lab was not quite deserted on Sunday afternoon. The glorious May sunshine, however, had made heavy inroads on the numbers of weekend regulars, and many doors were shut along the corridors. John Shoemaker ambled down the long corridor from the biochemical suite to the refrigerated space called the cold room, where some of his spare samples were stored. He was a graduate student in biological chemistry, one of the professor's research group, and he was behind, having misplaced a sample he'd been working with. This had thrown off a rather delicate piece of timing, so now he had to duplicate the entire sequence. He wished he were on the river.

The cold room was small: a storage cupboard with insulated walls. Glass vials stood in racks along the shelves, waiting in the frigid stillness. The door was six inches thick, with a heavy bolt like a meat-locker. He was faintly surprised that the handle was in the wrong position. The door wasn't bolted. He tugged at it. Then he staggered back, as though blown outward by a blast of freezing air.

There was a body on the floor of the cold room. He saw legs in blue jeans, smallish feet in scuffed Reeboks, a cotton T-shirt. One arm, flung upward, hid the face, but the contours beneath the T-shirt were female.

He shouted. His voice travelled a few feet and was smothered in the deep whine of a nearby fan. He ran into the corridor and yelled.

"Help!" The word dwindled hollowly down the empty hall. No one came.

He ran back to the body. He should call an ambulance, he thought. The police. But maybe he should try to help her first. Confused notions of hypothermia, of blankets, brandy, the kiss of life, crowded his brain. He stepped over her legs and squatted down beside her torso. Fearfully, he put a hand on her ribs, below the swell of her breast. He felt no movement. Nothing, not even a flutter. The body was ice cold under the T-shirt. Her pulse, he thought, touching two fingers to her left wrist. Nothing. Her forearm rested on her forehead: her right wrist, cocked at an extreme angle, palm outward, as if fending off a dreadful vision, was as stiff as concrete. Most of her face was hidden; only her mouth was visible, half open. He was glad he couldn't see her eyes. The hair, though, he knew that hair.

He pounded away to the nearest public telephone. It seemed like miles. Was she still breathing? He hadn't wanted to waste time trying to find out. Was that wrong? No, it couldn't be. She was too cold. The labs were full of telephones that rang all day long, but they weren't connected to outside lines. He'd shut the door to the cold room; maybe he shouldn't have, but it had seemed indecent to leave it standing open. And then there were the samples. Probably the little tubes would thaw when the police came, but he couldn't help that. What had happened to her? Suppose he'd come earlier and could have saved her? But surely anyone as cold as that had been dead for ages. Panic rose in his chest like a suffocating gas. When he got to the telephone he was gulping for air and stuttering.

In an agony of impatience he waited for the police by the front entrance. He had started to tell them how to find the cold room, then decided they would probably get lost.

"Isn't anyone here?" he called out despairingly after he had rung off. He heard an echo, then silence. Where were the police? The station wasn't far; why were they taking so long?

In fact, an area car arrived in less than three minutes, screeching through the roundabout at Trumpington

Road and stopping just outside the entrance to the department car park. Two police officers got out, a man and a woman. He watched them anxiously as they hurried across the car park. The woman was very young, a new constable, probably. He held the door open and led them back the way he had come. The man, who was older than the woman, asked him questions.

"When did you find her?"

"About five minutes ago, I suppose. Not more than ten."

"You touched the body?"

"Yes, to see if she was alive. That's all."

"And you think she's dead?"

"I—I thought so. She's so cold." He felt tears coming to his eyes and blinked them away.

The cold room did not open directly off the corridor but was situated within a dim recess where large pipes obscured the far wall. The cold room light that Shoemaker had left on shone into the recess from the left as he opened the heavy door again. He pointed without looking at her.

"She's in there."

The officers left him to wait in the doorway to the corridor and moved into the recess, to the entrance of the cold room.

"Go ahead," said the man. "Try not to disturb anything."

The woman looked at him. "All right."

Shoemaker could hear her light footfall as she

stepped into the room, then a rustle as she bent down.

"She's frozen! Stiff as a bit of cod!" she said in a low voice. Then, more loudly, "There's blood under her head."

"Right. Come away, then."

The two officers came out into the corridor. The woman spoke into her radiophone. Shoemaker leaned against the wall, feeling scared. The man produced a notebook and wrote something in it, then looked up.

"Who is she? Do you know her?"

At that moment Oliver Scudder turned the corner at the far end of the hall and saw the police officers. He recognized John Shoemaker, who waved at him urgently. What on earth's the matter, Oliver thought, and hurried forward. He didn't read much poetry, but now a line popped into his head: "not waving but drowning." Written by some woman with a man's name, he remembered vaguely. The police officers stood still and waited for him. Shoemaker pointed to the cold room.

"There's a dead body in there," he whispered. "That girl with the red hair."

Scudder's eyes followed Shoemaker's finger. He supposed there must be a mistake. The policewoman was blocking the entry to the recess.

"Let him have a dekko," the other officer said. "Maybe he knows her."

The woman stepped ahead of him through the

recess to the open doorway of the cold room, holding her arm out to prevent him from walking in. Oliver craned past her shoulder. He could see the body, the mouth, a bit of bright, carroty hair. "Good God. It's Wendy!" He stepped back, pale with shock. "Wendy Fowler," he repeated.

"I found her," Shoemaker whispered.

"What happened? Has there been an accident?" Oliver asked.

"I don't know," Shoemaker answered, still whispering.

The police officers were watching them. "Something like that," the older officer said.

The telephone call came while Edward was sitting in Detective Chief Superintendent Reynard Hardy's back garden in Cherry Hinton, drinking beer. Hardy's wife, Pandora, had left them to it. She had two flats of bedding plants: pansies, marigolds and alyssum, to plant in the small beds at the front of the house, and she was on her knees with a trowel full of moist, raked earth when she heard the shrill burring from inside. She wondered whether to ignore it. They probably wouldn't hear it from the far end of the garden. They were happy. And her gardening shoes were all over muck. She would have to take them off. She listened as the telephone continued to ring, sighed and set down her trowel, kicked off her shoes and sprinted for the door.

"Fox," she called from the sliding door at the rear of the kitchen.

He looked a question.

"It's the Godfather." She went back to her digging.

"Oh hell," said Hardy. He got up.

"The Godfather?" Edward said.

"That's my wife's little joke—because it's a phone call I can't refuse." He stumped towards the house. "I hope it's not overtime."

Edward waited, sipping his beer. He knew a lot of police officers and numbered several friends among the Cambridge constabulary, including Cutter, the Chief Constable, whom he had known since his early training days at Bramshill. But he knew none he liked more than Fox Hardy.

Their friendship, naturally, had begun on the job; they had worked together on several cases over the past ten years, including one murder inquiry that was still on the books. It had been a London murder, but the suspect had lived in Cambridge. He'd disappeared, gone abroad, Edward was nearly certain. He'd only been in England for a year. Now the exhibits that had cost so much time to gather and label and analyse and classify collected dust in a warehouse in Cricklewood. They would wait there forever in case new evidence turned up. And Edward and Hardy reviewed the case now and then, looking for anything they might have missed. It was like a splinter they couldn't tweeze out.

Superintendent Hardy was a large man, a head taller than Edward, broad-shouldered and barrel-chested. His sheer bulk could be intimidating, but his manner was mild. Long years on the force made a few men callous, even brutal, Edward sometimes reflected; more became cynics, especially in London—and the other big cities—where the sheer volume and intractability of the problems crushed out their youthful optimism. He knew careerists and politicians on the force, and he knew legions of long-time uniformed coppers who merely went through the motions: team players roused occasionally to anger by injury to their own, or to boisterous spirits by a victory, but by and large indifferent to the mass of ordinary citizens they served. Hardy was none of these. The people who crossed his path, on either side of the law, were still individuals to him: other human beings, who mattered. Edward's mind was the more agile of the two, as had been apparent when they took a two-week refresher course in medical jurisprudence, but Hardy was thorough, sensible and sane. Edward envied him his temperament. From time to time he himself was paralysed by disgust. The attacks were acute while they lasted and poisoned his view of the entire human race, excluding neither those he normally respected and cared for nor himself. When he was plunged into one of his black moods, no member of the species was worth a tinker's damn. Certainly not worth all the trouble taken. At those times his work became entirely mechanical.

In years past, a bruising game of football had sometimes served to dispel this humour. He would come away bloody and filthy, with every muscle wrenched but the poison leached from his system. Now, however, his body was getting too old for the cure. He had sprained his ankle and chipped a bone in his wrist already; the next time he was likely to break a leg, or his neck. It was something he had thought he might talk to Hardy about, if the opportunity arose. Maybe today, while Gillian was attending a lecture and having sherry with a crowd of historians. After a beer or two, perhaps then he would bring it up. Now they had had a beer, and enjoyed a pleasant hour deploring the bureaucratization of the police and the frustrating failures of the criminal justice system. There was plenty of time. He checked his watch. Unless, of course, the Godfather ordered otherwise.

He heard Hardy calling to Pandora, and then saw him leaning in the wide doorway. "Got a body to look at," he said. "Care to come along?"

Hardy's car was parked in the driveway. They left by the front door, passing Pandora, who had returned to her plants. A double row of small marigolds marched like a set of brass buttons down the narrow bed bordering the front walk.

"I knew I should have left it alone," she said, meaning the telephone.

"This may take a while," Hardy replied. "I'll ring you later. Your marigolds do look nice."

Edward, who hated marigolds but wouldn't for the world have hurt Pandora's feelings, looked on but said nothing. She tilted her head, squinting at him in the sunshine.

"How do you like them?" she asked, and then laughed before he could reply. "It's all right, love, I can see you don't. Where any of you fellows gets a reputation for a poker face I *don't* know."

"I'm not a gardener," Edward said, treading carefully, "but I like your roses." The first yellow blooms of a large old climber were opening against the wall of the house.

"Come along," said Hardy. "If you stand there for another five minutes you'll have no secrets left."

When they got to the chemical laboratories in Lensfield Road, there was already a constable at the entrance. He gave them directions. Edward pulled at one of the doors and was astonished at the effort required to open it.

"Something's wrong with the door," he said to Hardy. "Or I'm in much worse shape than I thought."

Hardy reached out a thick forearm and tugged. "Been neglecting the weights, have you?" He laughed at Edward's expression. "You're right. It's heavy."

Upstairs, the hall was full of people. Several police officers in plain clothes were already there and a man whom Edward took to be the police surgeon, since he was carrying the usual doctor's bag. Another man stood quietly near the doorway, a wooden box between his feet. Further away, a little crowd of students and faculty had collected as word trickled from floor to floor, from office to lab to coffee machine. A uniformed policewoman was preventing the anxious group from approaching the scene of the possible crime too closely; they pressed against an invisible fence and stared at the officers uneasily, like sheep watching sheepdogs.

The officers turned to greet Hardy, and the detective inspector, who recognized Edward, grinned at him.

"What? Called in the Yard already, have we?"

Then one man in the crowd of chemists, recognizing the arrival of a higher level of authority, pushed forward and confronted Hardy.

"I say, I've got some biological samples in there," he said, waving in the direction of the cold room. "They shouldn't be getting warm. If I could just nip in and transfer them to a refrigerator in the biochemical suite—" He stepped towards the door, as though it were settled.

Hardy raised a large hand, palm outward. "I'm afraid I'll have to ask you to be patient. I haven't assessed the situation."

"But the samples will be ruined!" the scientist said, his voice rising. "They represent weeks of work. They haven't anything to do with this accident!"

"All the same, nothing can be moved just now. Sorry," said Hardy calmly. He turned towards the entrance to the recess. "In there?" he asked his inspector.

The inspector nodded.

"Dead?"

"Dead as winkle-pickers. The photographer's nearly finished with the preliminaries."

The chemist retreated huffily. "This is ridiculous," he hissed, rejoining the knot of unhappy bystanders. "They've no idea how much damage they're doing."

Edward followed Hardy through the doorway, watching where he set his feet. They didn't go into the cold room but looked from the entrance. The photographer was swearing quietly. Like the rest of them, she had come dressed for a hot, sunny afternoon. Edward shivered. It was like standing in an open doorway on a winter day, the central heating warm at one's back while the chill air out-of-doors gripped one by the throat. A young woman's body lay supine on the floor, the legs sprawled wide, the chin up, one arm flung across her face. The room was perhaps five feet square, lined with shelves. Circular racks full of test tubes, like those at a medical testing laboratory, filled several of the shelves he could see. The door, half a foot thick, was presumably stuffed with some dense insulating material under its metal skin. It would act as an effective barrier to sound as well as heat.

"Not a bad place for a bit of dirty work," he muttered to Hardy. They returned to the corridor. They waited. Hardy conferred with the police who had arrived first in the area car. Edward chatted with

Inspector Walcott while he looked up and down the long hall. A row of fluorescent tubes, like sausage links, ran the length of the corridor and gave off a dull, glaring light. There were no windows.

The photographer came out and Banting, the surgeon, a stocky, greying man with Groucho Marx eyebrows, went in. Again, they watched from the doorway. He looked at the corpse. "Cold as a witch's backside in here," he said, opening his bag.

"How cold do you make it, exactly?" Edward said.

"I'll tell you in a minute or two."

"What are you looking at?" Hardy asked Edward, who was examining a device on the wall outside the room.

"A thermometer. Look. It's a continuous record of the temperature in the cold room. It's five degrees in there now and rising. Less than an hour ago it was zero."

"Zero!" the photographer said indignantly.

"Call it thirty-two, love, if it'll make you feel warmer," Banting chuckled. "But I know I'm freezing, in Centigrade or Fahrenheit." He nodded at Edward. "Five degrees in here now. The body's colder."

Hardy nodded. "We'll show that temperature record to the pathologist, if we need him."

When Banting had finished his examination, he came out stamping and blowing on his fingers like a man waiting for a taxi on New Year's Eve.

"Well?" Hardy said.

"If ever a body could be called a stiff, it's this one. Now then, suppose somebody popped you into a fridge and shut the door. Would you suffocate or freeze to death?" He shot a glance at Hardy.

"Depends on the size of the fridge," Hardy said.

Banting's eyebrows waggled. "And this is a big fridge. There's no sign of asphyxia. She's partly frozen, and I think she died of exposure, but I wouldn't swear to it. Wouldn't swear to anything before the autopsy. There's extensive bruising behind the right ear, not much blood, but it was a heavy impact. The body hasn't been moved since she died."

"You're sure?"

"Absolutely. The lividity's undisturbed."

"Any signs of a struggle?"

"Nothing blatant. No bruises on the arms; no scratches. You might find something under her nails, but there won't be much."

"Could she have slipped and fallen backwards, striking her head on something?"

"Possibly."

"So she might have fallen and then died of hypothermia while unconscious?"

"She might have. On the other hand, hypothermia might have caused the fall. What's certain is that she was alive when her skull received the blow. The contusions show that."

"Why would she have stayed in there long enough to get so cold?" Hardy said. "It doesn't make sense. She was only wearing jeans and a T-shirt."

"That's your job, chief," said Banting.

Hardy sighed. "A suspicious death, then. How long has she been there, do you think?"

"Ask an Eskimo."

"Take a crack at it, would you?"

Edward watched, fascinated, as the eyebrows, which had bounced upward at "ask an Eskimo" came diving down again.

"One to three days. That's the best I can do."

"Thanks, Doc."

Banting picked up his bag. "I don't like the smell of this." He walked away down the hall.

"Well," said Hardy, "let's go and spoil the Home Office pathologist's golf game. Oh, and we'd better tell Einstein and Company that they won't be getting their hands on those precious samples for a while yet."

The photographer went back to work in the cold room. "Can you find someone here to turn off the bleedin' air conditioning?" she called plaintively. A detective sealed off a section of the hallway with tape while Reagan, the fingerprint man, worked in the recess. Edward surveyed the familiar scene: the methodical activity of the police, the shifting crowd of observers. There were always the two separate groups: the inhabitants and the invaders, uneasily linked by the circumstances of a death. By a question.

He turned to Hardy. "What do you think?"

"Banting's not a pathologist, but he's no fool."

"No. There's something fishy here. We should have a good look at the door. Who was she, by the way? A student?"

"Not exactly. A researcher of some sort. I don't have the details yet. But according to the notes here her name's Wendy Fowler."

Edward stared in surprise. "Really? How extraordinary."

Hardy was all attention. "What? What's extraordinary?"

"I just heard about her yesterday. A friend of Gillian's was complaining that she didn't turn up for an appointment."

"What time?"

"Half ten Saturday morning."

"Chalk one up to Banting." Hardy looked at his watch. "That was about thirty hours ago." He made a note in his book. "I'd better give Cutter a tinkle pretty soon. It looks like a possible murder case, and he won't want to be the last to know. Besides, I'm short-staffed at present, and maybe he can pinch a few extra jacks for me. Their eminences are going to be breathing down our necks on this one." He put his book in his pocket and cocked his head at Edward. "I'd be glad of your company."

"Want another bag carrier, do you?"

Hardy grinned. "It's been too damned long since we worked on a case together."

"I could do with a change of air."

"Good. I'll ask the CC to put in a request."

"In the meantime, I'm here."

"What about your holiday?"

"It can wait. Your case won't. I can see the headlines already: 'Beautiful Young Scientist Brutally Slain in Cambridge Laboratory.' If it isn't solved quickly, you'll be digging latrines in a shitstorm."

SIX

Hardy beckoned to the young constable who had been holding the crowd at bay.

"Hullo, Pam. Where's the lad who found the body?" he asked.

"That bloke there, sir. The one with black curly hair and glasses. His name's John Shoemaker. He found her, but it was another bloke who identified her, the thin man with long white hair. His name's Scudder."

Hardy glanced down the hall and saw a slightly familiar face. "Oliver Scudder," he said quietly to Edward. "I know who he is. An observant chappie, by the look of him. And he's been in Cambridge since the year dot. He may be useful."

Reagan was dusting the door.

"Anything on the handle?" Hardy asked, without much hope.

"A lot of smears. Nothing we can use." He dusted the frame, picked up his wooden box and moved on into the room.

Edward looked closely at the door-fastening. It was a massive affair, with double bolts and a long, curved lever like a pump handle with which to slide both upper and lower bolts into twin slots in a heavy metal mounting to the right of the door.

"Could she have locked herself in?" Hardy asked.

Santini, the other SOC officer, was examining the inner door with a magnifying glass.

"No. The door opens from the inside even when the bolt is engaged. She couldn't have been locked in accidentally."

"Could the bolt have been tampered with before she went in."

"Doesn't look like it. No fresh scratches on the metal."

"And no prints of hers on the inside of the door," Reagan put in. "No indication that she struggled to open it."

"Who questioned Shoemaker?" Edward asked. "Did he say whether the door was bolted when he arrived?"

Hardy stuck his head into the corridor. "Turncliffe."

"Yes, Guv?"

"Did Shoemaker say anything about the bolt?"

"No. I didn't ask him about that."

Hardy turned back to Edward. "Let's go and have a chat with him now."

"Something here, boss," Santini said from the floor, where he was squatting, taking a swab. "It's oily. She could have slipped on it."

"What is it?"

"I don't know." He sniffed his swab. "Not olive oil. There's broken glass here, too. We'll take a good look at her shoes. Wait! I've got a label on this bit. It's torn. Some sort of diagram. What the hell?" He turned it this way and that. "A chemical formula, I guess." He chuckled. "Good. A little present for the lab."

"Any bloodstains besides the one under her head? Something hit her skull pretty hard, Banting says."

"I took a swab from that shelf there," Santini said, pointing to one of the grey metal shelves on the left. It was at the height of Edward's shoulder. "Found a bit of blood. Some skin will probably show up in the lab."

Hardy and Edward withdrew into the recess.

"So. Let's draw the picture," Hardy said.

"She walks in, drops the test tube or whatever it is, the oil spills, she steps on it. She slips and falls backward against the metal shelf, striking her head hard enough to knock herself out, after which she quietly freezes to death."

"All neat and tidy." Hardy was gazing at a large box with a glass front. The tops of two long black rubber gloves were sealed to two circular openings in the glass. They projected limply into the box like dead hands. "Look at this," he said to Edward. "Queer-looking arrangement, isn't it? I've seen something like it before; something to do with handling radioactive materials. But I shouldn't think they'd do that here."

"I've no idea," Edward said. "But if they did, they wouldn't leave the box standing about. Perhaps it's for handling chemicals that give off poisonous fumes."

Hardy thrust his hands into the gloves and they came to life with a reptilian wriggle. He gazed around the windowless recess and into the starkly lit cold room. "Odd place to be murdered," he said softly.

In the corridor, Turncliffe was taking down the names and addresses of everyone who had gathered to watch. It was a largely male crowd of graduate students, post-docs and faculty members; no undergraduates, male or female, were in the lab on Sunday afternoons, and the female secretaries were naturally off on weekends. The group had not dispersed, although they could see nothing of what was going on in the recess.

"McClure, fetch Shoemaker for us," Hardy said to his detective-sergeant, and moved off down the corridor out of earshot of the observers.

Shoemaker came, escorted by McClure. He looked nervously at Hardy.

"Now then, suppose you tell us just what happened," Hardy said gently. McClure had his notebook out.

"I came down to the cold room because I needed a duplicate sample," Shoemaker began.

"Hang on. Let's go back a little. What time did you get here today?"

"About noon. I came in because I was behind in my work. Otherwise I would have been on the river."

"And where were you working?"

"In the biological suite. It's along the corridor at the end on the right."

"Was anyone else there?"

"No. The professor came in later for a bit and then went out again. But he must have come back after I found her, because he's here now. He's the one who wanted to take the samples away."

"What's his name?"

"Tennison."

"But when you left the biological suite to fetch your samples, you were alone?"

"Yes."

"What time was that?"

"Three."

"You didn't see anyone in the corridor? Or hear anyone?"

"No."

"What about the door to the cold room? Was it bolted?"

"That's what I noticed. It wasn't. The door was shut, but the bolt wasn't engaged. It's always supposed to be."

"What did you think?"

"I don't know. That someone had forgotten, I suppose. I didn't think much before I opened it."

"And then?"

"Then I saw her. I thought she was ill, or had fainted or something. Then I touched her, and she was so cold I knew she was dead."

"Any idea what happened?"

"No idea at all. No."

Hardy looked at Edward. Edward said, "Is that room used much? Do people go in and out a lot?"

"Not really. It's not used much at all, actually."

"How much time might go by without anyone going in?"

"I'm not sure, but a few days, at least."

McClure's radio crackled. "The pathologist's on his way, Guv."

"Good. Let's have a chat with Scudder while we wait for him."

Oliver Scudder's office was on the same side of the corridor as the cold room. He invited the detectives in and sat down. Edward strolled over to the windows and looked out.

"It must have been an accident," Scudder said. "God knows she's had enough of them."

"What do you mean?" Edward asked.

"Floods," Scudder said tersely.

"Floods?" Hardy repeated.

"Three of them. Well, two, really. It was quite extraordinary. I've never known anyone with such a record of mishaps. I've been in this room for over fifteen years and never had a flood from the lab upstairs. Since she's been here there have been three." He pointed at his bookshelves. "Look at my journals. That happened just a few days ago."

Edward walked over to the shelves. There was a broad section of stained bindings, and he could see rippled pages. He touched the spines of the nearest books. They were still damp.

"Bit of a mess, aren't they? Tell us more about the floods," he suggested.

Scudder sighed. "The first one was in February. But that wasn't her fault; at least I don't see how it could have been; the water came from above her lab that time. There are great empty spaces between the floors, you see, with nothing to impede the flow."

"Why is that?" Edward asked, squinting at the ceiling.

"Because there's a massive network of pipes that runs all over the building between the floors, and there must be access to them. I'll show you, if you like."

"Later," Hardy said. "The second flood, when was that?"

"Not long ago," Scudder replied. "Early April, I think. She'd set up her rotavap—rotary evaporator—in her office upstairs and left it. But she hadn't wired the rubber tubes to the glass properly, and one popped off. It was connected to the tap, so water went all over the place. And through the floor, naturally. It was perfectly maddening, although I didn't sustain any serious damage that time. Roger Hill lost a lot of print-out and had some trouble with his keyboard."

"And the third happened exactly when?"

"Let me see. Today's Sunday. It was Thursday. Thursday lunch. A big plastic bag full of water broke. It was sitting on the floor by her bench. She was at lunch; so was I. I came back from lunch at college to find my office awash."

"What did you do?"

"I ran like hell upstairs, thinking it was the tap again and I'd turn it off. I saw Roger coming away; he'd found the bag. He was hopping mad. And then we met Wendy." Scudder paused, thinking of her. "She was unaware of what had happened, of course. Roger tore a strip off her. Quite understandable, but very unpleasant. Later she helped me try to dry out some of my journals. It wasn't much good."

Edward, who had returned to his post by the windows and was gazing down at a massive roof, turned round. "What's that roof down there? The one that looks bloated?"

"Lecture room one. It's for big first-year classes."

"What sort of person was Wendy Fowler?"

Scudder rubbed his nose and wound his long legs about the legs of his chair. "I didn't know her well, really. Not personally, I mean. Knew her work—it was good. Exciting, even."

"How do you mean?"

"She thought of good questions to ask. Other people were very interested in the answers."

"What sort of chemist was she?"

"Experimental, as opposed to theoretical. She did her Ph.D. with Reg Bailey, in coordination chemistry. He's away on leave this year. But then she became more interested in the organic fragments. She had a nice idea to link alkaloid molecules to make ligands for chiral recognition."

"Jesus Q. Christ," muttered Hardy, scribbling quickly. "How do you spell that when it's at home?"

"Oh, sorry. Of course." Scudder reoriented himself. "Not to be too technical about it, she was in inorganic chemistry, but then her interests shifted to organic, which explains why I'm familiar with her work."

"And you know nothing about her personal life."

"She lived alone, so far as I know. No husbands or children, at least. She was often in the lab in the evenings; people in her position have to be or they don't go very far. That would have been doubly true for her."

"Why?"

"Because she's a woman. Was, I mean. Women have to work harder than men to win recognition."

"Would you say she didn't have much of a life outside of her work, then?"

"No, no," Scudder said quickly. "I couldn't possibly say such a thing. I just don't know anything about it. She was a talented young woman, that's all."

"Aren't there many women?" Edward said. "I hardly saw any in the crowd."

"We have quite a lot of women students, now. Not like the old days, when there were only a few and most of them were crystallographers. Staff's another matter. We've only got one."

"Out of how many?"

"Forty-five."

"How did Wendy get on with her colleagues?"

"All right, I suppose. Reg Bailey—he was her supervisor—thought a lot of her. I don't know of anyone she was particular friends with, but she was in his research group when she was a student, and the ones who were in their first year when she was finishing her Ph.D. are still around. You might ask them. I'm afraid it's not the sort of thing I'm in the habit of paying attention to."

"Did she have any enemies?"

Scudder shook his head, bemused. "Enemies? It sounds too melodramatic." He waved vaguely at the office windows. "Hardly a Borgia palace, is it? Just a lot of rather dull men beavering away for modest salaries. There are antagonisms, of course, but enemies in the sense you mean? It's difficult to imagine." He raised an ironic eyebrow. "I suppose I might be the likeliest candidate. She's flooded my office twice. People have surely murdered for less. And there's Roger Hill. He's next door and his office has been flooded as often as mine. The last time . . ." Scudder hesitated, suddenly ill at ease. "The last time, he said he was going to strangle her. Figure of speech, of course," he added hastily.

Edward's eyes briefly met Hardy's.

"Did anyone else have reason to dislike her?"

"No serious reason that I've heard about. There was some grumbling upstairs about her having a whole bench to herself when her research interests were no longer primarily inorganic, and of course there are a few chaps who would rather not have women cluttering up the labs. Ron Bottomley doesn't care for her, I suppose. But he doesn't like anybody."

"Can you tell us where you were Friday and Saturday?" Edward asked.

"Yes, of course. Friday I was working in my office until half past seven. Then I went home. I was there until early Saturday morning. Then I drove to London. I was there all day; I didn't get home until after midnight. Then I went straight to bed."

"Anyone with you?"

"My wife. In London and in bed."

"All right. That'll do for now," Hardy said. "Now about that room where Wendy Fowler was found."

"The cold room."

"Yes, the cold room. Why would she have been there?"

"Presumably she was collecting a sample she'd stored, or was putting one away. I don't know. I shouldn't have thought her work would have required her to use it. But she could have been working on something I'm not aware of." He ran his hand through his white hair, suddenly looking very weary. "Oh Lord. What a dreadful thing to have happened."

"Thank you," said Hardy, getting up. "We may need to ask you some more questions, but we'll leave it for now."

"Will there be an autopsy?"

Hardy nodded.

"Which people keep samples in the cold room?" Edward asked. "Who uses it?"

"I haven't got a list. Not many people, I should think. Mostly the biological chemists, but anyone might. They leave various things in there—unstable compounds, perhaps, and sometimes collections of plant material."

"Have you got anything in there?"

Scudder shook his head. "No. But Tennison does. He'll be worried about the effect of the temperature variation on his samples."

"We know," said Hardy.

"Does he go in there often?" Edward said as they moved to go.

"I doubt it. Nobody does. Sometimes no one goes in there for weeks."

Later, after the police had gone, Oliver wandered down the hall to the biological suite. Tennison was still there and still fuming.

"They've locked up the whole blasted show," he told Oliver. "All my samples will be useless. What possible benefit they think there might be in wrecking my research, I completely fail to understand."

"There's been a death," Oliver said.

"I know. A damned silly accident. What was she doing in there, anyhow?"

"I think that's what the police want to know. What the devil's the matter with you? Wendy Fowler is *dead*."

Tennison deflated suddenly. "Sorry. I hardly knew the girl, and the fact is, I'm going to lose four months' work if I lose those samples. But I shouldn't be thinking only of that. What are the police going to do?"

"I don't know. But they're not assuming it was an accident. They asked me whether she had any enemies."

Tennison snorted. "What rubbish."

"That's what I thought. But—"

"But?"

"We didn't examine the body. They did."

Tennison frowned. "I still don't believe it. But if it was murder, then who's supposed to have done it? One of us?"

"I wonder how many people were here last night, or Friday night, for that matter," Oliver mused. "Were you?"

"Is the Pope Catholic? I've been here every day of the week since term started."

"We should see if anyone on the third floor was here. I don't suppose you noticed anything unusual."

"No, but I didn't go near the cold room. I left at nine." Tennison snorted. "The only unusual thing I saw was Bottomley. In the car park. I don't think I've seen him here on a Friday night since I arrived in Cambridge."

"How odd."

"He didn't see me, though. Poisonous weed, Bottomley."

"He used to be all right."

"Really? Before my time, then. You must admit he's one of the department's mistakes."

Oliver didn't deny it. He was thinking about Bottomley. Doubtless the police would ask him what he was doing in the lab on Friday night.

"If someone killed her," Tennison added, "which I don't believe for a minute, it must have been an accident."

Scudder nodded.

"Well, you and Roger are in the clear, at any rate. If you'd done her in, you would have drowned her." Tennison threw back his head and gave a short barking laugh. A printer began spitting out a sheet of data. He turned away and examined the graph, putting an end to the conversation.

Scudder left. People reacted quite strangely to death, he thought.

SEVEN

Edward rang Gillian at about six.

"You must be fathoms deep in shop-talk," she said. "You were going to be back an hour ago."

"Not only talk, I'm afraid. I've been on a bit of a busman's holiday."

"Oh God," Gillian groaned. "I don't believe it. Not a case. If I get my hands on your pal Hardy, you'll have another one. Are you coming home?"

"Yes, I'll be there in a bit. It depends on the pathologist's report. If you and Murray don't mind a late dinner, I'll join you. But I'll probably be tied up all day tomorrow and Tuesday."

"This was supposed to be a holiday! I hardly saw you for five minutes in London. Can't you leave

Hardy to get on with it? Is there nothing else in life besides your bloody cases."

"He's short-staffed, and this isn't a straight-up domestic killing. I know it was supposed to be our holiday, but Hardy asked me to help, and I'd feel like an absolute bastard if I said no. This case will bring a lot of pressure to bear. The good news is I'll probably be staying in Cambridge longer."

"I don't suppose you could finish your holiday first and then join in the fun?"

"I'm afraid that's not on. Cases like this don't wait."

"We're jinxed," she said gloomily. "Remember when we tried to go to Scotland and you had to get off the train? It was that idiot with the axe."

"Darling, don't take it personally. It's just life in the CID. And I've simply got to give Hardy a hand. Gilly, I'm sorry, there's something else you need to know. The victim is the woman Bee was talking about yesterday. It's Wendy Fowler."

"Oh Jesus."

"I am sorry."

"Where did it happen? Where are you?"

"At the chemistry labs in Lensfield Road."

"Oh God. Should I tell Murray?"

"Yes. It'll be in the papers tomorrow. You can break it to Bee, too."

"All right," Gillian said faintly. She put down the receiver.

"What's the matter? Should you tell me what?" Murray asked, looking alarmed.

"Oh God. First pour us a drink. A big one."

When Edward got back, he had the tight look about his jaw that Gillian had learned to associate with the start of a new case. He was burning with energy and moved impatiently about the tiny house as though he couldn't sit still. He was there but not there, his mind circling over the case, mapping the landscape: natural features, landmarks, major roads, obstacles.

Murray said and ate very little at dinner. Now and then he shook his head, in renewed spasms of disbelief. Gillian, who hadn't known Wendy, was less shocked and asked Edward questions. Edward ate absently but steadily. Refuelling, Gillian thought.

Eventually Murray said, "I asked her out, you know. Right after I got here. She said no."

Edward looked up. "Why do you think she said no?"

"Thought I was too old, I guess. She was perfectly friendly."

"Could she already have had a boyfriend?"

"It's possible. She didn't say so."

"Did you know her well in Vancouver?"

"She did a post-doc with a colleague of mine. Worked hard, had no problems. Firman thought she was exceptionally talented but a little pushy. Maybe he was reacting to something he would have thought was perfectly normal or admirable in a man. It's hard to say. If there were three computer terminals and four people, Wendy was never the one to be waiting for a turn. But I don't think she had real trouble with anyone. Just a couple of run-ins with some guys who treated the lab like a frat house."

"What do you mean?"

"Oh, the usual stupid stuff. Pictures of naked women on the walls. Telling dirty jokes."

"What did she do?"

"Tore the pictures down. Complained to Firman about the jokes."

"What happened?"

"Not much. They sniggered and muttered when she was around, nudge nudge, wink wink, made fun of her when she wasn't there. The atmosphere was a little sulphurous for a while. I told you about it at the time, Gillian, remember?"

"Now that you mention it. It was just one more incident in that awful fall term."

"When did she die?" Murray asked Edward.

"Sometime Friday evening—possibly while we three were sitting right here at dinner."

Murray winced.

"Whoever did it knew the building well," Edward went on. "He knew about the cold room and was probably well aware that it wasn't used very often. With any luck, no one would have found her for weeks."

"You think it was another chemist? That's absurd!"

"Is it? Why?"

"It just is," Murray cried and then slumped in his chair, disconsolate. "I guess everybody thinks that about the people they know."

"Well, at least you don't reek of the morgue," Gillian said to Edward when they went to bed.

"No. I didn't have to go this time."

"Small mercies," Gillian said. 'When do you have to be at the station tomorrow?"

"Eight."

"How's your friend Fox?"

"Fine."

"It must be an unusual case for him."

"Mmm."

Gillian tapped him on the shoulder. 'Earth to DCI Gisborne."

"What? Oh. Sorry. I was thinking about tomorrow."

"I know."

"I'm sorry about the next two days."

"Are you?"

"Yes, but—"

"I know. You haven't worked on a case with Fox Hardy for three years . . . Edward, do you never get sick of murder? Of having to deal with that kind of horrible filth?"

He lay on his back, looking at the ceiling.

"Sometimes. Usually when I'm in court, watching the defence play off their tricks. Some murders seem clean by comparison."

"They're that bad, the lawyers?"

"A few are." He sighed. "And the system is weighted in favour of the villains."

"How?"

"The rules of evidence. Don't get me started. It's a cliche that coppers think this way, but we've got reason." He turned his face towards her. "Listen. Sometimes, at the beginning when the first word comes in, I just don't want to know. I'm tired, I've already got fifty hours of paperwork staring me in the face, and I don't want to haul my aching bones out at two in the morning. But then I see the victim—the poor old bugger who's been beaten to death, or the young woman who's been strangled or stabbed. And I want to do something. I'm angry. I don't want the bastard to get away with it. That anger's invigorating. I put it to use instead of feeling helpless, like most people. I don't think society—any society I want to live in—can survive if people can kill and get away with it. When we catch a killer, we've done a job of work—and one that absolutely must be done."

"And that's enough to keep you going?"

"Some days. There are other things—the puzzles, for one. You know that part; we've talked about history and detection. But my puzzles have living pieces—families, informants, the killer. It's a game, sometimes. Then it feels good to win. And I'm not sorry for the killers, at least not often. When they're genuinely remorseful and desperate to pay for what they've done, it's possible to pity them, but usually they're trying to squirm off the hook. Sometimes they feel nothing for their victims. We nick them. That's the job. No regrets."

"At least the murder rate is still low here."

"Right," he said in the enlivened tone of someone who is making his point. "It makes all the difference. What's satisfying about the murder squad is that we *do* solve cases. We have a very high clear-up rate. We work like bloody lunatics—I don't have to tell you that. But then we're used to going on sheer adrenalin. It isn't so bad."

"Unless all addictions are bad." She laughed.

He put out an arm to pull her closer. "Are you calling me an adrenalin abuser? I can quit any time I want to."

"Prove it."

His hand slid over her breast. His mouth touched her ear. "I am. If you would just pay attention."

In the morning, Edward had a conference with Hardy, and they went over the report from Janes, the Home Office pathologist. He had come and inspected the cold room, the position of the body and the wound to the skull. Pending the autopsy, he had said the signs pointed to hypothermia as the cause of death, and that the blow to the back of the head had been too forceful and had struck her from the wrong angle to correspond to a natural fall in that confined space. His preliminary hypothesis was that her head had been bashed against the shelf by a strong, right-handed person. The blow hadn't killed her, but had induced severe concussion and fractured the skull. She had then been allowed to fall to the floor, and the attacker had walked out and left her to die there.

"The post-mortem results were definite," Hardy said. "Homicide. Janes found some bruising on her shoulders—fingermarks. And there was something under one of the nails of her left hand. A couple of threads. It's gone to the lab. She might have grabbed the killer's shirt. And there's something else," Hardy said. "Janes found a pattern of superficial abrasions to the skin that suggested to him that the body had been wrapped in some rough material, such as jute. Some coarse fibres were found at the scene and on the body: they've gone to the lab for analysis."

Hardy was loading his strong tea with lumps of sugar. Edward drank coffee, regretting that the pot Gillian had given him for his office was in London. The station coffee was stewed. Hardy had put an extra desk in his own office overlooking the car park.

"I hope that's all right. I've got a room just down the hall being set up as the murder room, but I know you like a bit of peace and quiet when you start banging your head against the wall."

"Burlap sacking?" Edward wondered.

"That would do."

"So she might have been carried to the cold room in a sack?"

"From where?"

"Surely not from outside the building. He would have had to be daft."

"Yes. But from another room, where he found her?"

"More likely. So what we must get on to is the building. We need a map of the place, and we need to know where she spent her time, and where the other people usually are."

Hardy was making a list. *W.F.'s habits*, he wrote. *Sack*. "Who was there Friday night? When and where did they see her? Anyone working out of hours is supposed to sign in and out; the book is being held for us in the office safe in Lensfield Road."

"Good. What about the time of death? Have we got a better fix on that?"

"At least twenty hours before she was found, but Janes wouldn't be pinned down any further than that. That would be seven p.m. Saturday. And she was seen alive Friday afternoon after half five. Say a span of 25 hours then, theoretically speaking, from Friday evening to Saturday evening. But Friday evening's still our time. She didn't turn up at an appointment Saturday morning, and we haven't found anyone who saw her Saturday at the lab where she would normally have been working."

"We may be able to narrow it down by using the temperature record. Let's see whether any temperature increases were registered between Friday afternoon and Saturday morning."

"Or decreases. He might have tried to freeze her more quickly."

"Who has access to the building?"

"If you mean keys, we don't have a list yet. But it may not matter. Anyone can walk in during the day, and they don't all know each other. The killer could have slipped in Friday afternoon and simply waited for his opportunity."

"So it could have been anyone who knew the building—even a first-year student."

Hardy nodded. "There are hundreds of those. We need to know who was in the building on the weekend. I'll assign two men to collecting names and times; let's hope that lot yields some leads, or we'll be sifting half of Cambridge."

"I'd like to ask Oliver Scudder to give me a tour," Edward said.

"Why don't you ring him? Or do you want to come to Wendy's flat with me first?"

"Where is it?"

"King's Parade. Bang across from the chapel."

"When are you going?"

"First thing." Hardy looked at the clock. "The team should all be here by now." He gathered up the papers on his desk. "Ready for morning prayers?"

They walked down the hall, side by side. Hardy passed Edward a copy of his notes on the autopsy. "There's another thing," he remarked, with a sidelong glance.

"Pregnant?"

"Bingo."

EIGHT

A little after nine-thirty, as Edward and Hardy left the station for Wendy's apartment, Gillian was walking across Parker's Piece. She hadn't been able to reach Bee before dinner the previous evening and had left a message on the answering machine, asking Bee to ring back as soon as possible. It was after eleven when Bee had returned home and received the bad news. Now Gillian was on her way to the house in Newnham where Bee and Pamela lived. The rest of the PIS group were coming over too, and she would tell all of them what she knew.

Parker's Piece was green and vast after the squeezed little streets. The town on the other side looked far away, as if outlined on a distant horizon. Bicyclists sped along the diagonal path to Hyde Park Corner, where the spire of the Catholic church pierced the bright sky. The cricket pitches, sheared to a green fur, were empty. It was all so familiar and dear that Gillian's spirits lifted a little in spite of her troubling errand. Her route took her south across the green and then along Lensfield Road, past the Scott Polar Institute and the chemistry labs. She stared up at the lab windows as she went by, looking for some sign of difference. There was none. The only departure from the norm that she could see was the presence of a police car in the car park.

Two horses stood in the grass near the river, and half a dozen cows grazed quietly in the morning sunshine. Small children raced up and down the playground in Lammas Land. She came to Grantchester Street in Newnham, a pleasant little village street where a tiny post office and a grocery were tucked into a row of low buildings fronting directly on the narrow pavement. There had been a change since her last visit, she noticed with amazed displeasure. The old Co-op grocery shop had been rebuilt, and above it there now rose a tall, ungainly addition like a monstrous wooden box delivered to the wrong address. It bulged out over the pavement as though carelessly crammed into a space too small for it. Gillian stared and then averted her eyes, wondering who had been sleeping when planning permission was given. She went on quickly and turned into Owlstone Road, a quiet residential street of close-set brick houses at the southwestern edge of Cambridge.

Pamela, Gillian remembered, had wanted a larger house and garden in Millington Road, but in the end Bee, feeling a little overwhelmed by Pamela's money, had dissuaded her. So much conspicuous consumption all at once, she said, would give her indigestion. So they had moved into a house near the end of Owlstone Road. There was a wood at the back, and beyond the wood, the river, flowing past the meadows into Coe Fen and the heart of Cambridge. This month, Gillian knew, the water would be crowded with red-painted punts every sunny weekend.

The house was deep and narrow, like its neighbours, and had been rather dark before Pamela had hired a team of carpenters to renovate the ground floor. They had knocked out interior walls, demolished the gloomy kitchen and extended the back of the house, adding French windows that opened on to a wide brick terrace. Heating pipes were installed under the tiled floor. Sliding doors separated the sitting-room from the enormous kitchen; when they were open, the entire ground floor was one big room, bright and warm from end to end. It was most unlike the England of Gillian's first visit in the 1960s, when every house in Cambridge had seemed to repeat the same arrangement of small, cold, box-like rooms.

Now, some years later, the upper storey was being enlarged and transformed. Bee was to have her own study at the back, overlooking the garden, and the spartan little bathroom was being replaced by a bigger one with a two-person tub and a skylight. In the meantime, the bedrooms were full of plaster dust and the downstairs WC was the only one that flushed. Bee said that since she had been to Kenya she understood Pamela's renovation schemes: they were all aimed at making her house in England more like her house in Nairobi, which was light and airy and deliciously warm all year round. "Her blood's too thin for English winters now, and she's damned if she's going to live like her Aunt Viv, creeping po-faced from room to room in that mausoleum on the Clyde, wearing three layers of woollies and carrying an electric fire."

Gillian rang the bell. She had met most of the group before, but she knew none of them well. Pamela, whom she knew rather better, was not a member of PIS but would be there as well.

It was Pamela who answered the door. She looked the same as ever; she had hardly changed over the years Gillian had known her, except for deepening crow's feet and her sun-aged skin, which now resembled the fine-grained leather of a Florentine handbag. Her hair was still honey-blonde, thick and springy. Now she wore it shaved short at the back with a mass of curls on top. She was tall and rangy, with a deep tan that stopped short below her collarbones. She squinted at Gillian, the blue-green flash of eye like a distant glimpse of water.

They embraced briefly.

"How's Bee?" Gillian asked.

"Shattered." Pamela led the way to the kitchen, where Bee and the others were gathered in a sombre group at the long table. An enormous Wedgwood teapot with a chipped spout stood in front of Bee, who poured a cup for Gillian and passed it down the table. Her eyes were puffy.

"I rang everyone last night and told them about Wendy, but we all want to hear the whole story from you, if that's all right."

"Irene's not here yet," Pat interjected. "Let's wait for her." Pat Merryweather was a heavyset woman of forty-five with hair that had gone grey early and completely. She wore it in a Prince Valiant cut, the fringe a perfectly straight line framing her square, unmade-up face. She had a Ph.D. in English from Cambridge but had grown tired of lurking in the shadowy margins of academe alert for the opening that never came. Now she was a therapist with a thriving practice. She was married, or had been the last time Gillian had seen her, with two half-grown children and a husband who was a Fellow of Jesus. She wore a shapeless denim pinafore dress that reminded Gillian of the farmers' wives pictured in children's storybooks.

No one protested at waiting for Irene.

"Did you know Wendy?" Pat asked Gillian.

"No, I never met her. But strangely enough I've heard her name before, from my friend Murray, who knew her in Vancouver. Did you all know her well?"

One or two voices murmured hesitantly and trailed

off. A movement went round the table as each woman considered her own answer and then turned her head to see how others might reply to the question.

Pamela, lean-hipped as a cowboy in her bluejeans, fetched more hot water and resumed her seat by Bee. "I didn't," she said bluntly. "She was here for dinner once or twice."

"I've known her for years," Vicky said. Gillian leaned forward to hear. Vicky's voice was a near-whisper. "Since she was an undergraduate. We were good friends. We went bicycling in Holland together, things like that. And we worked on the pro-choice campaign in 1988, when that sneaky bastard Alton tried to push through his private member's bill."

Vicky, who Gillian guessed was about thirty, was short and thin, with small bones and heavy, shining black hair. Her face was round and flat, her skin perfectly smooth and opaque, like a beautifully glazed plate. Her dark, widely spaced eyes lent her a deceptive air of innocent calm. Her clothes—wide black cotton pants, a tie-dyed silk T-shirt and gilded leather sandals—owed nothing to current fashion but looked stylish and cool. She was a freelance art restorer and lived in a tiny flat in a house north of the Chesterton Road.

"Wendy had a real gift for political organization," she went on. "She would have been an ace campaign manager. Bags of energy and a head for organization, and she could convince people to do things. She took a whole busload of people down to London for the march."

"So she was a political activist?" Gillian asked.

"Not really. At least she wasn't hooked on politics," Vicky replied. "After the fight over the Alton bill she dropped out. She was finishing her thesis that year, and she said she didn't have any more time for politics. If she was going to get anywhere as a chemist, she had to do chemistry and nothing else for a while. So she finished her thesis and then went off to do her post-doc. I didn't see her for ages, not until she came back last autumn."

"And then you brought her along to a PIS meeting," said Margaret. "That's when the rest of us met her." She looked round the table for confirmation. The others nodded.

Vicky cleared her throat. "She told me she wanted to do something for choice again, but she didn't have time to be involved in a lot of meetings and big campaigns. I knew we needed somebody—it seemed like a good idea." She seemed to be addressing the group now, rather than recounting history for Gillian. Was there a hint of defensiveness in her tone?

"Of course. We were all keen to have a new member," Margaret said warmly. Like Vicky, she looked about thirty and had been at Girton, but there the resemblance stopped. She was buxom and wore her hair in a thick flaxen plait that perfectly matched her fair-skinned, blue-eyed Nordic features. Her voice was high-pitched and clear, Gillian noted. It would be an asset in her job: Vicky taught at a language school in Norwich

Street. That was all Gillian knew about her, except that she lived in a communal house off Mill Road.

The doorbell rang.

"Irene," said Pamela. "I'll go."

Gillian was looking forward to seeing Irene again. She had been a founding member of the PIS. Now she and Bee were the only two left. It was Irene who had gone to the national women's conference and met Dr Sheila Abdullah and had come back, kit in hand, fairly bursting with the astonishing information that you didn't have to be a doctor to use the kit to test for pregnancy. That had been in 1973, as near as Gillian could remember. The group had formed instantly. Then they'd spent three months practising on each other and on pregnant friends before setting up shop in a ground-floor room in a derelict house in the Kite. Bee had described it to Gillian in a letter that year: the cracked window-panes and brown waterstains on the walls, the bitter cold in winter. There had been no running water on their floor; they had brought warm water in buckets from the first floor, and when the hot water supply was cut off made do with cold. They had complained, of course, but there had been no question of quitting. The service was too plainly needed. Then the council had taken over the building and housed "difficult" people in it. "That meant they had fights and broke the windows and the plumbing," said Bee wryly. There had been a question then about whether to stay, but it had been decided not long afterwards by the council, which sold the house. The PIS had moved briefly to the new women's centre and then to Grafton Street.

"Sorry I'm late," Irene said from the doorway. "I had to get bloody Patrick off. I can't make him pass his exams, but I can still get him out of bed."

She had a long, oval face and Titian hair, fading now but still glinting red-gold in the sunny kitchen. It hung bushy and wild to her shoulders. She was dressed in a mystifying assortment of garments in beautiful patterns, a style she referred to as ragbag chic.

"She's one of those people who can pick the right dress in a second-hand shop," Bee had once remarked enviously. "She can spend ten pounds and look as if she's been to Paris. When I try anything on in one of those shops, it doesn't matter *what* it is, I always look like a refugee."

She came straight over to Gillian and kissed her. "How good of you to come," she said in her deep raspy voice. "This is just awful, but I'm glad to see you. Have I missed anything important?"

"No. We were waiting."

She sat down opposite Gillian. Bee filled another cup and passed it down the table.

"I told Gillian we all wanted to hear the story from her first hand," Bee said.

"I wasn't an eyewitness," Gillian said.

"Yes, but you know what happened."

"I know what Edward told me."

"Do they have any idea who did it?" Vicky asked, her voice almost inaudible.

"Not yet."

"Let's have the story first, then questions," Pat said. "Agreed?"

The women sat still, tense and silent, as Gillian recounted the events of the previous day, beginning with the telephone call to Detective Chief Superintendent Hardy. "A graduate student found her, a young man named Shoemaker. He was alone and scared stiff, Edward said. He called the police, and they came right away, but she had already been dead for a long time."

"How long?" asked Bee.

"Probably since Friday night. Edward said the medical evidence wasn't as specific as that, but of course the fact that she didn't show up Saturday morning was significant."

"I talked to her on Friday," Bee said. "About bringing the kit."

"I did too," Vicky murmured.

"What time?"

"Just before lunch," Bee said.

"I don't know," Vicky said more slowly. "About five or six, I think." Her voice shook a little. "It was just a chat."

"Go on, Gillian," Irene said. "What do the police say happened to her?"

"There's a tiny little room in the labs that's insulated—like a walk-in fridge." Gillian drew a breath. This was the hard part. "Somebody bashed Wendy's head against a metal shelf in there, hard enough to crack her skull, and then left her there to freeze to death. Edward says it was probably supposed to look like an accident."

"An accident? She slipped and fell, that sort of thing?" Irene asked.

"That's right."

"But they know she didn't?"

Gillian nodded. "It's harder to fake those things than most people think."

"I don't believe it," Margaret said. "Who would kill Wendy? What for?"

"It's senseless and horrible," Pat said. Her fingers went to her throat and the grey wings of her hair swung forward as she ducked her head and sniffed loudly. Vicky huddled in her chair, her eyes squeezed shut, a hand over her mouth. Irene rummaged through her huge handbag and hauled up a bright red packet of cigarettes. She shook one out, then pushed it back and sat turning the packet over in her hands. Margaret looked at Vicky and pressed some tissues into her hand. Vicky dabbed at her eyes and nose. Pamela was holding Bee's hand and staring stonily at the teapot.

"Women ought to have their own cenotaphs," she said. "A tomb in every town for the dead."

"Where is she now?" someone said after a while.

"At the morgue."

"And what's your boyfriend doing?" Pamela asked.

Bee's glance—a plea—flickered to Gillian and away. She folded her arms tightly across her chest.

No arguments, Gillian thought. Not now. "I believe he's spending most of the day in the chemistry labs," she said neutrally.

"So they don't have a clue about who killed her?" Irene asked.

"Well, it was someone who knew the labs pretty well."

"But hundreds of people study chemistry," Pat said. "Over the years, thousands of people go through that building."

"Exactly," Gillian replied. "They have to narrow it down."

"But who would do a thing like that?" Margaret said. "Was it someone who knew her?"

"Nobody knows."

"He knows—whoever he is," Irene said.

"Could it have been a lunatic?"

Gillian looked down, fiddling with her cup. "Maybe. It's not likely. Most people are murdered by people they know, not by crazed strangers. But those are statistics. Right now, anyone might have done it." She looked up again. "If it wasn't a stranger, if it was someone she knew, her friends might be the most likely people to figure out who."

"But we didn't know her that well," Pat protested. "We weren't close friends."

"I was her friend," Vicky said, upset.

"Of course, Vick," Bee said quickly. "You knew her much better than we did. But I liked her. We all did. She was interesting, and funny . . ." She trailed of. "I'd call her my friend. But I don't know much about her life. I couldn't begin to guess who killed her."

"Isn't that the police's job?" Margaret asked.

"The job of the police," said Pamela, "is to maintain the status quo."

"The job description includes catching murderers," Gillian said, unable to keep quiet. "Don't you want that done?"

"If the problem is violence, then I don't think the police are the solution. They're just another aspect of the problem, one that's legitimized by the state."

"In my view," Gillian replied, "we can't get on without them. If we didn't have police, we'd be living just like peasants in the fourteenth century—constantly murdered and robbed by private gangs of bandits. But look, you said you didn't know Wendy, and I never even met her. Let's not argue about the police. Let's just do whatever her friends want to do."

"Fair enough," said Pamela, descending from her high horse with a surprisingly good grace. She looked at Bee, whose hands, gripping her cup, were trembling. "What do you want to do, love?"

"I want to catch the bastard," Bee said.

"The sooner the killer is caught, the better," Pat said quietly. "If he gets away with it—"

"He-or-she?" Margaret put in.

"You needn't bend over backwards to be gender-neutral," Pamela said acidly. "Most murderers are men."

"If he gets away with it," Pat repeated, "he might kill someone else. But I don't think I have any pieces to contribute to the puzzle."

"What do we know?" Irene said thoughtfully. "Probably more than we suspect. Let's think about that."

There was a pause.

"Do you mind if I take a few notes?" Gillian asked.

The women silently shook their heads, except for Pamela, who folded her arms and looked studiously neutral. Gillian extracted a few file cards from her pocket and laid them quietly on the table. Vicky stared at them. She cleared her throat and raised her voice slightly. "I'll tell you what I know about Wendy. She comes—came—from Peterborough. Her parents still live there. They run a little antiques business. Nice people; I've met them. Too nice, Wendy sometimes said—the sort of people who always pointed out the flaws in a piece of furniture before they let you buy it. Her grandfather has a farm in Norfolk. She was pretty close to him, I think. They were all amazed when she became a scientist and very proud of her. She was an only child."

"Oh God," Pat and Irene said together. There was another short silence, as every one of them thought about what it would be like to lose a child that way.

Then Vicky went on. "She was at Emmanuel. She was top of her year in chemistry, she told me that. She stayed on to do a Ph.D. She must have been twenty-four or twenty-five when she finished. I asked her once whether she'd had any trouble with the faculty—been patronized by the men, I mean, or had her bottom pinched, or anything. She said nothing very bad had happened. Some of the students were worse than anyone who taught her. But she learned very fast not to hang back, she said. You had to be adversarial or be crushed. She did her post-doc, and then she got a research fellowship at King's—they'd been dead impressed by her Ph.D.; I remember how excited she was."

"She was very ambitious," Pat said. "That was the first thing one noticed about her."

"And successful. Research fellowships aren't easy to get," Margaret added.

There was a general murmur of assent.

"What about her other friends?" asked Irene. "What about lovers? Did she have any? I know her professional history—she told all of us about that, and I know a bit about her politics, but if she had a love life, she said bugger-all about it."

"There was a crowd she went round with when she was an undergraduate. A bit jolly hockeysticks for me, but they were all right, really," Vicky said. "She was turned on by athletes. I didn't meet her until her third year. We sang in the same choir. We had a lovely time with Rossini and Bach cantatas and parts of the B minor Mass. Then we went to a few concerts together. She liked modern music, composers like

Shostakovich. I'd never heard any. I still have a record she gave me of Shostakovich quartets."

"Did she play?" Gillian asked.

"Cello," Vicky said. "But not seriously after she left home. She played duets and trios now and then with a couple of students she knew. I don't believe she saw a lot of them, and I don't think she had any friends who were closer to her than I was. I could be wrong, of course. But, I don't know, she never said much about her personal life. When I was worried about something she would listen, and she sometimes came up with pretty good solutions, but she didn't say anything about what was happening to her. It puts a bit of a crimp in things when people are like that—you feel like a whinger—you're always the one with the problems. I think she was just the same with other people she knew. She was crazy about her supervisor, Bailey, but it was a professional relationship. She didn't tell him about her personal life."

"She was reserved," said Bee.

"How did she fit in with the PIS?" asked Gillian.

There was an uncomfortable pause. Vicky looked unhappy. Finally Irene said, "You've hit a sore point. She didn't fit in all that well, but it seems unfeeling to say so, or to criticize her now." She pushed back her bushy hair and it immediately fell forward again, curling over her cheek. She pushed it away with an irritable gesture. "And the truth is, we handled the matter very badly."

The others nodded. Pat groaned. "For a group with two therapists in it, we did *not* do well."

"I'll sum it up for you," said Bee, who had been quiet for a long while. "She had no trouble with the test itself, or trusting her results; one would expect a chemist to handle that end of it with aplomb. And she wasn't afraid of the responsibility. Sometimes new members are. They're afraid they won't have the right information if someone desperate comes in, or that the test will be iffy and they'll get it wrong. But Wendy had no qualms. That was fine; she borrowed the files and learned all the information really quickly. She was quite ready to take charge. The problem was different. She didn't understand our style—just didn't get it. And it's important."

"We're all agreed on that," Margaret said. Vicky nodded.

"It was partly little things," Margaret went on. "Things we do that she never noticed, like arranging the chairs so the customers have the most comfortable seats and don't have to squint at a bright light or be visible from the street."

"But it wasn't just those details. You see, a lot of the people who come to us are frightened," Irene said earnestly. "Especially the young ones. They're scared. They don't know who we are or what powers we have. Half our job is *not* to act like authorities who are going to scold them, or tell them what to do, or keep them in the dark. They have a desperate need for information, and they have to feel at ease enough to ask questions about really embarrassing topics like contraception and abortion and do their parents have to know. What we try to do is to empower them to choose for themselves. To give them the information and let them decide. It's *their* lives. That's what 'choice' means." Suddenly she looked embarrassed. "I'm sorry, Gillian. I forgot you know all this. I didn't mean to give you my potted intro. I'm rattled, I suppose. The point I was getting to was that Wendy couldn't stop being head prefect. She'd bully them about contraception for their own good, and when they were vague about their periods she'd get impatient. 'You don't know!' she'd snap. And she told them what to do sometimes. It's hard not to, when they're being, from our point of view, not very bright about it."

"It was sensible advice, of course, and given with their best interests at heart," Bee added.

"That's where we fell down," Pat put in. "We didn't tell her. We didn't come right out and say what was wrong."

"We tried," Margaret said.

"But only in our own way. Not in hers." Pat looked at Gillian and smiled ruefully. "We were exquisitely indirect. So as not to hurt her feelings, of course. We talked at our meetings about how to treat people, and how to ask questions, and where to sit, all in a general way. We never said we were talking about her. And she never took the discussions personally.

Apparently, it didn't occur to her that this aspect of our work was important, and she didn't change her behaviour one iota."

"We should have been blunt," Irene sighed.

"How?" Pat shook her head. "We talked about that. If we'd done it as a group, it would have seemed like a mass attack. And no one wanted to be the critic." She turned back to Gillian. "At first we thought she'd catch on, and then, when she didn't, it seemed too late to tell her she'd been doing it wrong all along. Too humiliating."

"So what were you going to do?" Gillian asked.

"That's the awful thing," Bee said. "This week Irene and I—as the two founding members—were finally going to talk to her about it. We were going to tell her what the group thought. And we were dreading it."

"I thought she might never forgive me," Vicky whispered, "since I'd brought her to the group. I felt like Judas."

"I'll make another pot of tea," Pamela announced, breaking the tension.

"Bee's right. We all liked her, you know," Irene said. "What happened wasn't her fault. We hadn't come up against the problem before and we've always operated so informally that we simply didn't have a way of proceeding when hints didn't work."

"Has there never been anyone else who didn't fit in?" Gillian asked, wonderingly.

"Yes, but they felt it too, and left. Wendy seemed oblivious."

"She lived in a man's world," Pamela said from the stove, where she was heating the kettle.

"What *about* men? Did she have lovers? Did she ever talk about them?" Gillian said.

"Not a dicky-bird," said Pat. "At least not to me."

"She had a boyfriend before she went to Canada," Vicky said. "They were together for a couple of years, but they broke up before she left."

"Is he still around?"

"I shouldn't think so. He was German; I expect he went back to Germany to study."

"What was his name?"

"Fritz. Fritz Eisenberg. He came from near the Swiss border. But you don't think—"

"I don't think anything."

"He was a nice bloke. A rower, but not one of the hearties." Vicky smiled slightly. "A big, broad-shouldered chap. Wendy once said that he had the most beautiful arse she'd ever seen."

"Was there anyone in Canada?"

Vicky shrugged. "No one serious, she said."

"And after she came back?" Irene asked. "Did she have someone this year?"

Vicky looked troubled. "Yes, but she never told me who. And it will be breaking her confidence to tell you what I do know. She told me last week that she was pregnant. Contraceptive failure, she said. She didn't want anyone to know while she was deciding what to do. I did get the impression from something she said that the man—the father—was another chemist at the lab, but I wasn't absolutely certain. She didn't mean to tell me who he was, so I couldn't ask. Anyhow, she spends her whole life at the lab these days, so how would she meet anybody besides chemists?"

"Was she going to have an abortion?"

"That was what really surprised me. She wasn't sure. She hadn't made up her mind. I think she was surprised herself, that she'd even consider having the child. It would have made no end of a mess of her career plans. She had to be prepared to work sixty-hour weeks for the next few years or forget about shooting for the top rank. And yet she still needed to think about her decision. She said she finally understood what the word 'choice' actually meant. It was painful, she told me. She knew being a single mother would completely bugger up her life, but she wanted to do it anyway." Vicky sighed. "She hadn't told the man yet. She was going to. I asked her what she thought he'd say. She was positive he'd insist she should have an abortion. She was going to ask him to take her to Addenbrooke's and drive her home afterwards if she did have one, but she thought he might refuse, so she asked me to go if he wouldn't."

"He's married." Irene and Gillian said it simultaneously.

"He also sounds like a bit of a swine," Pat commented.

"That's what I said," Vicky answered, "and Wendy said she knew it. Basically, he was a shit. But he was amazingly attractive, and since she didn't have to live with him, it didn't matter. Or hadn't, till now." She cast an appalled glance round the table. "Maybe he's the one."

NINE

Wendy's flat was in a little row of Tudor buildings directly across King's Parade from the chapel. A steep, narrow flight of stairs ascended between two shops to a miniature landing garlanded with post-Tudor electrical improvements. Wendy's flat, to the right, was directly over a men's clothing shop selling scarves, pale blue shirts, striped ties, dark socks and other accessories of college life. The bay window above the street looked directly at the east front of the chapel, which rose, grand and glorious, elaborate and stately, filling the entire view like the *Queen Mary* looming over a rowboat.

The morning sun was on it now; the golden stone was clean and sharp between green grass and blue sky.

"Blimey!" Edward exclaimed. "What a view!" Then he looked startled, as directly below his feet a voice said crossly, "Oh shut it, Reggie, it was only a kiss."

Edward looked down. The window projected slightly over the pavement, and just below a couple was quarrelling, the young woman walking ahead, her face already invisible, the young man hurrying behind, his head only a few feet from Edward's shoes. A cyclist beetled past, and then several more pedestrians, their footsteps clearly audible. Edward was enchanted. It was like a Shakespearean comedy, he thought: the grand royal drama of the chapel combined with the rude mechanicals skirmishing stage front.

Wendy's room was a pleasant one, sparsely furnished with a rolltop desk, a couple of chairs, a crammed bookshelf and a sofa covered in crumbling leather. The desk and sofa were probably gifts from her parents. They would be arriving later this morning. Edward was glad it wasn't his job to meet them.

Hardy pulled open a desk drawer. "We'll have to sift this lot, but I don't see anything personal here. Just chemistry journals and papers. Some notes and diagrams. All very tidy."

Edward came over and looked. The top was rolled nearly all the way back, the pigeonholes open for inspection. Keys, stamps, paperclips, receipts, a note of a journal loaned to "Simon," with the date, a recent letter from her mother, suggesting that she visit soon. The flat surface of the desk was stacked with journals and pages of cryptic handwritten notes, presumably Wendy's. The men moved on to the kitchen. It was placed behind the room that faced the street, in the interior of the building. The single window looked directly at another window a few feet away. Edward glanced out. More windows, above and below, were set unevenly in the walls of the pinched little rectangle. He could hear jazz playing somewhere above. A dim face appeared behind the window-panes directly across from him, a hand reached out, and the curtains closed.

Hardy was looking at the dishes in the sink. "Two plates," he said. "Two forks."

"Could they be the remains from different meals?"

"If they are, she ate the same thing for lunch and dinner."

"What did she eat?"

Hardy sniffed and opened the cupboard door below the sink. "Chinese takeaway. The cartons are still here. She didn't eat much, by the look of things."

"But according to the autopsy, she had some sort of meal a few hours before she died. This might have been it."

Edward opened the fridge. Milk, half a loaf of bread, apples, cheese, and a screw-top bottle of French wine. There was a small, flat box at the back. He reached in and drew it out, holding it by the edges. It was a pregnancy testing kit. "Well, she knew she was pregnant, or at least suspected it," he said. "How far along was she?"

Hardy came over to look. "Two months."

"She knew, then."

"Not a kit you can pop into Boots' for," said Hardy. "It must belong to the Pregnancy Information Service."

"The one she was supposed to bring on Saturday morning," Edward agreed.

"Bag it up, will you," Hardy said to his sergeant, who had followed them into the kitchen. They looked briefly into the tiny lavatory, which was just by the entrance to the flat. It was bare and clean.

"Not the most convenient of locations," Hardy commented, "unless you're in a hurry when you get home."

They squeezed into the adjacent bathroom.

"One towel," said Edward. "One flannel. One toothbrush. No his-and-hers." He opened the mirrored cupboard above the basin. "A diaphragm."

"Hmm," said Hardy. He picked up a small basket of rubbish. "Hullo." He tilted it towards Edward. Nestling among the tissues was a second toothbrush. "His?" he said.

The last room was the bedroom, on the other side of the kitchen. It was darker than the rest, its windows facing a wall only inches away. They walked over and looked out at a sliver of sky above, and several windows at steep angles above and below, affording narrow glimpses of stairs, a desk and chair, a lighting fixture.

"Not a hell of a lot of privacy here, is there?" Hardy said.

"What sort of digs was she in before? After a student residence a place like this would feel like Crusoe's island."

Hardy strolled over to the bed and twitched the coverlet up. "And here are Friday's footprints," he said.

A pair of men's slippers poked out from under the bedstead.

There was nothing else: no clothing in drawers or cupboards, no stray socks. The sheets were clean.

Edward cocked his head, contemplating the slippers. "A row, do you think? She told him to clear out?"

"And they forgot these."

"And the next item is to find their owner. It shouldn't be difficult; her friends will know who he is."

"The question is, was he here for the Last Supper?"

"I'll get a list of the neighbours. Someone may have seen him."

"Right," said Hardy, moving towards the door. "They might as well have been onstage," he added, responding to the same theatrical quality in the view that had struck Edward. They went down the stairs into the street, leaving the sergeant to collect the evidence and lock up.

On the way to the car, Hardy chuckled suddenly.

"What's funny?" Edward asked.

Hardy gave him an embarrassed grin. He looked swiftly about, and seeing no one within earshot, muttered, "I'll tell you, but you mustn't breathe a word, or I'll never live it down. It was the diaphragm that reminded me. Pandora tried one once." He chuckled again. "I'll never forget it. Never. I heard a shriek from the loo, so I rushed in, starkers of course, to see what was the matter, and there's Pan, doubled up on the floor laughing. What's up. I ask her, and she says she tried to put the thing in, and it shot out of her hand like a greased pig, right out of the window into the garden." He chortled happily. "The neighbour's garden."

"And what did you do?" Edward asked, picturing the diaphragm whizzing through the air like a tiny flying saucer, and Hardy, huge and bare, racing to the scene of the crime.

"Do? Pissed myself laughing. When I could stand up I asked her if she wanted me to crawl under the roses like Sherlock Holmes and find it, and she said by all means and what was I planning to say when the neighbours came out to see what I was doing? Then she said she was never going to touch the stupid thing again, so we left it."

Edward shouted with laughter. "Did the neighbours find it?"

"We don't know." Hardy leaned against the car. His eyes were wet. "Pan tried to watch them from behind the curtains the next time they were out gardening—she sat on the edge of the basin until her bottom was numb and then gave up." He gave a final snort. "They've never mentioned it."

It was late morning, and the street was full of passersby. They took little notice of the police in their civilian clothes, though one or two noticed the car and glanced curiously about in search of the explanation.

"It's back to the factory for me. Shall I drop you in Lensfield Road, then?"

Edward shook his head. "I'll walk. I don't know the town the way you do. Wendy Fowler must have done this walk a thousand times."

"Cheers, then. I'll see you there this afternoon."

Edward strolled through the King's gateway and stopped at the porter's lodge. Wendy had received her research fellowship from King's and had lived in rooms provided by the college. The bursar, who had already been informed of her death, would know something about her; he would also know who lived in the flats with windows that looked into hers. The porter rang the bursar, found him in and gave Edward directions.

Twenty minutes later, a list of names in his pocket but no wiser about Wendy the person—"a very talented young woman"—he left the college and crossed the street again. He stopped in the shop below Wendy's flat and had an unrewarding interview with the sales clerk. The shopkeepers to the north and south had nothing to tell him either. It was time to think about lunch. He walked south past St Catherine's and Botolph Lane. When he arrived at Pembroke

Street, he stopped. A stream of cars flowed noisily and continuously up Trumpington Street and round the corner towards Lion Yard. A competing torrent rushed in from Silver Street, while a counterflow of bicycles came out of Pembroke Street and squeezed alongside the cars or darted suddenly and precariously across the traffic. As he waited for an opening, he looked up Pembroke Street at the queue of cars and saw Gillian standing on the narrow pavement. Oddly, she seemed to be inspecting the wall. Beside him, a miniature old lady weighed down with shopping glared self-righteously at the traffic and stepped into the road. The driver of a black Saab stood on his brakes and she crossed, tortoise like, a foot in front of the bonnet.

Edward followed and caught up with Gillian just as she started to move away.

"What were you doing?" he asked. "Searching for the secret panel?"

"Looking at the stone. Isn't it beautiful? All golden-pink, like peaches. It used to be as black as a coal-bin. It must have cost them buckets of money to restore it. Too bad they don't ban traffic along this road."

"The shops would go," said Edward. "No car park, no customers."

"They didn't have to put it smack in the centre."

"They probably didn't expect the number of motorists to double every decade. Let's have lunch."

They went to the Granta, which at a few minutes to noon was not yet crowded, and took their plates outside to the row of tables overlooking the millpond. Ducks paddled gently along the reedy shoreline.

"I never asked you about your lecture yesterday. Was it good?"

"It was terrific. Basil has the gift. I'm glad I could be here."

She didn't say anything more. Edward surveyed her.

"You look a bit shipwrecked," he said gently. "How was your morning?"

"Exhausting. Too much emotion. Conflicting loyalties."

"Tell me," Edward said, biting into his meat pie.

Gillian fidgeted with her fork. "Everyone was appalled. That goes without saving. The group respected Wendy, and they liked her, too, but she didn't fit into the way they do things. Only one of them was a close friend of hers—Vicky. She brought Wendy into the group. They felt bad because recently they'd come to the miserably uncomfortable decision that she had to change her ways or quit the group." She stopped and drank some beer, looking out over the water. Edward waited. "They felt really rotten about it. The trouble was, Wendy was something of a juggernaut, I think. Terrific at organization, smart, bursting with energy. But her attention was fixed on concrete results, as I suppose it was—had to be—in her professional life, and she was insensitive to the process, which for the group mattered as much as getting results. She was just too madamy, particularly with the teenagers."

"I don't quite understand. Can you give me a specific example? It would be helpful, because I haven't much of a handle on who she was. All I've got so far is a university answering machine that repeats 'talented young woman.'"

"All right. Why does the group exist? To help women make informed choices about their own bodies instead of being kept in ignorance and told what to do by 'professionals.' The test tells the woman whether she's pregnant or not, but if you then tell her what to do, or treat her like a fool, then you've given her the fact but you haven't made it any easier for her to think for herself. If you act like an authority and are accepted as one, then you haven't done the job properly. Take that business about names. It's one thing to introduce yourself—'I'm Bee'—and ask whether a customer minds giving her first name or an initial, but it's quite another to remain anonymous yourself and say briskly, 'Now then, what's your name?' sounding like Nanny. Wendy set up her interviews like a paternalistic doctor with a patient—precisely what the group wanted *not* to do, as a matter of principle."

"Why didn't they tell her?"

"They tried to—indirectly—so they wouldn't seem like an examining board with a failing candidate. It didn't work."

Edward shook his head, bemused. "I'm trying to imagine what it would be like to run the police force along those lines." He laughed. "It's impossible."

"But you complain about how rigid it is—the hierarchy, the authoritarianism. The PIS group is trying to keep away from that."

"I think hierarchy is natural. Like murder, it will out. The police just have too much of it. What else did you learn about Wendy?"

"I took notes for you. One item of undoubted interest: she was pregnant, and nobody, not even her friend Vicky, knows who the father is."

"Nobody?" he said sharply. "Not even a guess?"

"A guess, yes. He's probably in the chemistry department and almost certainly married."

"The secrecy?"

"That, and she asked Vicky to stand by in case she chose to terminate the pregnancy and the father wouldn't help with the arrangements."

"Was she in love with him?"

"I think their chemistry was physical."

"Organic, surely?" Edward said, grinning at her.

"Depending on which organs. Leave out the heart. Anyhow, it wasn't theoretical, or she wouldn't have been pregnant."

He shuffled through Gillian's notes. "One, who is he? Two, did Wendy tell him? Three, when? Four, did his wife know? Five, six, pick up sticks. I'd better go. Hardy will be wondering where I've got to. I'm due in Lensfield Road." He drained his pint. "Not that anyone there will divulge which wayward husband has been in bed with the talented young woman."

TEN

Arriving at the door of the chemical labs, Edward gave a mighty heave and lurched backwards as it swung past his nose. Today the door moved for mere mortals. Why had it been so heavy the last time, then? What had been the matter with it? His mind darting automatically down the trail, he tried to invent a connection between the murder and the door's peculiar behaviour. Nothing occurred to him.

Before going upstairs to find Scudder, he stopped at the accounts office and took a look at the register which was normally left at the front door. All those working out of hours were supposed to sign in and out and note the room in which they would be working. A safety measure, he'd been told: in the event of fire, the building's occupants would be found more quickly. The building was rarely empty in the evenings, he saw, turning the pages. But the corridors weren't exactly thronged with chemists. On Friday night, twenty people had signed in, and nineteen had signed out. Wendy Fowler had signed in at 7:40. She had written in a room number on the third floor. Probably the lab above Hill and Scudder's offices. Judging by their room numbers, none of the others had been working on the same floor. They worked late; only half had signed out before eleven. Scudder's name wasn't on the register, Edward noted, although he'd been in the building until half past seven. He ran his eye over Saturday's scanty list and closed the book.

He particularly wanted to see Wendy's office and her laboratory bench, but he also needed a more general picture: a diagram of Wendy's world. Like the rest of the inhabitants, she would have used the building according to her own pattern, probably appearing in the same places at regular intervals and using the same paths between them again and again. She hadn't used the cold room regularly; no one did. So the murderer could not have expected to find her there. He had to have brought her from elsewhere in the building, or have had the eccentric luck to be present when she went in for reasons that Edward had yet to discover. The fibres Hardy had mentioned indicated that she had been brought. If he could discover where she had been when she was attacked, he might also find useful evidence. Had Hardy's men found the sack, he wondered. Several had been sent to look for it this morning.

He wandered in the general direction of Scudder's office, noticing a peculiar hollow roaring sound. He'd heard something like it before. In the underground, that was it. The wind of a distant train thrumming in the tiled passageways. It was louder in some places than others, almost pressing on his ears. Had Wendy Fowler ever worried about being here alone late at night? The small number of names in the register conjured an image of desolate corridors like the long empty platforms of deserted tube stations.

Before knocking on Scudder's door, he checked the police tape across the entrance to the recess where the cold room was situated. A steady, ear-splitting whine came from a fan at the back of the recess. Across the hall, in a narrow room jammed with big bottles full of chemicals, a man stood behind a bench, facing Edward. Directly in front of him, a flame rose straight up in a brilliant column, perhaps a foot high. The man held a lump of glass on the end of a pipe and Edward watched, momentarily transfixed, as he blew into the other end of the pipe, and the glass, suspended above the flame, swelled delicately into an airy hollow like a transparent melon. Nearby, chemicals were bubbling and hissing in big glass flasks. Edward found himself thinking of Merlin and then of

Paracelsus. The tableau gave off a whiff of sorcery, despite its modern institutional surroundings.

Edward turned away reluctantly and walked on, noting the open stairwell and the students huddled over desks at the bottom. At the end of the corridor, a huge vat of liquid nitrogen rested in a corner; it was bigger than his hot water tank at home. The door at the end of the hall was standing wide; he stepped inside and saw an enormous laboratory filled with row upon row of benches. Students, some in white lab coats and some in street clothes, moved about or hovered over steaming flasks. An extraordinary din bombarded his ears. He steadied himself against it, as if leaning into a wind. A chattering, humming, rushing sound filled the air as water squirted from taps, and pumps sucked the air from desiccators. Little clouds of steam rose here and there. People shouted over rattling machinery, while several telephones were ringing at once. Edward could smell ether and something acrid. At the front of the room, seemingly oblivious of the racket and reek, a thickset, red-faced middle-aged man with immense ears sat at a desk marking a stack of papers. Edward withdrew and retraced his steps along the corridor, glancing at the glass-blower as he went by. He was now deftly drawing a slender neck, like a stem, from one end of the glass melon.

Scudder was waiting, his door open. He took Edward straight to Wendy's office at the front of the building.

"In the ordinary way, you see, she wouldn't have this

office. We're far too short of space. But Reg Bailey—she was in his group—is away this term, and he suggested she could use it. She's keeping an eye on his students until he gets back."

"Who has keys?" Edward asked, looking about. The room was different from Scudder's office, smaller, containing the usual academic clutter of books and papers, but lacking a fume cupboard and sink. A few glass vessels with tubes sticking out in all directions stood on a shelf, and the floor was crowded with cardboard boxes of files. A piece of flexible plastic hose snaked across one of the two desks.

Scudder shrugged. "Wendy, and Reg Bailey, who will of course have kept his own set. The custodian. There are probably other sets, but I have no idea where they are. You could ask the secretary of the department. It may not matter, though; lots of us don't lock our doors during the day—only when we go home at night."

"She would have locked her handbag in her desk, I suppose," Edward said, examining the drawers. They are locked.

Scudder squinted, remembering. "I don't think she carried one, at least not regularly. You're quite right, though, she would have locked it up. The secretaries are careful with theirs."

"Where did she do most of her work?"

"At her bench upstairs. She had her own bench in the lab with the students she was shepherding in Bailey's absence. She would have used the computer

here, as well. I don't know how she divided her time."
He looked at the printer. "There's a pile of print-out
here. A draft of her paper for the Oxford meeting, by
the look of it."

They locked the door behind them and went
along the corridor towards the stairs. A figure like a
devil's dairymaid materialized briefly and vanished
into a lab, bearing two smoking buckets. Edward's
head turned, following the apparition.

"Liquid nitrogen," Scudder said, matter-of-fact.
"It's in continual use. Oh!" He stopped, turned about
and opened a door. "Let me show you what I meant
about the space between the floors."

Behind the door, a dim, dirty space housed an out-
size galvanized metal duct. A cluster of fat pipes, like
part of a monstrous organ, hung overhead. A metal
ladder climbed the wall behind the duct.

"Those steps give access to the space between the
floors," Scudder said.

"There are more access points elsewhere in the
building, I suppose," Edward yelled over the noise of
another motor.

"Yes, of course."

The motor shut off with a sudden gasp. Edward
climbed the ladder in the interval of silence and
looked. A dusty space receded quickly into darkness;
pipes bulged dimly, as huge as mythical serpents. He
could see little in the dark, and he waited for his eyes
to adjust.

"You could crawl a long way up there," Scudder's voice said from below.

"A long way," Edward repeated. He could hear the largeness of the space in his own voice quality. Something glinted palely a couple of feet from his nose. He climbed another step and leaned. He could just see it in the dull light that welled up through the hatch. It was nothing to get excited about—merely an empty can of Diet Coke. He left it where it was and climbed down. The motor whined viciously, and they hurried out and shut the door behind them.

Scudder led the way upstairs. There was no one in the lab when they arrived.

"This is where Wendy was working on Friday afternoon," Scudder said. "I saw some students this morning who said she came in after tea and told them her experiment wasn't behaving properly."

"When was that?" Edward asked.

"About half past four. I believe she told them something rather peculiar had happened to it. This is her bench."

He went towards a bench in the middle of the lab. Edward stopped in the doorway, taking in the details of the room. It was the size of a conventional classroom, with four large windows. Venetian blinds, half shut, allowed slatted sunlight in to mingle with the cold glow of the fluorescent tubes overhead. There were nine long benches worn and stained by years of use and littered with equipment. Most were in great disorder, but Wendy's was noticeably neater than the rest. Rows of flasks were drying upside down on racks. Between the benches, the wooden floor was blotched and blackened. A cylinder of compressed argon gas stood on a dolly. The fridge was covered with postcards. He was conscious of noise again. The fridge hummed loudly, accompanied by the clickety-clack of a small motor on one of the benches. A faint roar like a distant motorway throbbed in the background although the windows were closed.

"A little dilapidated, isn't it?"

"This was the first part of the labs to be built; it's nearly forty years old now. Time-worn, you could say. The fume cupboards aren't up to modern standards, but it would cost five million pounds to put a new system in, so it won't be done unless somebody's poisoned. Most of these are communal benches; that's why they're so messy," Scudder said.

They looked at Wendy's bench.

"Can you tell me anything about this?" Edward asked, inspecting the apparatus.

"Hmm, yes. The students were telling me about it this morning. She was using a rotary evaporator to boil off the ether. That's this apparatus here. The rotary evaporator only heats the flask to 50 or 60 degrees Centigrade. Then she was going to transfer the residue to a distillation flask. But there was too much liquid left; she seemed to think there was at least as much as when she had checked it previously, before she left the lab for tea. So she took a closer look." Scudder hesitated, digging the knuckles of one hand into the palm of the other. "Oh dear. I'm afraid this is going to be troublesome. Apparently she smelt a rat. She took an NMR spectrum and got what she said was an inexplicable result, given the experiment she was doing. From what the students told me, I'd have to agree."

"Could she have made an error?"

"Of course." Scudder was emphatic. "It's *the* most likely explanation, even if it was the second time something had gone wrong. She'd been doing a long series of distillations, so there may well have been a mix-up. She would have been very annoyed, too, because she'd have had an awful lot of work to re-do it."

There was a flask in the rotary evaporator.

"Would this have been the one she was using?"

"I should think so. She began to repeat the experiment that same evening."

Edward thought. Wendy had been working at this bench after tea; perhaps this was the last place anyone had seen her. A day had elapsed since the body had been discovered, enough time for someone to come in and clean up any traces he might have left. But he might have wanted to make himself scarce. Forensics should have a go at the bench.

A telephone near the door rang, startling him. Scudder ignored it.

"Who might have tampered with her work?" Edward asked.

"No one, I hope," Scudder replied. He was distressed. "But, well, students do occasionally indulge in absurd pranks. If anyone has done so in this case, he'll be very reluctant to come forward now."

"I'd like to use the telephone," Edward said, moving towards it.

"That's not an outside line," Scudder said. "Use the one in my office."

Edward rang Hardy at the station and learned that he was on his way to Lensfield Road. He left word that there was more work for the forensics team and returned to Wendy's lab to wait for Hardy.

"I could have a look at her notes, if you like," Scudder said. "To see if she recorded anything about the experiment going awry."

"Thank you. That might be useful, but forensics should have a go at this lot first. By the way," Edward went on, contemplating Wendy's apparatus, "who's the glass-blower downstairs? He's rather mesmerizing."

"That's the floor technician. He's very talented. We were lucky to get him."

Just then two young men strolled in. They nodded to Scudder and looked curiously at Edward.

"Oh good," Scudder said. "These are the two I talked to this morning. Simon, Nick, this is a police officer from Scotland Yard. Detective Chief Inspector Gisborne. Tell him what you told me about Wendy's experiment."

"It was after tea. She said something had gone

wrong with it," the shorter and darker of the two said. "She went on about there being too much liquid left. Then she hinted that we might have added some— for a joke, you know. And we teased her about it."

"And did you add anything?" Edward asked.

"That wouldn't be funny. Simon and I thought she was, er, a bit over the top, you know, but then she took an NMR sample, and she was right, there was something very odd about it."

Simon had said nothing so far. Edward looked at him. He was fair, with brown eyes, slightly over-weight. His hair was long and shaggy, hanging over his eyebrows.

'Over the top? Why did you think so?"

Simon looked down, not meeting Edward's eyes. "We thought she'd made a mistake and didn't want to admit it," he muttered. "She'd just flooded the offices down-stairs again, and she was going on about the bag, too."

"Which bag?" Edward wanted to know.

"The water bag that split."

"Where is it now?" Edward asked.

"She kept it. She put it in that box under her bench, I saw her." He looked up swiftly. "I thought she was daft. Was her—her death really not an accident?"

"I'm afraid not." Edward lifted the lid of the box and glimpsed folded clear plastic inside. He made a note to have it collected.

"What did she say about the bag?" Scudder asked suddenly.

"She thought someone might have tampered with it, too."

Scudder looked startled. "Did she? What an extraordinary idea!"

Edward pressed on. "Do you know what she did with the chemicals? The ones that made her suspicious? Did she chuck them?"

Simon and Nick looked at each other. "I don't think so," Nick answered. "I don't know what she did with the flask after she took her sample, but I know she was going to use a new bottle of ether when she repeated the experiment."

"When did you last see her?"

"At about six. She went off somewhere. For dinner, I expect. She was coming back. She said she was going to work at her bench all night if she had to. But we left."

"At about half six," Simon said. "We went to the pub."

Neither knew where Wendy had gone.

Edward paced off the distance between the bench and the door, looking carefully at the floor.

Hardy appeared in the doorway, the station having passed Edward's message to him over the radio. "Forensics are on their way," he said. "What've you got?"

"A brace of witnesses. You'll want to hear this. Wendy Fowler was probably here most of Friday evening."

"You won't be needing me?" Scudder said, looking at his watch.

"Not just now," Edward replied. "We'll be here for a bit. Can we find you in your office later?"

"Yes, yes, or somewhere about. I'll be in the building." Scudder nodded and sped off down the corridor.

Edward took the two students through their story again. They spoke more freely in Scudder's absence.

"She asked us if anyone could have spoilt her work for a laugh," Nick said. "We thought it was a load of rubbish. There's—there was—a sort of joke going round, see. She was called the Sorcerer's Apprentice because of the floods. We feel like right bastards now, because we took the mickey out of her."

"And when you took the mickey, how did she react?"

"She was a good sport," Simon said miserably. "She laughed and told us to sod off."

Hardy sent them away. "You'll get your lab back later."

"Nothing on the sack yet," he said to Edward. "The building's a proverbial bloody haystack. Rubbish everywhere."

"It's a funny place, isn't it? More like an old factory than anything else."

"Did you go in by the same door today? Christ. I came near to decking my sergeant, it opened so much quicker than yesterday."

Edward grinned. "It caught me on the hop, too. Where is the good sergeant?"

"Having a chat with the lads who are looking for

the sack. If he can find them in this rabbit warren, that is."

They exchanged news. Hardy had a list of the people who admitted being in the building on Friday night. There were about thirty. Half again as many as had signed the book. Most of them were students or post-graduate researchers who had been running spectra on the NMR machines on the bottom floor. Most of them had already been interviewed, and so far none had seen Wendy after six on Friday evening. None of them had seen anyone wandering about with a large burlap sack. But then none of them had admitted to being on the third floor where Wendy's lab was, or to having business in the cold room. And no one had noticed anything odd.

"But then, as one of the chaps said, he isn't always certain of what's odd at three o'clock in the morning."

"And it's a big building."

When the forensics team arrived, Edward explained that, based on the register and the information offered by the students, the lab was the most logical place for the killer to have found Wendy and attacked her. He asked them to go over her bench and the path between her bench and the door, even though the path, at least, had already been contaminated by Simon and Nick, not to mention Scudder and himself. Then he and Hardy left them to it and toured the rest of the building with Scudder. They went up to the tea-room on the fourth floor, where the beige formica tables were empty, waiting for tea-time, and down to the shabby little student lounge in the basement with its hell's antechamber gloom and stink of dead cigarettes. They trod numerous and similar corridors from end to end, climbed stairs, rode up and down in lifts. The interior corridors were disorienting, like a maze of tunnels, despite the simple U-shape of the building. They inspected the library, a long room with a door at each end and rows of bound journals crammed into rank upon rank of towering shelves equipped with ladders reaching to their upper tiers. The silence was a relief. Elsewhere, machinery reigned: rattling, banging, humming, whining, tended by its keepers or standing alone in costly idleness.

"Will we get the bends when we go back upstairs?" Edward said, somewhere on the lower floors, trudging past metal leviathans penned behind interior windows like wonders of the deep, his submarine sensations reinforced by the dim light, the odd sense of pressure in the air and the continual low roaring sound like water in his ears.

"The building's bigger than I realized," Hardy said as they wearily climbed the stairs again.

"It is big," Scudder said, "but even so, it's not big enough."

"This is even worse than the station," Hardy commented, inspecting a dusty pile of old equipment. No cranny was unoccupied. Students were working in a tiny little room on the roof although it could be reached only by a set of claustrophobic, ladder-like stairs. There was even someone working on the roof itself, setting up a telescope.

"Atmospheric spectroscopy," Scudder said briefly, seeing their puzzled glances.

The nearby streets and rooftops of Cambridge lay spread beneath them. Hardy's eyes swept over the expanse. He wiped his brow. "A lot of ground to cover," he muttered.

"But if you're thinking of Wendy's patterns, you should be able to eliminate large sections of the labs," Scudder replied. "She would have spent her time in the south arm of the building; there wouldn't have been many reasons for her to go and see the physical chemists or the theoretical chemists. Like most of us, she would have had a rabbit run—office, lab, NMR machine, tea-room, library—round and round."

Back inside, Scudder darted through the open door of a handy lab and sat down at an empty desk. He sketched a diagram for them, showing which chemists occupied which parts of the building. The shorter and lower arm of the labs, the arm closest to Lensfield Road, was occupied by the physical chemists, while the theoretical chemists huddled at the bottom of the U, near the tea-room and the library. The organic chemists shared the larger south arm with the inorganic chemists, the huge undergraduate labs and the biochemical suite. A new structure, wrapped round a stub of the old and still under construction, was the exclusive domain of the crystallographers.

"All right. But she wasn't found on her rabbit run."

"No. But the cold room is in her part of the building, very near her office and one floor below her lab."

The lab was nearly empty. At the far end a young woman in a white lab coat was inspecting a piece of glassware, holding it up to the light. An unshaven student at the nearest bench was hunched over an *Aliens* comic, his distillation burbling beside him like a contented pigeon. He looked at them curiously, then went back to his reading.

On their return leg they stopped outside the closed door of Roger Hill's office and reviewed Scudder's version of the row he had had with Wendy. They also checked the nearby lab in which Bottomley had been when he listened to them. It overlooked a car park and a low cluster of buildings that housed a girls' school. Bottomley wasn't there.

"Was something the matter with the front door on Sunday?" Edward asked, abruptly remembering the mystery as they finished their tour at the entrance to the building. "It was much easier to open it today."

Scudder gave a sudden crack of laughter. "Oh, that. The make-up air supply is turned off at the weekend. You see, the fume cupboards are constantly sucking air out of the labs, along with the fumes, you know, and during the week we have big fans blowing fresh air in.

That's the roaring noise you hear. But when they're off, at night and at weekends, there's nothing to counteract the pull of the cupboards. I'm afraid the doors are sucked shut. He raised his eyebrows in comical dismay. "Some people can't get them open at all. It's embarrassing." He checked his watch. "Must go. Let me know if there's anything more I can do."

He scuttled off, murmuring something about a meeting.

Edward inspected the doors. "What a peculiar place this is. Mysterious floods, poisons everywhere—"

"Closets to freeze corpses in," put in Hardy.

"—Trick doors—it's like a fun house for detectives. I'm glad to have that ruddy door explained before I began weaving an elegant theory about it at five o'clock in the morning."

"News from headquarters. You have the Yard's blessing," Hardy said as they ambled back to Wendy's office. "Cutter's tickled. Wants to see you."

"How's Cutter getting on?"

"Getting on is just it. His back's been bothering him more and more lately. He's talking about retiring."

"But he's hardly fifty!"

"Fifty-four this year. And he's been a copper thirty-five years. Been running the shop for the past six. I hope he hangs on. He's a good boss. If he goes, I don't know where we'll be. Like as not, the next chap'll be dead keen on accounting. We'll all be running spread sheets on the computer while chummy's laughing."

"I'll go along and see him tonight."

"Do that. Bring him up to date."

Hardy had brought Wendy's keys. He unlocked her desk and opened the drawers. In the deep bottom drawer on the right, they found a sealed flask, with a small quantity of clear liquid in the bottom.

ELEVEN

Gillian and Murray ate dinner alone that evening.

"So this is what it's like?" Murray asked, passing the salad.

"The worst part is dinner," Gillian said, helping herself to a large plateful. "I grew up with the notion that having dinner together was the heart of family life. You sat around the table all together, you ate, you told stories, you discussed the issues of the day. If I have dinner alone, then so far as I'm concerned, I'm living alone."

"Is he gone that often?"

"All the time. Except when I'm only here for a week or so. Then he tries very hard to clean up his act. But the amount of overtime they do in the Metropolitan

CID is unbelievable. A seventy-hour week is normal for Edward."

"So what do you do about dinner?"

Gillian laughed. "Oh well, we've been through a number of phases. There was the very early, short-lived phase, when I didn't realize that no dinner was the rule rather than the exception. So I'd buy lots of lovely things and put together some divine boeuf bourguignon or whatever, and keep it hot till all hours. Then he'd stagger in at eleven o'clock and be too tired to eat, or he'd have had a pizza at nine and I'd want to kill him. Then I suggested that we cook together on weekends, but that was an utter disaster. Half the time he just wasn't there, and I'd have to do all the work or let the food go to waste. Frankly, he doesn't care enough about it to cook. He loves *eating* good food, but he'll open a tin rather than think in the kitchen. So now I cook my own dinners, and he eats on the fly. When he has an evening free, we go out for dinner."

"But he usually sleeps at home?"

"Oh yes. It's not a twenty-four-hour-a-day job, at least not most of the time. That part's fine. It's just that I'm hooked on my dinner ritual. Without that, it feels as if we're room-mates."

"You could have pizza by candlelight."

"Or beans on toast? Ugh. I have to have real food."

"How about a breakfast ritual instead?"

"Murray, what planet are you on? Leisurely breakfasts? Stop trying to solve this as if it were a chemistry problem."

Murray laughed and poured her some wine. "Well it is one, isn't it, if you can't talk to anybody without your enzymes chewing on some high-priced protein."

"Not to mention lubrication with alcohol. Anyhow, you told me that one of the reasons you broke up with Marilyn was that you couldn't ever have dinner with her."

"But she didn't spend the night, either. She went home to her husband and children. You're not going to break up with Edward, are you?"

"No, no. I'm not thinking about that. But I don't quite see where to go from here. We've been together for twelve years, if together is the right word. But continental commuting isn't easy. Every time I leave, it's a misery. But could I live with him and his bloody job all year round? I don't know. I can't decide. And then there's the question of my job. God knows, Murray, after last year I could kiss UPNW goodbye with pleasure. I love London. Maybe I could find a job if I pushed hard enough. Not a great job, but something I could live with for a while. I think about it in Vancouver when I miss him. But then I come over and spend a few weeks or months dining with the reality, and I think: for this I should give up the life I've made for myself? Cut my pay by two thirds?" She swallowed some wine. "That's a high price-tag for a sex life."

"Come on. It's not just a sex life."

"No. You're right. I'm just cross."

"But do you actually have to go somewhere from here—change what you've been doing? The distance must have been what you both wanted, or your affair would have fallen apart years ago."

"True. Changing it might be a disaster."

"What you and Edward are doing, it's modern romance, right? Your problem is the natural outcome of the feminist programme. Two careers, two lives."

"The problem with my modern romance is not feminism, it's airplanes. They're just not fast enough. It feels like such a lot of work to get here, and then I'm here, and we can't even have a goddamned holiday."

"But Gillian, Wendy's dead. Killed."

"I know that. I sound heartless, don't I? I'm not, really. I'm glad Edward's working on the case. I want him to catch the murderer. Of course I do. It's just that with his job, that argument is *always* applicable. There's always someone who's dead."

They ate their pasta in silence for a moment or two.

"Besides," Gillian added, "I'm not so sure he'd really like it if I lived here. How can I tell? How can he tell? It certainly wasn't his idea in the past."

"People change."

"Yes. But I don't know that he's changed that much. What was it like at the labs today?" she asked, changing the subject.

"All shaken up. Everyone was talking about the murder all day: where she was found and who was in the building on the weekend, and whodunit, of course."

"Any ideas?"

"Nothing specific. The 'outsider' theory is the most popular, as you might expect."

"You mean someone who's not part of the chemistry department."

"Exactly."

"But they don't think some mad stranger just wandered in and whacked her on the head, do they?"

"Not quite. I think most people tend to believe it was someone from another part of her life. Maybe even someone who followed her from Canada."

"A mad lumberjack, I suppose."

Murray smiled. "Ha. Well, it couldn't be a Mountie. That would never do."

"Wasn't there any gossip at all about people within the department?"

"A little. I don't know that many chemists here, remember. And they may have been cautious because I'm a visitor."

"And from Canada," Gillian said mockingly.

"Yes, it's a good thing Edward is staying here. When the lynch mob comes, he can shoot them."

"He doesn't carry a gun. Anyhow, what was the little bit of gossip you heard?"

"Roger Hill had it in for her. He's a passable scientist with an office on the floor below her lab."

"What sort of man is he?"

"The sort who calls you a poofter if you don't guffaw at his dirty jokes. Has a nasty temper. After a bag in her lab burst and the water flooded his lab, he told Ron Bottomley he was going to get rid of her. Bottomley's told everybody else."

"Get rid of her?" Gillian echoed. "That's—do people think he announced he was going to murder her?"

"No, no—rid the department of her."

"Could he?"

"No. He was just ranting. Bailey was her supervisor. He got her the research fellowship, and he's a much bigger fish than Hill. Those fellowships are hard to get, but once you've got one, you have to do more than spill a bag of water to lose it. Anyway, the story's more complicated than that. Bottomley's the one who really hates Wendy. And he's the one who started calling her the Sorcerer's Apprentice."

"The floods?"

"Right. But he wasn't flooded. His animosity has to do with Wendy's research. She got some extra funding for her project, which gave her the opportunity to do work that others couldn't—gave her an edge that made some people—including him—jealous. And she was moving into an area very close to his. He's been doing some similar work in chiral recognition, and he thought she was mining his claim."

"Chiral recognition—I don't know what that is."

"You don't need to. It's the hot new thing in organic chemistry. When she got the money Bottomley had a fit. He told several people that she'd stolen his ideas and used them to apply for the financing."

"Did anyone take him seriously?"

"Nah. He got the brush-off. He's not much liked. And Scudder told me he's always been a bit paranoid that way. Wouldn't tell anybody what he was working on until he'd finished—you know the sort of thing. Now he claims to be doing a book, I hear, but his colleagues seem dubious. Anyway, his accusations about Wendy are idiotic. I know Wendy picked up her lead when she was working in Vancouver, because I remember talking with her about it then. Bottomley may have been thinking about using alkaloids too, but, if so, he hasn't done much about it."

"Still, it would have been galling for him to see Wendy getting money and pushing ahead with the research. Do you think it can have anything to do with her murder?"

"All that happened in the fall. It's hard to believe he would stew for half a year and then do her in. He hasn't said anything about the subject for months. And he's a pale crooked little guy, like a frog. It's hard to picture him attacking her. Murder seems too physical."

"A pale little guy like a frog? If you tell me he subscribes to *Mercenary* and lives with his mother we might as well call Edward and tell him to swear out a warrant."

"I haven't got a clue. He could be a bigamist with ten children."

"Only if he's married to two stockbrokers or moonlights as a bank robber. Bigamy's too expensive for academics, like other forms of excess. We're doomed to lives of moderation. Have some more wine."

"It's so odd that we were sitting here talking about Wendy before anyone knew she was dead," Murray said, picking up his glass. "Small world, I guess." He paused. "Your friend Bee seems kind of armour-plated."

"Not when you get to know her."

"That wouldn't be easy. Does she have an extra British chromosome?"

"She's a sceptic where men are concerned. She doesn't let down her guard easily."

"I had that part figured. Wasn't she married once?"

"Yes. To Toby. A physicist. He's still around. He's remarried, Bee says, to a teeny-tiny, beautiful nurse from Thailand."

Edward came in late in the evening. Murray had gone to bed, so Gillian told Edward the gossip about Hill and Bottomley. She poured whisky into a glass and handed it to him. "You look beat."

"It's been a long day. I'm cream-crackered."

"Any progress?"

"The information's coming at us like snow in a blizzard." He swallowed some whisky and pulled off his shoes. "But it doesn't point in any single direction. I wish it did. We don't want any complications, thank you, not with this kind of case."

"What do you mean?"

"I mean it's the kind of case that we have to solve ASAP. As in nail it in twenty-four hours, not next week. Decent middle-class young woman, well-educated, brilliant future, distraught parents. And it happened at Cambridge. *In* the university. Did you see the papers today? We can't lock it up fast enough." He swirled the liquid in his glass. "So what can we say about Hill and Bottomley? Sounds like a dodgy accounting firm. Summary: Hill doesn't like women much; but if we sent men to jail for disliking women, how many Englishmen would be free? Don't answer that. He's a boor and has a bad temper. It's a start, but we need something concrete if we're going to devote any time to him. Bottomley sounds more promising. Say he's a bit past it, probably turns up his nose at female chemists. Then he has a hot idea, fame and fortune coming his way, but he's pipped at the post by young Wendy Fowler. He thinks she stole his intellectual property; probably imagines everybody's laughing at him. I'll double-check the interviews, but I think he has no alibi for Friday night. He could have been at the lab. What do you think? Will it get up and walk?"

"Check out the money. She had funding. If he tried to get money and couldn't, and then she got it, he could be very resentful."

"All right. We've got a jealous colleague and a phantom lover, so far. I wonder who else will turn up on the list."

"A psychotic Canadian."

Edward laughed. "Why?"

Gillian explained. "It's a good thing the Yard is billeted on Murray, he says, or he'd be suspect number one in the department."

"He wasn't in love with her, was he?"

Gillian was disconcerted. "No. He wanted to be, maybe. He told you himself that he asked her out and she said no."

"Do you think he was angry about it?"

"Rueful, that's all. Edward, what are you asking me for?"

"Nothing. Pursuing loose ends, that's all. It's a habit."

"Murray is not a loose end. He's been a close friend for almost twenty years."

"Was he ever your lover?"

"Am I still helping the police with their inquiries? No, he wasn't. I had just broken up with Michael when I met him. I was still in rehab. Then he fell in love and got married. By the time he was divorced, we'd been friends too long."

"What are you so tense about?" Edward drained his glass. "You like this sort of chat, usually."

"Interrogation isn't a chat. I like it if you're curious about me—not if you're asking me about my past because it's your job."

Edward rubbed his forehead tiredly. "Actually, I didn't mean it that way, that last question. I *was* curious, suddenly. But it didn't sound like that. Sorry."

"Me too." She poured herself a couple of fingers of

whisky. "Nightcap?"

He held out his glass.

"Have you found anything definite yet?"

"A sack. A constable found it this afternoon, in a heap of rubbish on the construction site."

"A sack?"

"She was carried in it."

On Tuesday morning Gillian went to the university library. Edward was at the police station with Hardy. It was the last day of his "holiday," and he would be working at least until seven. But if nothing broke, he said, he'd come back for dinner. Gillian had heard that before; she was making no plans. She hadn't expected to do much research this first week, what with settling in London and then rushing off to Cambridge for the lecture series, not to mention plans for Edward's intended time off. She'd brought all her materials, however, her chapters and her notes: she was equipped for long-term survival in the stacks of the UL.

She worked until three and then walked across Queen's Road and along the Backs to Silver Street. Bee and Pamela were waiting on the riverbank near the bridge, where a flotilla of punts, rentable by the hour, was moored.

"I'm going punting tomorrow if the weather holds," Gillian had told Edward as they went upstairs to bed.

"I thought you couldn't punt."

"Not well, but Pamela's an expert."

"She would be. I hope her pole gets stuck in the mud."

"There shouldn't be too many youthful enthusiasts thudding from bank to bank," Pamela said, shoving off towards the middle of the river. "Lectures aren't over."

The empty punts along the bank jiggled gently in the slow current. Gillian looked back and then settled against the cushions as Pamela found her rhythm and they moved upstream. The tourists on the bridge stopped to watch their stately progress. Gillian ignored them. In her sunglasses and a floppy-brimmed hat borrowed from Bee, she felt anonymous enough not to mind being part of a spectacle.

"We go for a punt nearly every year at about this time—whenever the early burst of summer comes—if it does come," Bee said. "I was going to give it a miss this week; I thought I couldn't enjoy it, but Pamela said Wendy wouldn't come back to life because we stayed at home, and we'd regret it if the weather turned foul later."

She was leaning back beside Gillian in the bottom of the punt, her legs stretched out towards the stern, where Pamela towered above them, squinting at the sparkling water, the long pole sliding upwards through her hands. They glided past a mixed flock of ducks, mallards and pigeons, between grassy banks where Coe Fen spread out behind the Fitzwilliam

Museum. Bee trailed her hand in the water and stared up through her sunglasses at the cloudless blue.

"How's Vicky?" Gillian said eventually.

"Stricken. She saw Wendy's parents after they identified the body. She said they were hardly able to speak. Wendy's mother's hands were shaking so badly she spilt tea all down the front of her dress. She sat there dabbing and dabbing at it with her napkin until a police officer came to drive them home. Vicky knew them; she'd been up to Peterborough with Wendy to visit them. Wendy's father said he kept thinking of the last time they'd been down to Cambridge, when she got her Ph.D. It was December—very cold, but bright. Bare and lovely, he said. They had a photograph of her in her regalia, smiling and shivering on Clare bridge. She already knew she was going to Canada, so they'd been joking about the winters there. It had worried them that she was going so far away, Vicky said. They'd been happy when she came back to Cambridge."

They slid noiselessly beneath the Fen Causeway; above them, the afternoon traffic drummed on the bridge.

"In Tsavo," said Pamela, when they were clear of the bridge, "I've seen elephant mothers mourning their dead babies. It's one of the saddest sights in the world to see a big old ragged-eared matriarch refusing to leave the body of her child, caressing it all over with her trunk, even carrying it if the group starts to move on. The herd is like an extended family—mothers, sisters, cousins, nieces and nephews . . . After years of watching them, I'm certain they grieve as humans do."

"What about the fathers?" Gillian asked.

"Adult male elephants don't stay in the group. They hang about the general vicinity and they mate with the females, but they don't rear the children or form permanent attachments. The matriarchs kick the males out when they're rowdy adolescents. Not a bad system."

"Plus je connais les hommes, plus j'aime mes éléphants," Bee said with a smile.

"Do you think Wendy's killer will be caught?" Pamela asked Gillian abruptly.

"Yes, I'm sure he will."

"Why?"

"Because it wasn't a random act. Something linked him to her. That link will be found."

"How's the investigation going?" asked Bee.

"All right. They've got plenty of leads to follow. But they're under a lot of pressure. They'd sure as hell like to know who her lover was."

They were beyond the edge of the town now, sliding between meadows and fields and the knobbly pollarded willows on the bank. A pair of punts appeared from round the next bend, overloaded with loud and cheerful sunburnt undergraduates. Pamela steered close to the outer curve, and the two crowded punts blundered heavily down the middle of the stream, the second one inadvertently catching up to the first and giving it a slight tap, whereupon the surprised punter nearly lost his balance. Then, to the vocal disappointment of both sets of passengers, he steadied again and shot the punt forward, escaping as the pursuit drifted sideways.

"Some things don't change," Gillian said as they rounded the next bend.

"They think it was the lover, then?" Pamela asked.

"Not particularly. But it's a possibility."

"If your lovers are male."

The noise from the other punts dwindled and died away. Gillian could hear the whisper of water beneath the punt.

"Why do men kill women?" she asked, only half aloud.

"Because they hate us," said Bee.

"It's about power," Pamela said. "Power over women. Murder's just another way to keep us in order."

"Do you think all men are potential killers, then?"

"Why do you suppose it took the police so long to catch Peter Sutcliffe? Because he was such an ordinary man."

"He may have been ordinary, but what he did was extraordinary. Men don't ordinarily kill women in handfuls."

"They ordinarily rape. They ordinarily batter. The statistics are public knowledge now. He just went a bit further. It's a difference of degree, not of kind.

Besides, all men profit by the murders, because the murders keep all women in a state of fear. Don't you think they know that, even when they masquerade as protectors? They're all implicated. That's why I don't want anything to do with them. You can't be with a man and not support the patriarchy."

"I don't agree."

"Obviously not," Pamela answered, with a deft thrust of the pole.

"Oh God," said Bee. "I thought we weren't going to talk about this."

"You think my views are tainted," Gillian said, "but my problem is that I think yours are without hope. If you say all men are evil and change isn't possible, there's nothing we can do. Besides, I think your view ignores the historical evidence."

"The historical evidence says that in all societies men have oppressed women."

"But not to the same degree. Some societies have been much less violent than others, for example. To me, that means we can strive for change."

"More women judges, that sort of thing? Then we end up playing their game."

"That's a risk all right, but separatism is a dead end. I don't mean women shouldn't be free to form their own communities if they want to, just that it's not a general solution to the problem of misogyny."

"Why not?"

"They're half the human race. We can't just ignore

them. At best it's an elitist solution, rather like the way rich women used to take refuge in convents." Gillian heard her voice rising and lowered it. "Besides, men aren't all the same."

"Yours is different, I suppose."

"Oh, leave Edward out of it. I wasn't referring to him."

Pamela was silent.

"Well why do *you* think men kill women?" Bee asked suddenly.

"I think men in our world grow up believing that they're superior to women, and that their sense of self-worth is based to one degree or another on hanging on to that belief and reaffirming it by controlling women. Some of them can throw away that prop. But the ones who need to believe it are in trouble, because it's false. They find female equality and independence very threatening. Some exclude us—like ones you could name at this university. Others rape or batter. The killers are the ones who can't recover their superiority by less extreme means."

"Do you think one of those killed Wendy?"

"I don't know. There are other reasons for killing people—men or women—practical ones, like money or prestige or keeping a secret. And there's also revenge. Wendy could have been killed for any of those reasons, or a mixture of them."

"I don't see how money could be it," Bee said.

"I don't either, unless it's something to do with

inheriting her grandfather's farm. But that's the sort of thing the police can find out."

"Speaking of the police, would you ask Edward something for me?" Bee said.

"What?"

"Ask him if they've found our doctor cards anywhere. When the PIS office was robbed, I thought our card file had gone with the rest of our things. But I've remembered since that Wendy had it. She wanted to go through the file, and she offered to update the cross-references."

"What does it look like?"

"It's a little green plastic box with three-by-five cards in it. Each card has the name of a Cambridge doctor on it and information about the practice. We collect data on doctors' attitudes to abortion and various methods of contraception, and on how they treat women in general. There are still a few dreadful doctors in Cambridge, though fewer than in most places, and we warn our customers about them. I mean, if you're a pregnant fifteen-year-old, you don't want to go to a doctor who's a right-to-life maniac, do you?"

"Tell her about that poor girl Irene saw this winter," Pamela put in.

"God, yes. A perfect example. It was a girl from Ely, a first-year student. She went to Dr Stoner. He's the absolute bottom. He wouldn't give her a test on the spot—sent the sample off to Addenbrooke's, told her that under no circumstances would he refer her for an abortion and that since she'd been fooling about, she should be prepared to accept the consequences. So she crept away and waited for the test to come back, couldn't do her work, she was so nervous. Then somebody told her about us, so she came along on the Saturday and had a test."

"And?"

"And she *was* pregnant, poor duck. So Irene talked to her and gave her the names of several doctors who would be sympathetic. She said she was pretty sure she wanted an abortion. Irene asked if she had anyone to turn to, and she said she could tell her sister and was going to talk to her boyfriend about it. But can you imagine, a doctor taking it upon himself to tell her she had to pay for her sin? And she's hardly more than a child herself. It's bloody mediæval."

TWELVE

The murder room was crowded. Cutter had yanked two detective-constables and a sergeant from another squad and given them to Hardy for the Fowler case. With Hardy's own group, including McClure, Detective Inspector Bob Walcott, the constables already working the case, two indexers and Edward, there were twelve bodies squeezed into the small room. The tables were arranged in a horseshoe, with space at one end reserved for the indexers, who would cross-reference every piece of fresh information that came in. Two telephone lines and an answering machine had been specially installed, and a photocopier commandeered. A large white board covered most of one wall. On it were posted the known facts of the case including

Wendy's name, age and pregnancy, along with photographs of the crime scene. The windows looked out on Parker's Piece; although it was still early morning, the room was already too warm.

Edward covertly inspected the team. Nine men and three women: the two indexers were women, as they usually were in London. McClure and Walcott he knew; the constables, fresh meat from CC Cutter or Hardy's home-cured, he was not yet familiar with. The third woman was the detective sergeant Cutter had sent. Since McClure would be running the murder room, she would presumably be hitting the street with the rest of the team. He wondered if it was her first murder inquiry. Murder was still a male preserve, by and large, a game of men catching men. Most police wanted it to stay that way. Hardy had admitted that his instinct was still to clap the women under the hatches—give them the paperwork—on major cases. What would he do with Sergeant Hilary Temple?

Right now, Hardy was outlining the case so far. The sack had been examined and several hairs similar to Wendy's had been found inside it, as well as some unidentified scraps of vegetation. Her last meal, a small one, had consisted of noodles, mixed vegetables and beef, matching the remains of the Chinese meal in her kitchen. There was no report from the forensic lab on her bench, but the analysts had been busy. Mass spectrometry and gas chromatography had identified the oily smear on the cold room floor as just what was written on the torn label, which, Hardy observed, left them no further ahead. It was a compound of no known history or use. The glass fragments belonged to a shattered ampoule which had contained the compound. There were splinters of glass and oily stains matching the compound on the sole of Wendy's right shoe, but the splinters weren't deeply embedded; she hadn't put her full weight on the foot. Consistent, Edward thought, with the killer having staged the slip.

Hardy was still talking. Twenty-eight people who had been in the tea-room on Friday afternoon and might have spoken to Wendy had been interviewed; none had had any information to offer, but there were at least another fifteen to interview. Hardy ran through the facts and then left it to Walcott to parcel out the morning's tasks. Hilary Temple got the Chinese restaurant, Edward noted. Not bad, he thought, whistling as he strolled down the hall to the room he was sharing with Hardy. She could have been stuck with the sack. Tracing the sack was the bottom of the job pile: boring, thankless, probably useless. What you'd call a cul-de-sack.

"Interesting bit about the glass on the sole of her shoe, wasn't it?" Hardy said, coming in behind him. "Cute."

"Cute as a rat trap. Let's hope chummy catches his own foot in it. I want to know what they found in her lab, though, and what's in the flask. It has to be the flask from her failed experiment."

"Yes, she must have put it in her desk to keep it safe: locked up, and not where anyone normally keeps their chemicals."

"When will we have a report on the contents?"

"This afternoon."

"Good. Then what about nipping back to the chemistry department in the meantime? Let's find out whether Bottomley or anyone else applied for Wendy's research money."

"It would be interesting if Roger Hill had. Is he just a bloke with a nasty tongue?"

"Has he been asked where he was Friday evening?"

"I went through the statements last night. He said he dined in college—Clare—and then went home."

"Any corroboration?"

"Not after dinner. He said he was home alone. He's not married. We can verify the dinner easily; someone may know what time he left. And he may have been seen when he parked his car at home. He lives in a cottage in Grantchester."

"I thought bachelors lived in college, swilling vintage claret."

"He dines in, so we'll assume he swills. He lives out because he has a dog he's potty about. An Irish wolfhound."

"Oh God, one of those damned things the size of Fenris. Send a DC out there, then. A big one. Let's see whether anything interesting turns up. We should check Bottomley's statement as well; he says he was reading a book all evening."

"What book?"

"A biography of Lavoisier."

"The father of modern chemistry." Hardy scratched his head. "I remember that from school—I don't know why."

"Probably because he was guillotined in the Terror. That was when the Tribunal made its famous remark, 'We no longer need scientists.'"

"Hmm," said Hardy. "I'm glad beheading has gone out of fashion. Now, what about Wendy's neighbours? Mostly graduate students, you said?"

"That's what the bursar told me. Behind her, in the flat that looks into her kitchen, there's a mathematics chap, and in the flats alongside, two history students and a research fellow in law. We could try them later today, after we've been to Lensfield Road."

"Let's see the students first. We're more likely to catch them now—in bed, like as not."

"Good. As a couple of hard-working public servants, we have a duty to go and knock them up."

"The mathematics man's name is Rose," Edward said. "Evan Rose."

After Hardy's second heavy-fisted tattoo, there was a reply.

"Bugger off!" a voice shouted from far within.

"Police!" Hardy bellowed.

"Go and be paralytic somewhere else!"

"Nice friends he's got," Hardy said, knocking a third time.

The door flew open and a skinny, tousled young man stared at them angrily. His clothes were so rumpled he had obviously been sleeping in them.

"Do you have any idea what time it is?" he demanded.

Hardy, who knew the time perfectly well, inspected his watch. "Nine-forty a.m."

"Are you sure? I just got to bed. It can't have been more than an hour ago."

"Quite sure. We'd like to come in and ask you a few questions."

"About what?"

"Wendy Fowler."

"The one who was murdered? What for? I don't know her."

"She lived in the flat right in front of yours. You can see into her kitchen."

For the first time, the young man looked disconcerted. "That was her flat?"

"We'll have a look at the view, if you don't mind, Mr Rose," Hardy said, moving forward.

Rose stepped back. Hardy walked into the tiny vestibule. Edward followed. It as a smaller flat than Wendy's. A powerful odour hung in the air: unwashed socks and something else Edward couldn't identify immediately. A squirrel's nest of papers, books, crumpled clothing, used cups and styrofoam containers surrounded the daybed, where the blanket had been pushed back, revealing grey and crumb-strewn sheets. He thought the kitchen would be worse, but it was relatively clean. Not used for much besides making tea, he surmised. They pushed back the limp curtains and looked across at Wendy's window. Her kitchen was nothing but shadows behind the glass, but with the lights on and the curtains open, anyone in it would be plainly visible. If both windows were open, conversation would be audible.

"You never met Wendy Fowler?" Edward asked, turning to Evan Rose, who stood behind them in the doorway.

"Didn't know her from Adam," Rose said, having regained his self-possession.

"So you didn't know that she was living in the flat across from yours?"

"No. I knew a woman was living there, that's all."

"How often did you see her?"

"Hardly ever. I'm not up and about during the day. I'm usually out in the evenings, and I like to work late at night, when it's quiet."

"Did you ever see her in her kitchen, through the window?"

"I hardly know. Spying on one's neighbours isn't particularly interesting."

Edward said patiently, "You might have seen her

by chance, if she walked into her kitchen when you were in yours."

"I keep the curtains closed. The people who had the flat before she did used to prance about stark naked."

"Did you ever see anyone with her in the flat?"

"I told you, I keep the curtains closed."

"What are these for, then?" Edward asked, picking up a small pair of binoculars that stood on a shelf next to an open packet of tea-bags.

"The opera," Rose said coolly. "I'm a student, you know. I'm always in the gods."

As they left the kitchen, a swift brown movement caught Edward's eye. He stopped. A ferret scurried across the carpet. Rose held his arm out and down, and the ferret leapt up and climbed to his shoulder, where it sat and glared at them.

"You woke her up," said Rose. "Now Mrs Thatcher's in a bad mood."

"Rose!" said Edward, breathing deeply when they reached the bottom of the stairs.

"It did pong a bit. Worthless little beast."

"Rose or Mrs Thatcher?"

Hardy grimaced. "A lovely couple."

"What about those opera glasses? I saw him—or someone in his flat—twitching the curtains when we were here yesterday."

"I dunno. But from his window he could see into the bedroom of one of the other flats. That might have provided more interesting performances than Wendy's kitchen."

The next flat, beside and below Wendy's, was occupied by two women, both graduate students in history at King's. Only one of them, Vrinda Kumar, was at home; her room-mate, she said, had gone for an early swim at the pool and would return soon. They both would be glad to help if they could. Her hair was thick and black and shiny; her skin was brown and clear like strong tea.

The news of Wendy's murder had been all over King's College Monday evening, she said. After dinner, she had seen several knots of students gathered near the gate, looking across at Wendy's window. She had met Wendy once or twice but that was all. She was quite willing to show the detectives her bedroom, which faced Wendy's. The room was very small, and she remained in the hall while they went in. There was little furniture: a narrow bed, a scratched wardrobe, a low table with a lamp a wooden chair. A piece of blue silk draped over the table and a photograph on the wall over the bed provided the only life and colour in the room. Edward looked at the photograph. It was an aerial shot, an exquisite pattern of green strips and squares embroidered with water.

"Rice fields?' he asked her.

She smiled and nodded. "I'm writing my thesis on women and the green revolution," she answered.

The window was small and set high in the wall.

Wendy's bedroom window was some distance to the left and several feet higher up.

"Not much of a view from here," Hardy said, "but look at Rose's window."

Edward squinted upward. Rose's window was at right angles to theirs, but he would be able to see part of Vrinda's bedroom if he leaned close to the glass.

"Have you ever seen Wendy going in or coming out with a man?" he asked.

Vrinda never had. Nor, they were unsurprised to learn, had she ever happened to look up from her window and see anyone looking down from Wendy's. The angle was too steep to see into the room.

"Your window doesn't have a blind," Edward said.

"No," she said, "it's so small, and it doesn't face anyone else's. Why should it have one?"

"We've been in the other flats," Edward said. "I think a blind would be a good idea."

She looked at him, her eyes wide with sudden fear. "Has someone been watching me?"

"We don't know that anyone has," Edward answered. "But it's best to be on the safe side."

She looked even more frightened. "Not the murderer?" she whispered.

"No, no. Not at all," Edward said, mentally kicking himself. But how could he have put it so as not to frighten her? "We don't know that the murderer was ever in Wendy's flat, and if he was, he couldn't have seen you from there."

"Why did you mention this at all then? You are here to investigate a murder; why are you frightening me with rubbish about Peeping Toms?" she asked sharply.

"Policeman's instinct," Hardy said, coming to Edward's rescue. "We're conditioned to look at things in ways other people don't. Most people walk past a school and see children and classrooms. I see a building with half-a-dozen entrances and exits, inadequate lighting, and sixteen places to hide in the shrubbery. A security detail's nightmare. You see?"

She listened impassively, her arms folded.

"I will put up a blind today," she said when Hardy had finished, but her manner was no longer friendly. It was plain that she wanted them to go. There was no sign of her room-mate.

"She thinks we're dirty old men," Edward said after the door had closed.

Hardy chuckled. "Made a right balls-up of it, didn't you? We should have sent DS Temple. A woman would have had no trouble."

"Let's give her the room-mate."

"Done. Not much hope of a lead there, though. Who's the last neighbour on our list?"

"The law student, Jeremy Martingale."

Hardy snorted. "Never met a Jeremy who was any bloody use to anyone."

They had climbed a flight of stairs and turned a corner and were now at the back of the flat, which faced the street, like Wendy's. Edward tapped on the door. It was opened by a blond young man in a dressing gown. He was thin and good-looking, and smelt pleasantly of soap. He seemed rather pleased than otherwise when Edward explained their errand and invited the detectives in for coffee. It was no trouble, he said, the kettle was just on the boil. They followed him to the kitchen, where Edward noted the bag of coffee beans and the electric grinder as well as a tall glass coffee pot with a silver plunger.

"I can't say our paths crossed often," Jeremy was saying as he poured boiling water from the kettle into the pot. "I don't suppose we had much in common. But of course I knew her. One does meet such a lot of people. It's a tragedy, what happened. Rather clever, wasn't she?"

"Apparently," Edward said, avoiding Hardy's eye.

"She did like music. I know that. I ran into her once at a concert. What was it? The Arditti Quartet, yes, that's right. We took the train home together. We had a bit of a chat about the British legal system. I'm in law, as I suppose you already know."

He brought the coffee into his sitting-room and they settled at a table by the window. It wasn't a bay window, like Wendy's, but the same spectacular arrangement of stone and sky was his to look at.

"Rather super, this view. Wendy's window is even better, of course."

"You've been in her flat, then?" Edward asked.

"Oh yes, but before her time. A friend of mine had digs there last year." He poured coffee into Edward's cup, and Edward sipped it gratefully. It was excellent, hot and strong. Hardy, by preference a tea drinker, ladled spoonfuls of sugar into his and filled his cup to the brim with cream.

"The British legal system," Edward prompted.

"Yes, well, she thought the whole system was wrong-headed. She said the adversarial system turned justice into a game in which the lawyers were the only winners. She thought that truth was a casualty of the system, and that scientific inquiry was a more appropriate model for the courts to follow than mediæval combat. It's not a view I subscribe to, of course, but she offered a rather spirited defence. I remember she said that rape cases in particular had hardly progressed beyond trial by ordeal."

Edward felt his interest quicken. This was a glimpse of the real Wendy, he thought, not just the "talented young woman." So much for Hardy's useless Jeremys.

"What else did she say?"

"That's all I remember, I'm afraid. It was months ago."

"I don't suppose she ever talked about her private life? Troubles at work, boyfriends, lovers . . . ?"

"Never. I would have thought it quite odd if she had."

"Did you ever see anyone with her? Coming out of her flat, perhaps?"

Martingale hesitated. "No."

Edward heard the hesitation. He waited.

"But I know she had a visitor." Abruptly, Martingale stood up. "In the spirit of scientific inquiry, allow me to show you my bedroom."

They followed him to the back of the flat. The bedroom was on the left, facing Wendy's building. A queen-size bed covered with an enormous hand-stitched quilt occupied most of the floor; patterned carpets were layered over the rest. A carved chest with mother-of-pearl inlay stood in the corner. The window, unlike Vrinda's, was set low in the wall. A thick velvet curtain was pulled across it. Martingale drew it back, and Edward and Hardy looked out. Wendy's window was placed slightly further back and about three feet below them. Edward estimated that he could see about a quarter of the room, including a corner of the bed.

"That's Wendy's window," Martingale said, pointing, "as you must know. Last year, when my friend Geoffrey was living there, he popped over one morning before breakfast; I'd had someone spending the night with me. My friend, who can be a bit of a rotter at times, particularly first thing in the morning, said he'd just popped in to see the top half. Of what? I said. 'Of the bottom I saw last night,' he said. He wasn't half pleased with himself. It wasn't very nice, really; but he did warn me, you see. So I had the curtain made up."

Why is he telling us all this? Edward thought. Theatre? He's got both of us hanging on every word. Then: No, he wants to be sure we don't think he's a Peeping Tom. He's making a better job of it with us than we did with Vrinda. The humour of it suddenly struck him and he bit back a laugh. Who would have guessed that Wendy's windows would have caused so much embarrassment to so many?

Martingale was speaking rapidly. "But I occasionally open the window to air the room. One evening, when I did, I happened to see Wendy with a man in her room."

"How long ago was that?"

"A month ago, six weeks perhaps."

"Would you recognize him again?"

"Undoubtedly."

"You had that good a look at him?" Edward said curiously, wondering how long Martingale had stayed at the window.

"Only a glimpse, but I wouldn't forget. He was frightfully good-looking. Too Apollonian for words."

"She's becoming interesting," Edward said as they crossed the street. "She had the right idea about the legal profession."

"And didn't hesitate to express it where it might cause offence."

"He didn't seem miffed."

"He wasn't mourning, either."

"No. But he did tell us about his window. If he

hadn't wanted to help, he need never have brought it up."

"True. He's redeemed Jeremys everywhere." Hardy squeezed his bulk behind the wheel of the car. "If Gillian and her friends are right, Romeo shouldn't be hard to find. How many blond gods can there be in the chemistry department?"

"He could be a musician."

"No. He's a chemist. Then we can find him." Hardy laughed. "A quid says we have his name today."

"How?"

"Ask the secretaries."

THIRTEEN

As Edward and Hardy had seen on their tour, the organic chemists' secretary had an office in a small space on the same side of the corridor as the cold room. It was crowded, like the other rooms, but the plants grouped by the window asserted a difference of atmosphere. A bulletin board was covered with postcards. The secretary, a pleasant-faced woman in her forties, looked up from her typing, her eyes widening with interest when the detectives identified themselves.

"Is the Professor of Organic Chemistry in?" Hardy asked.

"Professor Kintyre? Yes, he's here today, but he has his own secretary. You'll have to ask her whether he's in his office just now. Are you investigating Wendy's death?"

"That's right."

"Well I do hope you catch him soon. It's horrible thinking he might still be somewhere about. What kind of lunatic would do that to an innocent person? Poor girl. With all her future in front of her."

"Did you know her well?"

"Only a little. But she had a spark. She was going far, anyone could see that."

"Did she have any particular friends in the department?"

The secretary thought for a moment. "Maybe Alan Kennedy. Ron Bottomley says they're chums. But he's a gossip, is our Ron. I don't believe half he tells me."

"Is Kennedy in?"

"He's here today, but he has a lecture right now."

"And Bottomley?"

"You could try his lab. It's just along the hall."

"Oh, and by the way," Hardy added casually as they turned to go, "could you identify anyone in the department—not an undergraduate, this man would be older—described to you as a big blond, handsome, muscular, probably works out with weights?"

"Why, that would be Alan Kennedy," the secretary replied instantly.

"You're quite sure?"

She pointed. "His office is right down the hall. The weights are under his desk."

"He's very fit?" Edward said.

"Fit enough to do a one-armed handstand," she answered. "I've seen him. He will leave the door open." Her eyes twinkled. "He's also a health fiend. Brushes his teeth all day long."

"You mean here, at work?" Hardy said, nonplussed.

"That's right, after every meal. Even after tea!" She laughed. "He's American, of course."

In the corridor, Hardy experimentally ran his tongue over his front teeth. "If I brushed my teeth every time I had a cuppa, they'd be worn down to the gums by now. I'd have a set of chompers in a glass by the bed. He must be raving."

They found Kintyre's secretary.

"He has the Professor of Biological Chemistry with him now. I'm not quite sure when he'll be free."

"Right. When he is, would you tell him we'd like to have a brief chat?" Hardy gave her the number to ring at the station.

She nodded briskly. "I'll let you know as soon as he's available."

They drove back to the station and parked in the lot behind it. Hardy opened the door and unfolded himself.

"Christ, I'm glad I don't drive one of these match-boxes for a living; I couldn't stand up at the end of the day. Let's see what McClure has for us."

McClure, a thin, flabby man like an over-cooked noodle, was in the middle of the murder room, talking into the telephone. The indexers were working in one corner, cards spread out on the table and cups of tea at their elbows. A constable was pecking at the typewriter. McClure put down the telephone.

"What've you got?" Hardy asked.

"Nothing on the Chinese takeaway yet; DS Temple hasn't come back. But that card file on the doctors DCI Gisborne wanted, we've got it. It was in Fowler's office."

"Has the lab report on the flask come in?" Edward said.

"No analysis of the contents. But there are two sets of dabs on it; one of them's the victim's."

"And the other set, are the prints good ones?"

"Beautiful. A textbook set, Reagan says."

"That's good news, Guv," said the constable, who had stopped his two-finger typing to listen.

Edward laughed. "It usually means they're worthless. Rule number 1OA in the detective's handbook: a great set of dabs belongs to anybody but the villain; if they're no bloody good, they're his."

"I could do with a cup of tea," Hardy said.

Edward snapped his fingers. "Tea and a toothbrush for the Super," he said, "and I'll have a look at the doctor file."

McClure jerked his thumb at the constable. "Here, Bob, fetch that box for DCI Gisborne." He turned to the telephone, which was ringing again.

Edward opened the green plastic box. The surface had a rough texture, useless for fingerprints. Not that he thought there would be any prints of interest;

either the box had nothing to do with the murder, or, if it did, the murderer hadn't found it. Edward was inclined to believe the former.

The box was two-thirds full of three-by-five cards, with the names of the doctors arranged in alphabetical order. The notes had been handwritten by several people in a variety of inks. Edward flipped through them, reading a card here and there, and then started at the front, reading each one. It didn't take long; the information on the cards was clear and concise: the name of the doctor, cross-referenced with other doctors in the same practice, the address and telephone number of the practice, and brief comments, usually prefaced by a note of the year. A few of the comments were old, but most dated from the past five years.

"What's in there?" Hardy asked, loading his tea with sugar.

"Pungent commentary," Edward said, looking up briefly. "The sort one never sees in official documents."

"Give us a sample."

Edward flipped towards the end of the pack. "Try this: 'Rendell. Revolting man. Will refer for abortion but avoid for contraception; wields speculum like a bootjack.'" He scanned a few more cards. "Or this: 'Goodman. Avoid this practice, no good doctors in it, 1986,' and later, 'Horrible practice, avoid at all costs, incompetent and unsympathetic.' Here's another one: 'Won't fit IUD, diaphragm or cap; dishes out the pill without asking for medical history, etc.'"

"Sweet Jesus, haven't we got any good ones?"

"Bags of them. Here: *'Cross, A. Pro-choice; good with vulnerable teenagers and women with language difficulties.'* But it's the bad reviews I'm interested in."

Edward read rapidly through another two dozen cards while Hardy sipped his tea. He whistled. "Listen to this: *'Stoner, T. Hits an all-time low. Member of pro-life group; thinks unwanted babies are God's reward for lack of self-control. Will not give pregnancy tests or refer for abortions; clumsy and arrogant, 1989.'"*

"Whew!" said Hardy. "Where do they get their information?"

"From the patients. Now suppose you were Dr Stoner or perhaps Rendell or Goodman, and you found out that these comments, or something of the sort, were on the file in the PIS office. How curious would you be?"

"You mean the burglary. If I'd been told about the file, would I want to suss it out? I just might, especially if I knew anything about the counselling centre. It's wide open—not much of a risk. But there's nothing to say it wasn't an ordinary nutter. Why?"

"Timing. The PIS was broken into within a day or two of Wendy's death. Coincidence?"

"Possibly not, but with a secret lover somewhere under our noses I'm not going to round up half the GPs in Cambridge. Until we run out of leads on Fowler's bedmate, in my book it's a coincidence."

McClure tapped on the door, then stuck his head in.

"There's something just in. One of the lads interviewing students says he's found a bloke who was in the tea-room Friday afternoon and overheard Wendy Fowler arrange to meet a man at six o'clock that evening. A chemist in the department. His name's Alan Kennedy."

They were back in Lensfield Road within the hour. The interview with Professor Kintyre didn't take much time. He stood upon his dignity a little, unwilling to imagine that a violent criminal might be lurking behind any familiar face, but he was businesslike and cooperative. He had no knowledge of Wendy Fowler's friends and didn't suppose she had what the police would call enemies. She was a research fellow, a position of three years' duration. The research fellowships cost the department a considerable amount of money, since the colleges refused to contribute anything towards the research facilities. They housed the fellows and paid their salaries, but the department was expected to find bench space and pay for the chemicals and so on. It had been going on for a long time, but it was an unsatisfactory arrangement. It caused resentment now and then, owing to space limitations, and department members sometimes felt that the money might be better allocated to their own projects. But in general the inconveniences were tolerated because the fellows were good.

"Was Wendy Fowler doing research in the same area as anyone else in the department?" Edward said.

"Yes, she's in an interdisciplinary field, with interests in organic as well as inorganic chemistry. She had an interesting idea about a particular problem that Ron Bottomley had been working on for some time. It was a clever idea she had, and she received industrial backing to follow it up. That's nothing out of the way."

"Had Bottomley applied for funding to work on the same problem?" Edward asked.

Kintyre rubbed his massive bald head. "Well, yes, now that you ask. He'd applied somewhat earlier, with a different idea in a related area, but he was turned down."

"Why?"

"Oh, well, one never quite knows, really. But his approach to the problem was perhaps not as inventive as hers . . . He hasn't published much in the past ten years . . . The committee may have thought he wouldn't get on with it. But then if he'd submitted her proposal, there's nothing to say he would have been funded. You see, they like to give money to the high-flying young scholars—to try them out, you know. See what they can do."

"Bottomley must have been resentful then, when Wendy got the money?"

"Erm, at the time, yes, I suppose. He did utter some rather ill-judged remarks. But that was months ago. nothing to do with this business. That would be a preposterous idea."

"What sort of remarks?"

Kintyre drummed his fingers on the desk before answering. "He said that she had stolen his research."

"Preposterous?" said Edward as they skirted a huge metal cylinder that was blocking part of the hallway. "If murder was as unlikely as all that, I'd be out of a job."

Kennedy was in his office. His big blond head was bent over his desk, and they saw him through the open door before he realized they were there. He lived up to his description. The fine blond hair was cut short but retained a slight wave, the strength of the arms was visible below the short sleeves of his shirt. It was an interesting head, Edward thought: both brutal and refined. The skull was large and heavy, set on a thick column of neck, but the nose and ears were small and delicate, the mouth a rosebud.

Hardy knocked at the open door. Kennedy looked up. Edward saw a slight movement of the muscles at the hinge of the jaw, a definitive symptom of severe tension in the Gisborne guide to human behaviour. But Kennedy's manner was cool.

"You wanted to see me?" he said, in a tone of faint surprise.

"You were a friend of Wendy Fowler's" Hardy said after closing the door behind him and sitting down across from Kennedy. Edward strolled to the window and stood with his back to it, a position from which he could clearly see Kennedy's face, while his own would be a dark silhouette against the glass.

"Yes. She was a bright kid. I liked her a lot."

"You thought highly of her—as a chemist, I mean?"

"Absolutely."

"You worked together, then?"

"Not really. Her area's related to mine, but it isn't the same. We never worked on any specific projects together, but we discussed our research pretty often."

"Did you meet outside the laboratory to discuss your research?"

"Sure. I guess so. We had lunch a few times. What about it?"

"Did she ever talk to you about personal things? About her private life?"

"No. It wasn't that kind of relationship."

"No boyfriend troubles, no problems with anyone at the lab?"

"No."

"Have you any idea why someone would have killed her?"

"I don't have any idea at all. It's hard to believe it wasn't an accident."

"It wasn't," said Hardy. "What did she want to see you about at six o'clock on Friday?"

Alarm flashed in Kennedy's eyes, but he replied evenly, "Her research. She was having a problem with her distillations that puzzled her."

"According to our information, there was something particular she wanted to see you about. Not just her research."

"Then your information is wrong," Kennedy said. He leaned forward, emphasizing his denial. His hands were below the desk surface, on his thighs. Edward saw them move slightly, as though to wipe sweat from the palms.

"Could you tell us about that meeting?"

"She didn't stay very long. Twenty minutes, maybe half an hour at the most. We talked about her work. That's all. Then she went off. To get some dinner, I think she said. Then she was going back to work in her lab."

"So you knew she would be in the lab that night."

"Yes," Kennedy said. "So what? She worked in the lab at night all the time. It was no secret."

"You didn't have dinner with her?"

"I went home for dinner."

"What time was that?"

"I don't know. I often work late myself. It must have been between seven and eight when I got home. You can ask my wife."

"Thank you," said Hardy. "We'll do that."

"So you didn't see Wendy after half past six Friday evening?" asked Edward from his place by the window.

Kennedy turned towards him, narrowing his eyes against the glare. "No."

"You didn't go to her flat that evening?"

"Definitely not. I've never been in her flat," Kennedy said coldly.

"You weren't having an affair with her?"

"An affair? That's ridiculous. What gave you that idea This is the 1990s. A man and a woman should be able to carry on a professional friendship without people making these assumptions. It's insulting."

"Do you think he was lying?" Hardy asked, opening the door of the car. A smell of hot plastic flowed out.

"'The louder he talked of his honour, the faster we counted our spoons.'"

"That's good. Who said that?"

"Emerson. Gillian quoted it one day when she'd been reading about Lloyd George and the English middle classes."

"My grandfather used to say that Lloyd George was the greatest prime minister we ever had."

"And mine thought he was a dangerous demagogue. Now, what about our missing spoons? I'd like to put Kennedy in that flat Friday evening. If we can do that, his story will unravel."

"Martingale might shake him. Kennedy said he was never in her flat, but Martingale's seen him there. At least, we think he has. We need a positive ID."

"Exactly. And let's see whether DS Temple has come up with something at the Chinese restaurant. Any brick we can knock out of that wall Kennedy's built will help."

"Now then, what about Bottomley? We've caught Kennedy in a lie, it seems, but this Bottomley fella had a grudge. He had dinner in his college, but he was alone in his room, he says, for the rest of the evening."

"Alone with Lavoisier. I know. We'll just have to see if we can dig up a witness who saw him somewhere else. Anywhere, but preferably at the chemistry labs."

Hardy leaned against the car, reluctant to make contact with the baked upholstery. It was mid-afternoon, and they hadn't parked in the shade. He mopped his brow with a crumpled handkerchief. "And then there's Roger Hill."

Edward threw his jacket on the rear seat. "All we've got on Hill at present is that he made an intemperate remark after his office was flooded."

"And that he was seen coming out of Wendy Fowler's office immediately after the flood occurred."

"Yes. We should look into that. Has he or anyone else been seen mucking about with Fowler's chemicals or her lab equipment? I'd like to know a bit more— have something to spring on them—before we start asking questions. We didn't have enough to rattle Kennedy. And he's a much more viable suspect."

FOURTEEN

When Gillian returned to Earl Street at the end of
the day, she settled down at the little desk in the sitting-room and began to write a letter to her mother.

> I was so glad to have seen the dogwood trees
> when they were in bloom. Walking through
> that little stand at the top of the field, with all
> the flowering branches quivering in the wind,
> was like walking back into childhood. Do you
> remember the story of the Twelve Dancing
> Princesses? . . .

She had walked through that wood, on its little
rise in the great valley of the Hudson River, in every
season all through her childhood, and she could still

recall every step of the path along the edge of the field. She knew the places where the moss grew in plump green cushions, and where the ghostly Indian pipes appeared after rain, the tree that the wild grapevine climbed, the shiny-leafed patch of poison ivy. In some mysterious way she felt that she, who she was deep within, had been formed by her repeated journeys to the wood: by the path itself, by its adherence to the subtle contours of the hillside, its prospect of domestic field and low, distant hills.

The field, long left untilled, was waist-deep in warm grass in summer, splashed with gold and white wildflowers, and knee-deep in snow in winter, with skeletal brown seed heads poking through the crust. At the upper end, a wall had once divided field from wood; a tumbled line of stones remained, where garter-snakes sunned themselves, pouring like water down the nearest crack when her footsteps disturbed them. The image of the dogwood trees in flower went back to when she was four or five; it remained fixed in memory as a sudden surfacing of consciousness: of knowing her own delight in the beauty of the world.

In the midst of her reverie, Murray came padding down the stairs in his slippers.

"You're home," Gillian said in surprise. "I didn't know you were here." She watched him. "You look weary."

"I didn't sleep very well last night. I haven't had a good night's sleep since the news about Wendy. I wake up in the dark and think about her."

He dropped on to the sofa and sat, massaging his forehead where the hairline had once been and repeatedly smoothing the thin, curling strands of hair above his ears. "Not that I knew her intimately, but I did know her. She was a little piece of my life. It's different when you read about gang murders in Los Angeles or a prostitute found dead in an alley. When it's people you don't know, you can keep thinking it will never happen to anyone you *do* know. But this thing with Wendy reminds me of how vulnerable we all are. And then I wonder if I only feel bad about it because what happened to her brings home my own mortality. I start feeling guilty, and then I think I'm going nuts. Survivor guilt is normal, I'm Jewish, I should know. But I still feel very disturbed. Don't you?"

"I feel angry. It's different because I never met her."

"The lab is a pretty weird place right now. The story's getting around that it had to be someone who knew the place." He crossed his leg over the other and rubbed his calf as if it ached.

"It's nearly six," said Gillian. "Do you want a sherry?"

"No, thanks. Not yet . . . You know, chemistry is all about order: the beautiful arrangements of atoms and molecules and their repeated patterns of behaviour. It's a way of talking about the world that seems reductive to people who don't understand the vocabulary, but to a chemist, to a research chemist, anyway, it's beautiful, an almost miraculous way of seeing more and more order in what was formerly chaos. Do you know what I mean?"

"Yes, of course I know what you mean. History is about the same thing at bottom: arranging 'the past' into an order we can describe. We're not as tidy as you chemists, of course. Sometimes reading different historians on the same subject reminds me of the six blind men and their elephant."

"I remember a story a biologist friend of mine read somewhere. It's about a new student. His professor gives him a fish and tells him to look at it: just to look and write down everything he can see. So he looks at the fish all day, and he thinks he's learned everything he could learn from looking. The professor comes and checks his notes and says he's missed the most obvious and important characteristic of the fish. So the student looks at the fish for another whole day. And he sees more—things that he'd overlooked the first day. By the end of the day, he's sick of the fish, but when the professor comes, the student has missed the key item again. So he has to spend a third day with the fish. He's at his wits' end when it finally dawns on him: the fish is bilaterally symmetrical. That's the fundamental fact of the fish's anatomy."

Murray leaned back and sighed. "I love that story. The fish could be an amino acid, or anything else— anything you really want to understand. It's about making sense of what you see. You have to have order, but the order in biology or chemistry—any science—isn't absolute. It's not as though the core never changes and we just keep fiddling with the margins. A new, fundamental insight can reconfigure an entire field of knowledge."

"Yes, and seeing is ordering. Without order, we're blind."

"Exactly. And that's how I feel right now. I think about Wendy's murder, and I feel blind and stupid. I'm groping in the dark all of a sudden. I'm supposed to know where I am, but everything feels unfamiliar. It scares me, and I don't know what to do. Human beings can't live in a chaotic universe. They have to have order, however imaginary or fragile." He looked at her sadly. "I guess that's the attraction of Edward's job. Instead of feeling the way I do about Wendy's murder, he goes out and does something—catches the murderer. He restores order."

"Of a kind. What the mathematicians would call necessary but not sufficient. What order can be restored to Wendy's family?"

"Still, I wish I could do something to help."

"You can keep your ear tuned to department gossip. You might turn up something useful. You put Edward on to what's-his-name, Bottomley, didn't you?"

"Well, yes, for whatever it's worth." Murray shifted his weight restlessly and then got up. "But listening is passive." He paced the carpet. "I want to *do* something."

"Ride out with the posse?"

"That's right."

"Tell Edward, then. He always says the police would be helpless without public cooperation."

"When's he coming home?"

Gillian ruffled his hair affectionately. "Go play with your molecules. There's no beautiful order in Edward's timetable."

Edward was in the murder room. DS Temple was back, and she had information. To start with, she'd gone to the police photographer and obtained a set of colour snapshots of Wendy.

"I thought people would remember the hair, if nothing else," she said. Her own hair was a nameless brown.

She had taken the photographs with her to each of the Chinese restaurants in Cambridge, and when no one remembered Wendy, had left a print behind, to be shown to the members of the staff who worked in the evenings but hadn't yet arrived when she visited in the morning. After lunch, she had returned, and at the Chengdu, a small upmarket Szechwan restaurant that had been open for just over a year in Regent Street, she'd found a waiter who remembered Wendy.

"He's a kid, sixteen, speaks good English. He's got a sharp eye. She came in every couple of weeks, he said, usually on a Friday night, and ordered food to take out. I asked him whether anyone was with her, and he said she came in alone, but that he often had the impression that someone was waiting for her, because of the way she would keep looking out of the window when the restaurant was busy and it took a little longer than usual to get her food. I asked him how much food, and he said too many dishes for one person. Then I asked if Wendy had been in last Friday, but he wasn't there that night. His sister stood in for him. Maria Lee. She doesn't work in the restaurant all the time; she has another job with a software company, but she helps out in the evenings when she's needed. So then I went to see her where she works.

"She's twenty-three. Can't stand the restaurant trade, wants to move up in the world. But she helped set up the Chengdu; she told her parents what would sell in Cambridge, and she wasn't far off the mark. They're having no trouble paying back the loans."

"Did she tell you the whole family history?" Hardy asked, amused.

"We did talk for a bit," DS Temple answered, unperturbed.

"And during this, um, prolonged conversation, did you learn anything about Wendy Fowler's whereabouts last Friday night?"

"I certainly did. I showed Ms Lee the photograph, and she recognized Wendy straight away. She'd seen her before. Wendy did come to the Chengdu last Friday, at half past six or a little sooner. She seemed preoccupied, Ms Lee said, and in a hurry. When the food came, it was packed in little white cartons and the cartons were put in a paper bag. Wendy paid and rushed out of the door. Then one of the cooks came out with the rice, in another carton. It had been forgotten. So Ms Lee went out to the street to find Wendy. She caught up with her a few doors down; she was walking towards the centre of town, and there was a big blond man with her. Ms Lee says she would probably recognize him if she saw him again."

"And how did they react when she caught up to them?"

DS Temple looked at her notes. "She said Wendy thanked her, 'but I think if I'd handed her a brick instead of the rice she wouldn't have noticed.' The man walked on ahead, didn't say a word."

"Good," said Hardy. "Terrific." He turned and contemplated the white board. "So now we can place Wendy Fowler outside the Chengdu at 6:30 Friday evening. Probably with Alan Kennedy. We can presume that she went home after that, because the cartons were in her kitchen, and she ate some of the food. Then she returned to the lab. We know she missed an appointment on Saturday morning." He wheeled about and looked at Temple and McClure. "Did Alan Kennedy go to her flat with her? Did they go back to the lab together? Where was Kennedy on Friday night?"

"It's time to interview his wife," Edward said.

"We could put him in a line-up and let Maria Lee identify him," DS Temple said. "She thought she would know him again."

"Not yet," Edward said. "If the increase in temperature registered by the cold room gauge is any indication of when Fowler went in, it wasn't until nearly eleven o'clock. We want a bit more data on the rest of the evening before we chuck Kennedy into a line-up."

"She might have been unconscious much earlier," Temple said.

"Her head hit the shelf in the cold room," Edward answered.

"But what if she was out cold before that?"

"How?"

"Something he put in her dinner. He was a chemist, wasn't he?"

"Nothing's showed up in the analysis of the stomach contents. And she went back to the lab at 7:40. Or did she?" Edward said, stiffening. "We only have her name in the book. Someone else could have signed it for her. And we haven't worked out how she came to be inside the sack. There wasn't much of a struggle in the cold room." He nodded at Temple. "You may be on to something there."

She flushed slightly but merely said, "What next?"

The telephone rang. McClure picked it up.

"McClure . . . What?" He groped for a pen.

A half-hour before, Tiffany Levitt, six, her golden retriever and her father Philip had set out for a walk through the little wood behind Owlstone Road. Tiffany's parents had separated three months earlier, but Tiffany's father came to see her every Tuesday afternoon and every other Saturday. They went to the park and usually bought fish and chips from the van that stopped in Selwyn Road. Sometimes they took Farah, Tiffany's dog, for a walk. Tiffany held the leash unless they saw another dog coming, when Philip would take hold of it until Farah stopped pulling.

This afternoon, they walked along the narrow, twisting path under the trees. Farah trotted beside them, sniffing every leaf.

"Matt's got lice," Tiffany said. "Mrs Lewis sent a note. Do you know what lice are, Daddy?"

"An insect," Philip said vaguely.

"They suck your blood."

"Ugh," said Philip. "That's not very nice of them, is it?"

"And then they have babies," Tiffany added, gleefully knowledgeable. "Hey!" Farah had rocketed off the path, dragging the leash from her fingers.

"Farah!" Tiffany shouted.

"Here, Farah," her father echoed.

But the dog, usually obedient, ignored them. She was about fifteen feet off the path, pawing at a drift of dead leaves. She whimpered.

Probably a dead rabbit, Philip thought, hoping the dog wouldn't bring any bits for Tiffany to inspect.

"Farah!" he called insistently. She wouldn't budge. "Wait here," he instructed Tiffany, and plunged off the path. The dog was whimpering loudly.

Tiffany followed close behind him. When he came to the dog, he grabbed her collar. "Come," he said firmly. The dog resisted. "What the hell's the matter with you?" he said, irritated and puzzled.

"Daddy," said Tiffany.

"What? I thought I told you to wait for me." He was standing in a little mound of branches. But under them was some kind of muck. There was a terrible smell in the air; he'd just noticed it.

"There's some fingers over there." Tiffany pointed.

He looked. Just past him, past the spot where Farah had been pawing, he saw a hand, pale and bloated. A small hand, a woman's.

"Is it a grave?" Tiffany asked, awed.

"We have to go home now," her father said.

FIFTEEN

Gillian awoke to the sound of the shower. It was still dark. Confused, she listened for a moment and then felt the bed beside her. The sheets were cool. Edward hadn't come to bed. She waited, dreaming a little and then waking again to the shuddering clunk of the water pipes. The shower had stopped. A few minutes later a door opened and footsteps padded softly along the hall and down the stairs. She was half asleep again when the footsteps came back up and into the room.

"What time is it?" she asked.

"About five," Edward answered. The edge of the bed dipped under his weight.

She reached out, touched a damp back.

"What happened?"

"Did they let you know I wouldn't be home?"

"Yes. What was it?"

"The wheels came off. A body's been found in the woods near the river. Behind Owlstone Road."

She came wide awake. "By Bee and Pamela's house?"

"Not more than a few hundred feet from it."

"Who is it?"

"A young woman. No ID. She'd been there for a couple of weeks."

"Oh," Gillian shuddered. She knew what that meant. "It must have been awful."

"Filthy."

She heard him swallow.

"Want a drink?" he said.

"No, thanks. It's a bit early."

"God, I wish I could squirt whisky up my nose. Pickle myself in it. Just to get the smell out of my nostrils." He took another slug and crawled under the sheets. "I'm going to sleep for a few hours before I go back to the station. Sorry I woke you."

"Is it connected to Wendy's murder?"

"Ask me when we've put a name to the face. What's left of it."

He curled up on his side, his back to her. She tucked her knees in behind his.

"I missed you tonight."

"Good."

In five minutes, his breathing changed. She lay

quietly until six and then slipped out of bed and into her dressing-gown and tiptoed downstairs.

When Edward got up, she gave him coffee.

"How are you?" she asked.

He blinked and squeezed the back of his neck with one hand, tilting his head cautiously to one side and then the other. "I feel reptilian. About a hundred million years old and covered in scales."

"Iguanodon or tyrannosaurus?"

"Nothing with rex in its name."

"I could hurl a couple of eggs into the frying-pan— if you eat your young, that is."

He winced. "Er, I think I could manage some toast, if it's not too much trouble."

"Coming up."

She cut two slices from a loaf she'd bought at the bakery in Newnham and turned on the grill. Toasters were not among the basic equipment provided by college rentals. She chuckled.

"What's funny?"

"I was bitching to Murray about never having dinner with you and he suggested that we have long intimate breakfasts instead."

"Gazing across the table through our nictitating membranes."

"Yes. There's more coffee in the pot."

"Good. I couldn't survive on the station brew today." He poured himself a second cup and drank. She made the toast, spread it liberally with butter and marmalade and then sat down across the table from him.

"You can tell Bee we found that card file on the doctors she was asking about. It was in Wendy's office."

"That's good. She'll be relieved. Did you read the cards?"

"With pleasure. Like Cecily Cardew, they call a spade a spade."

"They don't have Assistant Commissioners looking over their shoulders."

"Or public inquires."

"Do you think the burglary is connected to the murder?"

"Let's say it's not the most promising lead we've got. But after today, who knows? This new body, if it's connected, may alter the whole picture."

Murray shuffled in, yawning hugely. His hair stood up in three little tufts.

"Triceratops, I presume," said Edward.

Murray blinked at him.

"Here's some coffee," Gillian said. "Consumed by extinct reptiles everywhere."

"Have mercy," Murray said. "You've been up longer than I have."

The telephone rang. Gillian looked at Murray, who raised his arms as if to fend off an attack. She went to answer it.

"Gillian!" Bee's voice said loudly. "There's the most unholy commotion in our road. Police cars, and reporters and horrid little men with cameras. We got home late last night and missed everything, but the neighbours say a body was found in the wood behind our house. A woman's body. A little girl who lives a few houses down found it when she was out walking the dog. Does Edward know anything about it?"

"Yes. He was there when the police went yesterday."

"Who is she?"

"They don't know yet."

"What's he told you?"

"She'd been there for a couple of weeks."

"God. And we didn't know. Can you come over this morning? Pamela's got to teach, and I want to talk. This is ghastly."

"Sure."

Gillian hung up. Edward was standing up, ready to go.

"Did you ask him how you could help?" Gillian asked Murray. Murray looked sheepish.

"He wanted to do something, he said last night. So I told him to ask you if he could," she said to Edward.

"Fingerprint your colleagues for me, would you? Then we could match their prints to the ones on Wendy's lab equipment." Edward laughed, then saw the disappointed expression on Murray's face. "If there's anything, I'll tell you. We can use all the help we can get."

He moved towards the door. "Why didn't Vermeer paint a 'Woman with Coffeepot'? There is no more beautiful sight. What did I do with my shoes last night?"

"They're by the front door, Kemo Sabe," Gillian replied.

He was gone.

"Hi ho, Silver," she murmured, sitting down again.

Murray squinted at the street door. "Who was that masked man, anyway?"

When Gillian arrived at Bee's, Owlstone Road was fairly quiet. A few neighbours were standing about and murmuring, but the police had closed off the path into the wood, and there was nothing to see. Most people had left for work, and the children had gone to school, where there would no doubt be some sort of announcement made, since the place where the body had been found was not very far from the school grounds.

Irene was at Bee's, too. She had tied her unruly hair with a dark ribbon and was looking severe, despite her fluttering layers and fringes.

"How could it have been there so long?" she wanted to know.

"It was buried. In a shallow grave, Edward said. It was covered with dirt and then branches and leaves were put on top. He thinks an animal must have been digging at it recently—with the spell of hot weather we've been having it would have begun to smell— and that's why the dog found it."

"Ecch," said Irene, shutting her eyes.

"I feel as if I'm living in a war zone," said Bee. "Bodies everywhere."

She wasn't wearing any make-up, and Gillian fancied she could see, beneath the rounded contours of cheek and jaw, the hollow look Bee had when she was unhappy.

"They must be linked somehow, Wendy and this other one. We can't suddenly have two murderers barging about Cambridge, doing everybody in."

"But who is she?" Irene said.

Gillian sighed. "Jane Doe."

There was a loud thump from upstairs.

"What was that?" Gillian asked, startled.

"The plumber." Bee grimaced. "Renovations stop for no man—nor woman either. Otherwise, they never get started again."

"Let's go and sit in the garden," Irene said. "I want to smoke."

Bee looked at Gillian. They had both been smokers once.

"I think I'll have one too," said Bee.

There were chairs on the terrace. The sun had warmed the bricks, and clusters of golden wallflowers blazed against the wall. A faint scent of honeysuckle was in the air. Irene lit her cigarette and Bee's.

"That's better," she said.

Bee coughed. "Oh Christ," she said and coughed again. Her eyes watered. "Here, take this damned thing," she said to Gillian, blindly extending the cigarette. "How did I ever manage to smoke a whole one?"

Gillian took it, watching the smoke curl in the sunlight. It felt so natural in her hand, still. She suddenly thought of Michael. Funny, she'd thought of him twice this week, after months, or was it years, of not thinking of him at all.

She and Michael used to sit in bed and smoke after making love. She remembered his face, lit by the red glow. Blue eyes, wild, curly brown hair. Sixties hair. Where was Michael now? "Remember how much people used to smoke in the movies?" she said.

Bee stopped coughing. "Now they swear," she said. "What are you doing with that cigarette?"

Gillian looked down. "Just holding it. I don't want to smoke it. I just like the feel of it in my hand." She watched Irene exhale two thin streams through her nostrils. Girls had practised that in front of the mirror when Gillian was in school. "By the way, Edward said to tell you they did find your card file on the doctors. In Wendy's office."

"Thank God," said Bee. "It would have been a real nuisance to collect all that data again. When can we have it back?"

"As soon as they solve the case, I guess. I'm not sure. I keep wondering about that burglary."

"So do we. Maybe Dr Stoner did it. He hates our guts."

"Why?"

"Because we warn our customers about him. He's the last doctor in Cambridge a pregnant woman should go to. Even if she wants the baby. He's a tyrant and a clumsy old goat. If you want an abortion, forget it. He's a member of SOB."

"SOB?"

"Save Our Babies. They're anti-choice fanatics."

"Oh. But does he know you tell people he's no good?"

"Oh yes, we know he knows. Someone told him, and he called us up and threatened us. He ranted and raved and said he'd take us to court. That was several months ago. We haven't heard from him again, but he's an enemy of ours, no question."

"So you think he might have burgled the PIS office?" Irene said. "To steal the cards? That's silly. What good would it do?"

"Maybe he wanted to see what we said about other doctors. Maybe he thought he could sue if he had the evidence."

"But he didn't get the cards."

"No. But he might have taken the book. Who else would? He probably thought the information he wanted was in it. Or something else he could use against us. And then he took the money so we'd think it was an ordinary burglary."

"And why did he take the kit, then?" Irene said, still dubious.

"General trouble-making and bloody-mindedness. Because little girls shouldn't play with grown-up doctors' toys."

"Well," said Gillian, "that may all make sense to you, I don't know, but it doesn't connect the burglary to Wendy, unless you think he's got everyone's name from your book and is going to kill off all the PIS members one by one."

"I wouldn't put it past him," said Bee darkly.

"Our names and the numbers are in it," Irene said, for the first time sounding a little uneasy.

"Is SOB like Operation Rescue?" Gillian asked.

"What's Operation Rescue?"

"They blockade clinics—illegally—to prevent women from getting in. They scream abuse and intimidate doctors by picketing their homes."

"Christ! We don't have anyone like that here," Bee said.

"Not yet," Irene added. "Our lot are very holy. Vigils and pious pronouncements and attempts to turn the clock back to coat-hanger days. But no violence. I've sometimes wondered whether it's because the revolutionary potential of women having real control over their fertility just isn't as obvious here as it is in America, where women's economic position has shifted more, and where people think in terms of revolution anyway."

"We're a less violent society," Bee said.

"We have a lower murder rate," Irene answered,

"but do we have a lower wife-battering rate? I don't think so. And the anti-choice brigade has the same agenda here as everywhere. When they get vulnerable teenagers in their clutches, the pressure they put on them is really vicious. SOB are opposed to contraception, too, especially for teenagers. Their agenda is all about controlling sexuality, not about saving lives. We think of them," she added parenthetically to Gillian, "as the Sons of Bitches, politically incorrect though the term may be."

"They don't care if the mothers die," said Bee, "only the babies."

"Still," said Gillian, "even if Stoner is an SOB that doesn't make him a murderer."

SIXTEEN

After leaving Bee, Gillian put in several hours at the university library before attending Basil's third lecture and then going on to tea at Jesus College. Murray had been invited, with guest, and had suggested that she should be the guest. "The bursar's organized it," he'd said. "A number of Fellows will be there, and visiting firemen like me. Maybe you'll meet some interesting people. You can keep me company and see the Fellows' garden," he'd added, wheedling a little.

"All right," said Gillian cheerfully, thinking it would be a blazing afternoon. "Damn the ozone layer, full speed ahead."

She met Murray in Earl Street at three-thirty and went upstairs to change. When she came down she was wearing a flowery summer dress from Liberty, the sort of dress that brought to mind Edwardian afternoons and the word "frock," with its air of chaste frivolity.

"You've gone native," Murray said, opening the front door.

"Yes, I've probably been here too long." She gestured at the hot blue sky. "It's the sun, you know. We're not bred to it."

Murray laughed. "Oh yes we are. New York summers were a lot hotter than this."

"How would you know? You were out on Long Island."

"You think Long Island wasn't hot in the summers? Let me tell you, I remember some real stinkers."

They crossed Christ's Pieces and turned into King Street. In Jesus Lane the automobiles fumed. The college hid behind a high, sooty brick wall. They turned up the walk leading to the gatehouse, and the sound of the engines receded.

"Isn't it pretty?" Murray said, peeping into Cloister Court.

"This was once the nunnery of St Rhadegund," Gillian said. "The Bishop of Ely helped himself to the buildings and revenue and turned it into Jesus College—for men, of course. "

"The women are back now."

"So they are. And it only took five hundred years."

They went into the garden. Thirty or forty people were eddying slowly about the lawns and flowerbeds, nibbling biscuits and drinking tea. Cups and saucers clinked, and conversation overlaid the drone of the traffic in Jesus Lane.

Gillian saw a historian she knew and was quickly drawn into a discussion of the Gulf War and its historical background. They soon strayed far from the UN and Kuwait, however. Her acquaintance was a Mediævalist, and the background that came under his scrutiny extended to the contentions of the Byzantine and Persian empires, the Crusades, the Black Death, the Mongol invasions and the capture of Baghdad by Genghis Khan's grandson, whose warrior herdsmen had much the same effect as the Vandals had had on Rome.

The heat and talk made Gillian thirsty. "Goodness, it's hot! If this keeps up you'll be growing oranges instead of apples, and no one will go to the Riviera any more. Whatever became of English rain?"

"An American voice! How wonderful."

Gillian turned. The remark, piercing the general tea-party hum, took her by surprise. It had come from an exquisitely turned-out woman of about thirty. She was very blonde, and two inches taller than Gillian. How often had Gillian been told that nobody really looks like the models in *Vogue*? This woman could have stepped right off the pages. Gillian felt the impact and tried not to mind.

"I'm Samantha Kennedy," the woman said. "You may have met my husband, Alan." She nodded at a man, just as blond and taller than she, who was talking to Murray and another man a short distance away.

"Samantha," said Gillian. "I'm Gillian Adams."

"Just call me Sam," she said. "Everybody does. People at home do, anyway. People here have trouble with it. It's too short for them to pronounce."

Samantha Kennedy must have been a homecoming queen in her college days. She glistened all over, from her burnished cap of blonde hair to her dewy eyelids and glossy lips, her silky dress and long nylon legs and little Italian sandals, fragile as eggshells. She glistened with confidence and expensive skin care: a polished look that came only with money and disciplined attention.

"Where's home?" Gillian asked.

"Santa Fe. You ever been there? It's the most beautiful place on earth." Her voice was wistful. "Our house—my family's house—is up on a hill. The air's like crystal, and the desert in spring—it's like magic. The flowers seem to come from nowhere—you see it happen every year, but you still can't believe it."

"You're interested in flowers? The college gardens are exquisite in May, don't you think?"

"Sure," Sam said without enthusiasm. "But everything's so boxy. So little and shut in. People from the south-west are used to open spaces. Where are you from?"

"How do you answer that question when you've moved around?" Gillian asked. "Nobody's all that interested in your life story. I live in Vancouver."

"But you sound American. Don't tell me I'm wrong about that."

"I grew up in New York State, and I went back there to teach after studying here. My mother's Canadian, though, from Toronto, and I lived there for a few years too. How long have you been in England?"

"Two years. Alan's been here much longer, of course. We were married two years ago, and that's when I came over. When were you a student here?"

"Twenty years ago—in the dark ages."

"Dark ages?"

"Before the men's colleges admitted women undergraduates. I was here for three years, doing my doctorate in history."

"And then you went back home," said Sam. "You weren't bitten by the Cambridge bug. Alan was."

"There's a more generalized British bug. I've got that, judging by the amount of time I spend over here."

"Well I don't have it, but I'm stuck here."

"What do you do?"

"Hardly anything," Sam said crossly. "I went to law school; I had a job with one of the top firms in New Mexico. I'm not exactly stupid. But I can't practise here. I thought I might go into real estate—my mother sells real estate at home, and I know a lot about it, but the system here is ridiculous. Besides, when you think about it, selling houses isn't very interesting. People who do it like to think they're professionals, but it's no different than selling anything else. My mother always says it's like selling shoes—you just have to find the one that fits. Alan wants me to study law here; he thinks then I'll want to stay. But it means practically starting all over again. Besides, I don't want to be a dinky little solicitor, and being a barrister means London. And of course he won't commute to Cambridge. Oh no." She sighed. "Usually I can make him see things my way, but he hasn't budged an inch on this. I'll get through to him sometime, but meantime I spend half my life getting my hair done and taking exercise classes, and I'm bored out of my tree."

"It sounds pretty dull," Gillian said, watching Sam's extremely full pouty lips closing over her pearly little teeth. Was that what they called the Paris lip?

"It's excruciating," Sam went on. "Oh, hell! I can't tell you how good it feels to talk to somebody from home about it. I can't say everything right out to English people, it sounds too rude, and I've said it a million times to Alan—he doesn't listen. When I first came here, I thought it was real cute, you know? I like old things, and we were invited around to people's houses. But now I hate it. It's like I just don't exist. The people here think Cambridge is the whole world, you know? The men don't think you're human if you're not at the university. They treat you like a bimbo or wallpaper that can cook. And the wives are just polite. You can't get to know them at all."

"So what are you going to do?" Gillian asked curiously. Sam's description of Cambridge was not a new one, and her looks probably made things more difficult for her. She most likely scared the wits out of half the men. Gillian didn't ordinarily think of lips as sexual organs when she was listening to people, but she couldn't stop thinking of Sam Kennedy's lips that way. Obviously that was the effect that collagen injections were intended to have. Maybe she was born with those lips, though. Maybe Alan Kennedy married her lips. Physically, Sam and her husband were quite a striking pair, showier than was typical of the species.

"I don't know. I want Alan to come home and teach in the south-west. But he loves it here. He doesn't want to leave. Cambridge, Cambridge, that's all I hear. It's a thing with him. We fight about it a lot."

Who would win, Gillian wondered. This was a strong-willed woman, and used to having her own way. People that good-looking usually were. He had a job, but if her clothes were any clue she had money of her own.

"Do you have children?" she asked.

"A little boy. He's almost a year now. He's cute as a bug, but I can't spend my whole life with him. I've got way too much drive—I'd probably be trying to make him pass the bar exam when he was six, or something. I've got a sweet young Portuguese girl who lives in." Her jaw tightened. "But I adore him. If I leave, he goes with me."

Gillian didn't doubt it. She looked across the lawn at Alan Kennedy, thirty feet away. He fidgeted, shifting from one foot to the other, and his eyes periodically darted about the group on the lawn. He had the look of a hunted man.

After she and Murray had left and were walking back down the Chimney to Jesus Lane, she said, "You spent quite a bit of time talking to Alan Kennedy. Is he a friend of yours?"

"A colleague. He's a chemist from California."

"You don't know him well?"

"No. I've met him a few times, seen him at conferences. He's a whizzbang chemist, but I don't like him much, really. He's too egotistical and self-absorbed. He's not interested in people unless they're useful or in his way. Why do you ask?"

"He seemed very edgy. I wondered if you'd noticed it when you were talking to him. I picked up on it because his wife pointed him out to me."

"Queen Samantha? I'd be nervous if she were my wife."

"Really? Why?"

"She makes me think of Turandot."

Edward, meanwhile, was not thinking about Alan Kennedy. The interview with Kennedy's wife had been put on hold while he and Hardy dealt with the body in the woods. They had found out who she was without much difficulty. Her parents had reported her missing two weeks earlier. They lived in Grantchester.

Her name was Cynthia Perdreau, and she was seventeen years old when she died. Her name and description had popped up almost instantly when the police had checked the missing persons file. There had followed the tragic business of notifying her parents and having her body identified.

Then the autopsy, the further scouring of the wood for evidence, the review of the missing persons report. The telephone calls, the attempts to poach a few more detectives, the re-scheduling of assignments, cancellations of leave. Edward looked at the photograph they had borrowed from Cynthia's desolate family. It was a recent picture, not a formal portrait but a close-up taken by her father when she'd passed her driving test. She was smiling, sitting at the wheel of the family car. It was a round face, pretty with the bloom and liveliness of youth but unremarkable. Brown hair, bright blue eyes, a few freckles on the pale skin. No longer a girl but not yet a woman, Edward thought. There was something uncertain in the expression, something still blurred about the contours of mouth and chin. She had passed three A levels, her parents said, and was studying for a fourth while she worked part-time in a flower shop. Had she ideas about her future, Edward had asked. She hadn't made up her mind, they'd told him, but she'd been determined to train for something that paid well and offered some chance of advancement. She was good with figures; she thought perhaps something in accounting. Her parents were willing to support her while she studied, though with another child coming up to fourteen, it was a strain on the pocketbook.

They were nice people, Edward thought, recalling the painful interview. Not particularly expressive. The kind that help when there's trouble and mind their own business the rest of the time. Now they were in shock. In Edward's experience, there was nothing that could prepare parents for the news that a missing child was dead. Hope resisted probability until the bitter end, and even beyond. They had been terribly frightened when she disappeared. There had been no quarrel, and they were certain she hadn't run away. She wasn't that sort of child. At first they'd imagined an accident. When that was ruled out, they were baffled and increasingly afraid.

They had asked the police to check on her former boyfriend. The police had done so promptly, but the investigation hadn't turned up anything useful. The romance had dissolved a couple of months earlier and he claimed not to have seen her since. He was temporarily unemployed, he'd told them, having recently left a position with a pharmaceutical company. He lived in Histon. Her parents hadn't seen him since Cynthia had told them the relationship was over. She'd said very little about him since, had seemed a little blue and anxious but not overwhelmingly distressed. They'd seen no reason to worry about her. Both parents had been very relieved when the romance ended; not, they said, that they knew anything specific against him.

"Not our sort," they'd said quietly. And he was too old—twenty-seven—for a girl of seventeen. But she was quite independent for her age, and it was easy to see what the attraction was for Cynthia, her mother admitted. "He was rather smashing, in that sulky way girls like." They thought he hadn't much future and had considered forbidding her to see him but had decided not to risk it. "Friends of ours tried that with their daughter, and she up and married the lad. She's divorced now, of course, only twenty, with a baby and no job prospects. The father's gone off—she won't see a penny from him for the child." Cynthia's mother's lips folded inward and the corners of her mouth turned down. She and Cynthia's father had waited for "love" to fade, she said. And it had, it seemed.

There was a file on the disappearance. The earlier interview with Cynthia's parents had been less detailed than Edward's own. There had followed a lot of tedious inquiries: the flower shop, her school, the family doctor, her friends and neighbours. Nothing. She was a nice, ordinary young person with no strange habits or obvious troubles. And she had disappeared without a trace.

Edward read the report through and then talked to the young detective-constable who had interviewed Tod French, the boyfriend.

"Did he seem unhappy about the break-up?"

"No. He was calm—as though it was all finished and done with."

"Why did they break up? What exactly did he say about it?"

"Not very much. Just that he wasn't interested in her any more."

"So he broke it off?"

"That's what he told me."

"Was she upset?"

"He said if she was, she didn't show it."

"But they had had a sexual relationship. Was it her only one, I wonder. What sort of fellow is he?"

DC Paris looked at Edward eagerly. "I wondered about that myself. I've thought about it. If she didn't run away, I mean, now we know she didn't, but when I was thinking about him we didn't know—it looked to me as if she'd gone off somewhere, to London, maybe, because the bloke dumped her. I thought maybe she was upset and he wasn't letting on."

"Go on," said Edward, whose mind had skipped back twenty-odd years to a shabby little interrogation room in south London. It was his own suspect; he was asking the questions, his first time. Had this little toe-rag conspired with his friends to rob his own grandmother and knock her senseless, or had he known nothing about it, as he claimed? Edward had thought and thought while the boy hotly denied any part in the crime. Later, with experience, it became easier to tell when people were lying. Not always, of course, but usually. *Why* they were lying was another matter. You could fill a shelf of psychology books with the reasons. Yes,

Edward acknowledged with an inward grin, DC Paris, young DC Paris, all blue eyes and crisp black hair, would have studied his suspect with some intensity.

"You thought about him. What opinion did you form?" he asked, matching Paris's earnestness with formality.

DC Paris cleared his throat. "A smart bloke, not very chatty. He didn't object to being questioned, but I don't think he liked it. You couldn't call him a hostile witness, but he said as few words as possible. Answered yes or no."

"Was he frightened?"

"Not so's you'd notice. Despised me and my job, I'd say. A bit of a chip on his shoulder, maybe; I asked him if he had a new girlfriend, and he sort of huffed and said it was none of my business. He passed a comment about spoilt rich girls at Cambridge. Then he said Cynthia wasn't like that."

"She wasn't rich."

"No, but a cut or two above him. His flat's not much. He's a bit of a flash dresser, though."

"Anything else?"

"Well, I don't know, sir. He wasn't very worried. About her disappearing, I mean."

"How did he account for it?"

"He just said girls did as they liked these days. They didn't tell their parents what they were up to. He couldn't have cared very much about her, it seemed to me."

At the end of the day, Edward looked at his notes. Perdreau had been progressing satisfactorily in her studies. She was well thought of at the flower shop in Bridge Street, where she did some book-keeping as well as sales. French had met her at the shop after work now and then, but Cynthia's employers hadn't seen him for weeks. He was too old for her; her father should have put his foot down. Young people had more independence today than was good for them. French never took her out anywhere nice, they thought. But he was quiet and well dressed, they'd say that for him.

In the murder room, the big white board on the wall was filled up with data. The autopsy had revealed that Cynthia Perdreau had had an abortion shortly before she was killed. The abortion, they now knew, had been performed at Addenbrooke's on Friday, April 19th, five days before she disappeared. She had been at home all weekend and had stayed home Monday as well. On Tuesday she had gone to work; the next day, the 24th, she had worked a half-day, in the afternoon. She had left work at five p.m. At eleven, her parents had telephoned the police.

"Let's review what we've got," Edward said to Hardy. He swallowed some coffee and put the cup down. "If we don't wrap this up in a day or two, I'll be forced to buy a coffee pot."

"All right. You start." Hardy dropped three lumps of sugar into his tea and stirred.

Edward said nothing.

"Go on," Hardy said, stirring violently.

"What about the other two lumps? You usually take five."

"Pam said I should cut down." He gazed gloomily at the mug. "Bloody hell. There's no decency left in this life when a police officer in the upper ranks can't have proper sugar in his tea." He scrabbled in the top left-hand drawer of his desk and found two toffees. The wrappings were dusty. He offered one to Edward.

"No, thank you. They make my teeth hurt."

"Mine, too. Cheers." He popped one into his mouth. "Go."

"The autopsy. She was hit on the head with a heavy branch. Two blows, close together. Fragments of bark in the wounds. Killed instantly. No signs of a struggle. She wasn't molested. Some alcohol in the body; no other drugs. A healthy young woman. Didn't tell her family or their GP about the pregnancy."

"Right. SOC says she was killed close to where the body was found—twenty feet away, on the path. Then she was carried, not dragged, to where she was buried. She'd had a bit to drink but wasn't too ripe; she was taken unawares. In that area, if she'd screamed, it's likely someone would have heard her. Conclusion: she knew her killer. She went to the wood with him, or he met her there. We'll have to get on to the boyfriend. We'll need to go back over all the ground DC Paris covered when she disappeared. He did his job; I don't mean he didn't; we worked that case harder than we might have—the parents were so sure she hadn't run away. But it wasn't a murder inquiry."

"I've seen the file. Tod French wasn't very forthcoming. We need to shake a few apples from that tree."

"And where was she the night of the 19th? She told her parents she was staying with a friend, but that friend—and her parents—said she wasn't there and wasn't expected."

"She was last seen leaving work at five in the afternoon on the 24th; she never came home. So she was probably killed that evening. Where did she have a drink first? And what about the burial? How did our villain arrange that? What did he dig with?"

"Santini thinks a spade. We should have a look in the river for it. Wherever he got it, he wouldn't have wanted to carry it out of the wood again. Might as well advertise on the telly."

"And why there, I wonder. Why that particular spot?"

"She lived in Grantchester. She usually walked home along the river, unless the weather was bad." Hardy spread out a map of Cambridge. His large, sausage-like finger traced a line from Bridge Street down King's Parade and across the Fen. "Her most direct route would take her through Lammas Land and Newnham, very close to the wood. Her parents said she liked to walk in the meadows, looking for birds. Maybe she walked in the wood, too."

"You're saying that our villain knew her habits and stalked her?"

"I don't know. It would be a funny place to meet a girl unless she was in the habit of going there."

He must have had a plan, unless he goes everywhere with a spade over his shoulder."

"Hmm. I wonder whether any of the good citizens of Owlstone Road has an unlocked garden shed."

SEVENTEEN

Edward rang Earl Street early in the evening. Another night like the previous one, he and Hardy had agreed, and they'd both be worse than useless. Gillian had told him she'd be home all evening.

"What would you say to a glass of beer in about half an hour?"

"I'd say yes."

She went back to her file cards. How much cross-referencing did she want to do? Research, it seemed to her, sometimes boiled down to this decision. One could spend one's entire life cross-referencing, devising schemes of classification that would trap every fact, every theory, in an ever-denser web. The snag was that the book would never be written or if written would be unreadable. But the compulsion to classify sprang from the need to hold impossible quantities of information in order. Too little cross-referencing, and faulty memory would toss the book to a howling pack of critics. She had almost two feet of file cards already. How much was enough? A yard? An ell? A rod? A furlong of file cards. How long was a furlong? The word came from furrow, she knew that. How long was a furrow? She reached for the dictionary, abandoning her file cards.

"This is an unexpected treat," she said when Edward arrived, laden with several pints of beer.

"As you remind me now and then, there's more to life than death. Besides, I'm knackered. And there's something I want to tell you."

"Absolutely wonderful beer. What is it?"

"Theakston's Old Peculier."

Gillian laughed with pure pleasure. "I love England."

"It's from the free house at the end of King Street. I had to sample it."

"How's the case going? Or cases?"

"Oh, the station's a madhouse. We couldn't double the team, but we have twice as much work to do. The indexers are going round the twist trying to catalogue all the new information."

"They have my heartfelt sympathy," Gillian replied, tilting her head at the desk in the corner, which was covered with cards, as was one end of the sofa. The other end was piled with books and a messy stack of photocopied articles.

"How are you getting on with your political hostesses?"

"They're an exhausting bunch. They had far more zip than anybody I know. The race has deteriorated. Anyhow, depending on whether I enlarge the scope of the book or not, I have either too much material or too little. I'm shuffling my deck of cards while I decide. What did you want to tell me about?"

"The girl in the woods. Her name was Cynthia Perdreau; she was a seventeen-year-old from Grantchester."

"Didn't you tell me one of the chemists who didn't like Wendy lives in Grantchester?"

"Roger Hill. His house isn't far from hers. That's one interesting point. But the one I particularly wanted to mention is that she had an abortion not long before she died."

"Oh."

"Her parents didn't know about it."

"I wonder if she went to the PIS for a pregnancy test."

"That's what's on my mind. She didn't go to her family doctor."

"Do you have a photograph? Why don't I ask Bee and the rest of the PIS whether they remember her?"

"That would be very helpful. We'll have a word with the Cambridge GP who saw her, but if she went to the PIS for advice first, we want to know what she told them. See what you can find out, will you? The main question, of course, as McClure so gracefully put it this morning, is who put her in the pudding club."

"Charming. Do you think the man might have been interested in keeping her quiet?"

"It's one possibility."

"She may not have told the PIS anything much, but I'll see. I'll snout around tomorrow. I'm fed up with my file cards for the moment."

Edward refilled his glass. "You know, we've had hardly a minute since you got here."

"I've noticed."

"I was going to ask you," he went on, "while I was here and we had a bit of time—hollow laugh department—what you want to do about your job. What you're thinking about it. I don't mean to press you—it's your choice to make. I just want you to know that I'd like it if you came to live in London. All the time." He turned his glass in his hands, frowning. "I'm a swine about London, about sticking here, I know that. But I can't help it. Some people don't transplant. It would be a disaster."

"I know."

"Anyhow, I've been mulling it over since the autumn, but there's been no moment that seemed the right one to discuss it. This one's probably not the best either, but I didn't want you to imagine I hadn't given it any thought."

To her own dismay, Gillian felt her eyes brim with tears. Edward was horrified.

"What have I said?"

"It's not you," she said rubbing the tears away as they slipped out. "It's just that I don't know what to do. I don't even know whether it would work, living here. It's an impossible decision. I don't want to go on leading two lives, I'm too tired. But I don't want to choose, either. Where would I get a job in London? The last time I looked, there weren't any, and there were ten brilliant people turning over every stone trying to find one. I can't just stop working." She gave him a watery smile. "I'm just as selfish as you, you see."

"No. You've had a miserable year, you haven't had a sabbatical in far too long and you're facing a choice I won't make. The best I can say for my swinish self is that I won't force you to make it either. But I know what I want." He leaned across and filled her empty glass. "Here, have a drink. "

"I've read that pigs are good companions," said Gillian. "Clever, and quite clean, too. Pot-bellied pigs are the best kind, I believe."

Edward looked down at his waistline. "If I keep eating Murray's dinners, I'll certainly be one of those."

In the morning, when Edward returned to the station, there was a message waiting for him. It was from Jeremy Martingale. He had rung up to tell Edward that he had seen the man who had been in Wendy's flat. Would Edward return his call as soon as possible?

He answered on the first ring. He was in a state of

excitement. "It's quite extraordinary," he said, his voice hitting a high note, "I just saw him walking in the street—down Tennis Court Road. It was the same man. I'm absolutely certain." He paused dramatically.

As he would do at the right moments in court, Edward thought.

"So I followed him!" Jeremy continued.

"And where did he go?" Edward asked.

"The chemistry labs! He's a member of the department. I even know his name!" Jeremy sounded pleased with himself.

"And what would it be?" asked Edward, amused.

"Alan Kennedy."

"And you've seen this man in Wendy's flat?"

"Yes, I have. And I can identify him for you any time. In fact I found out that he lectures tomorrow morning in the big lecture hall at the labs. I could meet you there if you like."

The morning conference produced a fresh harvest of information. They now had the analysis of the contents of Wendy's flask. There was indeed ether peroxide in it, which confirmed that her analysis had been correct, but they still didn't know why the peroxide was there. The other report, on the forensic evidence from her lab, was more interesting. Fibres that matched the sack had been found where the wall met the floor near the door jamb, and a broken strand of red hair had been removed from the wooden floor, where it had been caught on a splinter. Some fragments of as yet unidentified greenery had also been collected. Her bench showed no signs of disturbance.

Interviews with those present in the labs on Friday night and at the weekend had produced one student who had gone up to the third floor on Friday evening. The door to Wendy's lab had been open, and he had seen her at her bench, alone, as he passed by. He was certain it had been about half past eight, an hour before he went home. This piece of data was duly marked on the board. Edward was relieved to have her presence early in the evening confirmed. It was logical to assume that she had signed in herself and was there, since she'd told Simon and Nick she'd be working all night if necessary. But if no witness had turned up, the team would have had to pay some attention to alternative possibilities, a time-consuming and probably useless diversion. The register revealed that she was careful to sign out on the occasions when she had signed in. Based on that fact, and their witness, they could assume that she had signed in at 7:40 and stayed until whatever time she was assaulted in her lab. And they now had narrowed the time-slot by nearly an hour.

"What do you make of the lab report?" Hardy said, as he and Edward were mapping out the day's efforts. "It looks as if you're right—she was attacked in her lab, not in the cold room. She went towards the door of her lab and was attacked there. Presumably, he wanted her away from her bench, to avoid leaving a mess he couldn't clean up. The struggle was over quickly. No bloodshed. He must have been pretty sure he could immobilize her fast, and I fancy Kennedy would be, but there's no indication that he coshed her before she hit that shelf in the cold room. Do you think he put a gun to her head? He's American, he might have one."

"In England?"

"They don't like parting with their guns, I'm told." Hardy had more questions. "And why would Kennedy have attacked her in the lab? Suppose he's afraid Fowler's going to tell his wife that she's pregnant with his child, and he thinks his wife will leave him, taking his son and all that lovely money with her. Wouldn't he have killed Fowler somewhere else, where suspicion would be less likely to fall on him?"

"But suppose she was going to tell his wife right away—that night, even. After he left her flat, he panicked. And maybe he knew about Bottomley's little tricks and thought we'd suspect him."

"Why not wait in the dark and run her over in the car park? Wouldn't that have been easier?"

"Maybe he didn't want to dent his BMW." Edward stared at the photograph of Wendy on the board. "I think Sergeant Temple had the right idea: she was unconscious before she arrived in the cold room. But not from a blow. I think a chemist could manage that."

"Clap something over her mouth and nose, you

mean? Not too hard to do if he's someone she knows, I suppose, especially someone as powerful as Kennedy."

"He wouldn't have to be all that strong. Suppose her attacker came to her lab and said there was a fire in the building. She'd rush to the door, unsuspecting, and he'd be waiting for her."

"I still say it's likely to be Kennedy. She would have been suspicious of Bottomley if he'd come bursting into her lab at night with some tale about a fire. She knew he hated her."

"What if he—or whoever it was—told her there was another flood downstairs? She would probably have believed him."

Hardy pondered this for a moment. "And if it was Hill, he could have pretended to be angry," he said. "They say that the brain deteriorates as it grows older, but yours still seems to work, Gisborne."

"Now and then."

"What have we got on Hill so far? Dinner in college checks out; he left at about a quarter to nine. He drove home, was seen walking the wolfhound past the Red Lion at a quarter past and coming back again just before ten. It's a conspicuous dog. After that, he says he was at home. He doesn't have a garage, the car was parked outside. His next-door neighbours were out in the garden; they say he couldn't have driven the car away before eleven without them noticing it."

"So if he went out, he walked. Along the footpath back to Cambridge. How long does that take?"

"It's a mile from Grantchester to the edge of Cambridge, on the footpath. Then maybe another mile to the labs, no, not as much as that. Certainly under two miles, as straight as he could go."

"Say a good half-hour, then. He would want to be inconspicuous."

"He could have been back by half past ten, at the earliest."

Edward looked over the DC's notes. "The neighbours seem to have been very cooperative."

"So Paris said." Hardy heaved himself out of his chair. "All right. Back to Alan Kennedy. We know she was alive at half past eight. She left the lab at six, went to the restaurant, went home—probably with Kennedy—then went back to the lab. She signed in at 7:40. He went where? Home?"

"I'll find out this afternoon," Edward said. "I'll ask his beautiful wife."

"I suppose that leaves me with Cynthia Perdreau's boyfriend. The Yard always takes the plums."

Edward considered how to proceed. He now had a witness to Kennedy's presence in Wendy's flat. A witness who would impress a jury. Kennedy had lied. Why? To conceal an affair or a murder? It was time to ask his wife a few questions. According to Gillian, she was a woman of forceful character and apparently independent means who was finding the whither-thou-goest formula hard to swallow. And they had a son. Kennedy would have good reasons for hiding his infidelity.

Or infidelities. How many affairs had he had? Edward drove out on the Barton Road. Hardy was busy with the Perdreau case. Was there any link? Did Kennedy's taste include seventeen-year-olds? Samantha—Sam—was a beauty-contest blonde, Gillian had said, except that she looked too smart to enter a beauty contest. Gillian. She didn't find the whither-thou-goest formula very palatable either. "And why should she?" he said, as the rooftops of Newnham College peeped over the trees off to the right. To be fair, he had never considered whither thouing off to Canada. It simply hadn't occurred to him at the beginning that after a dozen years he would find a part-time romance unsatisfactory. Indeed, for years, it had been just what he wanted, leaving him free to work the extraordinary hours that his job demanded and he chose to give, unconcerned about the effect on anyone else. He was well aware of the consequences such hours could have. The divorce rate among detectives was no secret. And it was not only the hours. The clannishness of police officers—their tribal rituals—had put a few marriages on the skids. His own hadn't survived. That was ancient history, now. Raine had remarried eighteen years ago; her children were nearly grown. He thought of her seldom and without rancour. His mother had kept in touch; otherwise, he wouldn't even know about

Raine's children, he supposed. He had been in his twenties then. An earlier self. The energy he'd had! To work a fourteen-hour day and down pints at the pub until it closed, to come off a gruelling night shift and go straight into a football game—no wonder Raine had left. He'd had no interest in holidays or domestic trifles; he hadn't wanted children, at least not right away; the force had absorbed all—and it was a not inconsiderable amount—he'd had to give. Why had they married? Sex, really, and family expectations. His memories of sex with Raine had faded now, lost their sensual detail, but it had been good, he remembered that. At least it had been good until they were too angry to want it. An image, long forgotten, flickered suddenly on the surface of his mind: Raine's body, the first time he had seen it, its extraordinary whiteness in the dim room, the almost shining white of a newly cut apple.

It no longer mattered. He was not the type to dwell on the past. His uncharacteristically reflective mood had to do with Gillian and wanting her to move to London. Suppose she did. Would it work? Had he changed enough since the disaster with Raine? When he met Gillian, he'd been single for almost ten years. She'd been staying in London for the summer, doing research; she was going back to her job in Canada. And so it had continued: visits, longer or shorter. The shorter visits had been easiest; he'd pruned his working hours except when it was impossible. When she'd begun staying longer, he'd gradually reverted to his usual habits. He hadn't guessed then that later he would want, need, be tempted to demand a radical change.

Edward suddenly noticed where he was: speeding south on the M11. He'd headed for London like a homing pigeon. He slowed and then touched the accelerator again. He'd have to get off at the next exit. Anyhow, Sam Kennedy could wait. She might not even be at home. What was happening to him now? He wasn't sure. He worked as hard as ever; the job still required it, and the edge of his interest was still keen. But it wasn't enough. He could remember a time when Gillian's presence in his life had thrown him off balance, when he had retreated into his work with something like relief even as he missed her. Now, although he found it hard to alter his habits when she was here, the balance was somehow wrong when she left. He shut down, like an office when everyone had gone home, leaving only the answering machines on.

It was recent, this feeling. Or, more likely, his awareness of it was recent. He suspected it had started when his father died. She'd been in Vancouver. He had wanted her to come to the funeral, but it was a difficult time of year for her, and he hadn't liked to ask. He hadn't asked. And he'd missed her, regretted it for months. His father hadn't liked her at first. He'd rejected everything American. The Americans had waited too long to enter the war—both wars— and they'd ruined English culture. Edward could still hear his father on the subject. They were loud, ignorant, vulgar; they mistreated the language. When young, Edward had learned American slang for the pleasure of annoying his father. When his father assumed that Edward had chosen Gillian for similar reasons, Edward had done little to disabuse him of the notion. There had been an element of truth in it, he had to admit, although a very small one. Gillian referred to his trying parent as Colonel Mustard and did her best to be philosophical. In the end, her quiet wit and good-humoured refusal to be intimidated had won him over. But he hadn't changed his mind about Americans; he'd merely treated her as an exception. Edward's mother, less prejudiced, and pleased that Edward had found something to care about besides the Yard, had always liked Gillian.

His father hadn't been pleased when he joined the Yard. Neither of his parents had cared for the idea. His father had tried to put his foot down. Edward had—brutally, he recognized now—pointed out that after twenty years of neglect it was a bit late to start coming the patriarch, and they hadn't spoken for a year. His mother had engineered the reconciliation. She had been affectionate in an absent-minded style when he was a child; it was only when he joined the Yard, stood poised, perhaps, on the brink of a permanent detachment, that she abruptly gave him her undivided attention. Such was her charm that he was quickly captured, even as he observed it happening and told himself he was a fool. He did not give up the Yard—he'd closed his ears to that siren song—but he had found himself wanting to please his mother in other ways. And so he made the overture to his father. They had travelled a bumpy road since then, but it had become smoother after he met Gillian. It hadn't occurred to him before then that it was possible to find his father funny.

She was having a hard time thinking about leaving her job. The old one-sided system had certainly been simpler. She would not have been head of the history department at a university on the other side of the globe. She would have stayed home and—and what? Ironed his shirts? He couldn't picture it. His mother hadn't ironed shirts; the cleaning woman had done it. Even Raine hadn't; she'd sent them out. And she stayed at home, but that hadn't saved their marriage. So much for the old system. He would not insist that Gillian leave her job. He couldn't. But he could use his powers of persuasion, try to convince her that she would be happier in London. The other side of the balance was formidably heavy—her job, her friends, her house . . . Surely she could find a job in London, perhaps not right way . . . She would make less than half as much money here, and she wouldn't be head of a department. She might regard that as a plus, however. A house like hers was out of the question, but he—they—could afford a bigger flat. He would look into it. And then there was his work. It was a pity that he'd been chasing that child-killer when she arrived. He'd hardly seen her. It had not been an advertisement for the pleasures of life with Edward Gisborne. He would take some time after this case was finished. They would go away somewhere. Maybe even Italy, if that was what she wanted.

He took the A10 and cut back through Hauxton to the Shelfords. Having thought of these things to do, he was suddenly confident. He sang under his breath as he drove. "I'm off to my love with a boxing glove, ten thousand miles away."

EIGHTEEN

There was a car in the drive at the Kennedys' house. A new Audi 100. Sam's car, presumably. They already knew that Alan Kennedy drove a BMW. Money, he thought. If it was her money, Sam Kennedy would be able to walk out without looking back. If she were given a reason. The house was suburban, with a detached garage and a manicured garden. He parked behind the Audi and looked about. From where he was standing, he could see between the garage and the house to a slice of lawn and flowerbed at the rear. A blonde woman and a little naked curly-haired blond child were sitting on the lawn, playing with a striped rubber ball. He heard them giggling. Not the scene he'd expected. He walked to the front door and rang the bell.

A plump, short teenager with stylishly cut black hair and a dark complexion opened the door. She was wearing jeans and a T-shirt with the name of a ski resort printed on the front. Had she gone there with the Kennedys? She spoke English fluently but with a pronounced accent. The Portuguese live-in. He followed her to the back of the house and she went outside to fetch her employer. It might be worth questioning the girl too, Edward thought, but not until he had heard what Sam Kennedy had to say. Why did people wear those shirts with the names of silly places on them, he wondered, irrelevantly.

Sam stood up, brushing a few blades of grass from her white trousers. She left her baby with the girl and came in through the sliding doors. She was tall, as tall as he, very blonde, with an extraordinary mouth. Like Brigitte Bardot's, thought Edward, who had awoke to such things when Bardot was the reigning sex symbol. She was tidy and cool and mistress of the house; if he hadn't seen her with her baby, he would not have imagined her capable of that playful affection.

She held out her hand. "Samantha Kennedy. What can I do for you?" A flat American voice, the sort his father wouldn't have liked. She was sizing him up and wasn't troubling herself to conceal it. Definitely not a shirt-ironer.

He explained that he was making inquiries concerning the Wendy Fowler case and, getting his bearings, asked her a preliminary question or two about her history and how long she'd lived in Cambridge. After a few brief replies, she interrupted him.

"Why are you asking these questions? What's this got to do with me?"

"We're trying to establish Wendy's whereabouts during the hours before she was killed. She had an appointment with your husband at six that evening."

"Really?"

"We're not exactly clear yet as to what she did later, or at what time they parted."

Sam's eyes flickered. "Why don't you ask him?"

"We have," Edward said, not elaborating. "What time did he arrive home Friday evening?"

She frowned—considering whether to answer or to send him packing, Edward thought.

"A little after eight."

"Was that unusually late?"

"No. He's usually back sooner, but he's been as late as that before."

She was angry, but whether at him or her husband or both Edward didn't know.

"Did he have dinner with you?"

"Yes." She stopped.

Edward waited.

"He didn't feel well," she said reluctantly. "He didn't eat very much, and he went to bed early."

"And what did you do?"

"I went out," she answered, her voice cold. "And before you ask, I went to a neighbour's. They were having a party. We were both supposed to go. Alan didn't want to, so I went without him. You can have the address if you want it."

Edward made a note of it and asked her what time she'd returned home.

"About midnight, I guess."

"And was your husband in bed then?"

"Of course," she said sharply. "Why? You don't think he had anything to do with Wendy Fowler's death, do you? That's ridiculous." She glared at him. "What is all this?"

"Did your husband ever talk about her?"

"Certainly not. Why should he? She wasn't a student of his."

"They had a close working relationship, we understand."

She glanced down at Edward's card. "Let's not beat around the bush, Chief Inspector. You think he was banging that skinny little carrothead, don't you? He has better taste."

"So you've met her?" Edward said.

"Sure I met her. Department parties. I've met practically the whole chemistry department. Lucky me," she said satirically.

She wasn't just angry, Edward saw; she was furious. The police would not be Alan Kennedy's only interrogators. How could he use this anger, he thought, what could he find out? Poor Samantha. Her hair, her nails, her skin, all those boring hours at the gym, perfecting her beauty, and her husband was sneaking off with another woman, an ordinary-looking one at that. And she knew it. Though perhaps she didn't know she knew it.

"I'd like to talk to your au pair," he said. "What's her name?"

"Flora. Are you spending all your time checking on my husband, or do you have any other brilliant theories?"

"We're checking every possibility. We're quite open-minded at the moment," Edward said. Sam, who had been standing between him and the sliding door to the garden, hesitated a moment and then stepped aside. He walked across the lawn to where Flora was sitting. Sam came after him and snatched up the baby. Sensing her disturbed state, the child began to whimper. With a visible effort, she murmured soothingly to him. "It's time for your nap," she said and left them alone.

Flora looked at Edward uneasily. He explained his purpose and wrote down her name and particulars. She was eighteen and had been working for the Kennedys for six months. Samantha had hired her through an agency. She expected to stay for a year. Was she satisfied with her employers, Edward wanted to know. Sam was fine, Flora told him. Generous with her days off and was paying for driving lessons. She shifted uncomfortably and looked towards the house.

Did she remember what time Alan Kennedy had

arrived home on Friday evening? About eight, she thought. He and Sam had had dinner soon afterwards. And what had happened after that? Samantha went out, she told him, and Alan Kennedy shut himself in his room.

"Did he stay there for the rest of the evening?"

"I think so," said Flora. "No, but really I don't know. I went to my room to watch the television. In March Sam bought me a television for my own room. I closed the door. I don't know what he did later."

"What time did you go to your room?"

"About nine o'clock. I put the dishes in the machine after dinner; then I went to my room."

"Did you hear Sam Kennedy come back?"

"No. But when I sleep, I don't hear anything." She smiled a little, embarrassed. "I sleep very deeply."

"You didn't hear any cars coming and going?"

"My room is at the back of the house, by the garden. The cars, they are on the other side, in the garage. I don't hear them."

"What sort of relationship do Samantha and Alan Kennedy have?"

She plucked a blade of grass and then another. "Is it necessary for me to answer you?" she asked.

"I can't force you to answer, if that's what you mean," he said.

"No. I mean why must I—do you understand?" she asked, looking directly at him for the first time.

He answered with care. "You mean that you don't

feel comfortable answering personal questions about Samantha Kennedy. That you want to know whether my reasons for asking are important enough to sacrifice her privacy. She's a good employer—almost a friend, perhaps?"

"Are they important?"

Who was interrogating whom? Edward thought. "I don't know yet," he said. "We don't know who killed Wendy Fowler; Alan Kennedy was with her earlier that night. And he hasn't told us the truth."

Flora nodded. "He is a liar," she said.

"What do you mean?"

"He lies to his wife," she said.

"About?"

"Women."

"How do you know?"

She shrugged. "I know the signs. My father did the same." She gave him a look that was a mixture of shrewdness and distaste. "And I do the laundry. There are hairs. Sometimes smells."

"What colour were the hairs?"

"Some brown ones, I remember. And sometimes red ones."

"Does Sam Kennedy know?"

"She has not told me. But she isn't happy. They fight. She wants to go home to America. He wants to stay here. He doesn't want to lose his wife and son. Or her money, I think. He is a fool," she added. She threw away the bruised blades of grass. "You are a man," she said suddenly. "A detective. You must know something. Why would a man with a wife so beautiful, who works every day to make herself beautiful for him, why would he behave like that? She has had needles in her lips for him! Why would he go with the other girls? Why would he try to kiss me in the kitchen when his wife is out with the baby?" she asked softly, angrily.

He glanced involuntarily up at the windows. Sam Kennedy stood in an upstairs window, her child on her shoulder, watching them. He sighed. "His wife's beauty has nothing to do with it," he said. "It is a different need. But not all men—"

"No?" Flora said. "I will see, won't I?"

"One last question. Could Alan Kennedy have left the house and returned while you were in your room Friday evening without your knowledge?"

"Yes."

"Do you think he did?"

She shook her head. "I don't know. But he is a cold man. If he did something bad, it would not be sudden. Not like a man shooting people in the street. He would make a careful plan."

"I don't suppose," Edward said as they walked slowly back towards the kitchen, "that you remember what he was wearing on Friday."

"No. His clothes are not interesting enough to remember. Always the same shirts, white, blue, pink. But he wears a clean one every day. The laundry comes on Thursday afternoons, so the one he wore on Friday will be in the laundry bag."

There was a room, little more than a cupboard, off the kitchen, where the washing machine and spin dryer resided. A wicker basket half full of baby clothes stood on the floor in front of the washing machine; a second, lidded basket was tucked behind the door and a heavy white drawstring bag leaned in a corner. The room was tidy and clean but windowless, and when Flora opened the door, Edward could smell a baby by-product odour of banana, sour milk and urine, underlaid with a sharp whiff of bleach and the sweet commercial perfume of powdered soap. Flora pointed to the bag, explaining that Alan Kennedy's shirts and the sheets were sent out, while she did the rest of the laundry herself. Last week's accumulation had been attended to on Monday, so he would be unable to inspect any garments worn on Friday with the exception of Kennedy's shirt.

He pulled the mouth of the bag open and took out the contents piece by piece. Four sheets, six pillowcases, all in floral prints, were at the top. Today, Thursday, was the day for changing the beds. Beneath were seven plain, well-made man's shirts, collar size $16\frac{1}{2}$, in white, pink and pale blue oxford cloth. He looked at each shirt carefully. Near the bottom of the bag, he found a pair of trousers and a checked shirt rolled together.

Flora looked puzzled. "I haven't seen that shirt in

months," she said. "I know it because it's different from the other ones he usually wears."

Edward scrutinized it with extra care. There were no hairs or jute fibres that he could see. But he took the checked shirt and the trousers away with him for the lab to look at. He had a notion that they had come from Wendy's bedroom cupboard.

NINETEEN

Entering the tea-room late that afternoon, Murray was absurdly nervous. His heartbeat was rapid and his palms were sweaty. He checked again that his plastic bag wasn't protruding from his pocket. It would look funny, and the eagle-eyed tea-ladies might pounce on him. For some mysterious reason, they didn't allow plastic bags— or any sort of bag—in the tea-room. The tea-ladies didn't allow papers or lab coats, either. He saw a heap of bags and papers by the door, as usual. He stuck a clammy hand in the right pocket of his baggy trousers and felt the plastic bag squash under his knuckles.

"Don't be an idiot," he muttered to himself. "There's nothing to it." He followed Ron Bottomley to the counter. Bottomley took tea and Murray took a watery cup of coffee. "Do you think there's anything that can be done about the coffee?" he asked Bottomley, looking sadly at his cup.

"I'm a tea-drinker myself," Bottomley said. "Is the coffee off today?"

"Every day," Murray said.

They found seats at the far end of a table. When Murray had been lying awake the previous night, he had passed the time concocting a question to ask Bottomley: a question about a chemical problem that was plausibly connected to Murray's work and that Bottomley might know something about. He asked it now and was rewarded by a slight lowering of Bottomley's guard.

"That's interesting," he said, and mentioned some recent papers on the subject.

Murray had already read two of them, but he asked Bottomley to elucidate. Bottomley hunched forward over his teacup, clutching it with short, spatulate fingers. His protuberant eyes glistened. Murray's instinct was to lean away. Bottomley was an unattractive little man. But it was a pity that he did so little research, that he had lost the drive or the confidence or whatever it was he'd lost. His explanation of the article was perfectly clear, and his further speculations were intelligent. He was almost pathetically eager to instruct. Murray nodded and listened and murmured appreciative noises. At the end of twenty minutes, Murray had nearly abandoned his original intention. He wondered whether Edward ever had qualms.

"I wonder how the murder investigation is progressing?" Bottomley said suddenly.

Murray started. Was Bottomley reading his mind?

"They're prowling round the labs all the time," Bottomley went on. "It's rather difficult to concentrate."

"Just doing their job," Murray answered, sticking to platitudes.

"They'd do better to look elsewhere," Bottomley said.

"What do you mean?"

"Naming no names, I can think of somebody's wife they ought to interrogate."

"To ask her where her husband was Friday night?"

"To ask where she was." Bottomley giggled. "Hell hath no fury, isn't that right, old boy?"

Murray looked covertly down the table to see whether anyone else was listening. But their table was already deserted.

When Bottomley was ready to go, the tea-room was almost empty. He stood up, but Murray didn't move.

"I'm just going to sit and think for a few minutes," Murray said. It was a little odd, perhaps, to want to sit and think in the tea-room, but he couldn't leave, or he'd miss his chance.

If Bottomley thought it was odd, he didn't say so. He walked away towards the exit, depositing his cup and saucer with the others on the counter. The tea-ladies rattled loudly as they cleared up. Murray watched him go. He hadn't noticed before that one of Bottomley's shoulders was so much higher than the other. His arms swung unevenly at his sides. But he moved quickly enough. Murray waited until he was gone, one eye on the counter where Bottomley's cup waited among dozens of other, identical cups. It would never do to get the wrong one. Fortunately, Bottomley's, being the last to be set down, was protruding slightly over the edge of the counter.

There were still three other people in the tea-room, apart from the tea-ladies, who were invisible from where Murray sat, but distinctly audible. They were laughing about something. He could hear water running. It might be safer to wait until the room was entirely empty, but then it might be too late. He'd better get on with it, or the tea-ladies would get the cup first.

Murray got up, carrying his own cup in his left hand, his white plastic bag balled up in his right fist. Luckily, the chemist sitting nearest the counter had his back turned. He might get up at any moment, though. The other two were sitting further away and were absorbed in conversation. Murray reached the counter and set down his cup and saucer. A tea-lady eyed him as if checking for contraband or stains on his shirt. He smiled weakly. She marched up to the counter and looked into the room, to see if everyone had gone. Observing the stragglers, she checked her watch and pursed her lips. Taking no further notice of Murray, she turned back to the tea urn. Another tea-lady was busy putting the biscuits away. They're probably locked in a vault every night, Murray thought. It was now or never. Below the level of the counter, he opened the plastic bag. Then he drew a tissue from his pocket. He couldn't look round; his back screened the counter from the other chemists. He prayed that no one was getting up. He laid the tissue over his fingers and thumb and picked up Bottomley's saucer. There was a tiny sip of tea in the bottom of the cup. He hoped that wouldn't matter. He slid the cup and saucer into the bottom of the bag. They clattered as the cup tipped and rolled off the saucer. The tea lady at the urn swivelled about and looked at him. He waved a feeble farewell with his empty hand.

Feeling more like a shoplifter than a detective, he moved gently away from the counter, carrying the bag below her line of sight. Then he heard crockery clattering. She must be gathering the last cups. Nearly at the door, he glanced back, his prize dangling inconspicuously by his side. As she leaned out over the counter, her eye fell on the bag. She sniffed loudly.

He fled.

Edward found Hardy brooding over the mounds of paper on his desk, a cold cup of tea at his elbow.

"Well, Brer Rabbit," Hardy said, looking up.

"Well, Brer Fox. I've had an interesting conversation with Sam Kennedy and an even more interesting one with her au pair. What have you been up to?"

"Up to? Up to my arse in paperwork."

"Anything new?"

"Lab report on the bag of water. The bag didn't split; it was cut open. Probably with a small pair of scissors."

"So Wendy was right. Someone was playing dirty tricks. Any dabs on the bag?"

"Any? They must have passed it round with popcorn in it. We've got prints from four or five different people."

"Any we know?"

"Fowler's. And we've got one match to the dabs on the flask."

"Bottomley's, Hill's, or is there somebody else with a grudge?"

"No bets. But what's the connection with the murder? Of course she might have caught X at his little tricks. If she'd told the department, he would have been fired."

"Not unless she could prove it."

"Maybe she could. Maybe she walked in on him in her lab on Friday night—caught him tying knots in her hose."

"They could have had an argument in the lab, I suppose. But if he didn't plan to kill her, why did he have the sack with him? Just happened to bring it along that night?"

"He didn't have to," Hardy said smugly. "It was in the cold room already!"

Edward sat down. "You're way ahead of me. All this came in while I was out?"

"That's what you get for dallying with blonde

mantraps. Who do you think you are? Humphrey Bogart?"

"Definitely," said Edward. He seized a pencil and took a deep drag on it, squinting at Hardy. "Here's looking at you, kid."

"That was terrific," Hardy said.

"I know." Edward chucked the pencil at him. "What's this about the sack then?"

"The sack belonged to a man called Fisher in the biosynthesis section. It had some plants in it he was using for his work on alkaloids. It's been sitting in the cold room for a couple of months. He was off at some conference or other this week and only just got back. When he heard about Wendy, the first thing he asked about was whether his sack was still in the cold room."

"Such devotion to research," Edward remarked. "What flows in their veins? Liquid nitrogen?"

"He was shocked," Hardy said. "I skipped that part."

"At least we don't have to spend weeks tracing the damn sack in case someone remembers chummy buying it. That's a comfort."

Hardy grinned. "Just what I said to McClure."

The sergeant stuck his head in the door. "Taking my name in vain, Guv?"

"Are the lads all here?"

"The murder room's bursting at the seams."

"Right. We'll be in in a minute. Meanwhile, you can tell them that there'll be no weekend leave."

Hardy turned back to Edward. "I went to see

French. He wasn't at home, but one of the neighbours said he was usually down the pub at that hour, so I went and found him there. Didn't have any mates with him, he was just sitting in a corner, inhaling his pint. A few of them, I'd say."

"And?"

"He stuck to his story. He gave me a few details. He hasn't seen Perdreau since they broke up in February. About February 20th, he says. He put an end to it; he was thinking of looking for work in London or further away. He wasn't interested in having a girl at a distance, and he wasn't going to support Cynthia 'or any woman' while she studied, so it was best for her to stay with her Mum and Dad. He said there was no reason to keep seeing her, rather giving me to understand that the bloom was off the rose. He claims he wasn't aware she was pregnant at the time. She never told him. He says he knew nothing about the abortion. He wasn't happy that she'd had one without consulting him."

"What if he'd known?" Edward asked. "What would he have done?"

"He wouldn't have married her." Hardy looked at his notes. "'How would I know it was mine?' he says. I asked him if he had reason to think that Perdreau had other boyfriends. He didn't know, but he seemed to think in a general way that you couldn't tell, with women."

Edward was reminded of what DC Paris had told

him—that French had said women did as they liked these days. "Then what did he want?"

Hardy shrugged.

"What did you make of him?"

"It's hard to tell. But the world owes him a favour, he knows that. What was Mrs Kennedy like?"

"Stunning. I didn't think women like that existed off-screen. A Swedish Bardot."

"It's a wonder you came back at all, then."

"Maybe it is," Edward said. "For the first minute or two, she could have clubbed me over the head and tied me up in her laundry bag and I would hardly have noticed."

Hardy raised his eyebrows. "Do you think she's been clubbing anyone? I shouldn't have thought her charms would have stupefied Wendy Fowler."

"No. But I think she'd be capable of eliminating her competition. And we've only got her word for when she arrived home."

"I see. You'd better give me the rest of it. And if she has to be interviewed again, *I'll* go." Hardy added in a fatherly tone, "Some jobs require the maturity and detachment of a married man."

"Get knotted," Edward said amiably.

The windows were open in the murder room, and the blinds drawn against the glare of the late afternoon sun, but it was stiflingly hot. Edward hoped Hardy would keep things moving. He shut his eyes, listening to the digest of the team's recent efforts. Bottomley was a bachelor, fifty-four years old. He had never been married. He had rooms in Queens' College, where he'd lived for the past eighteen years. He had indeed been to dine in college, but further questioning of other members present on Friday evening revealed that a Fellow on Bottomley's staircase had seen him leave his rooms just before nine o'clock. The Fellow hadn't seen him come in again, and neither had anyone else.

"So he could have walked right down the road to the labs. It wouldn't have taken him more than ten or twelve minutes," Hardy said, "unless he took a very roundabout route. He's lied about staying in all evening. It's time we asked him a few questions."

They moved on to the Perdreau case. Hardy had been to see the surgeon and the GP who'd referred Perdreau for the abortion, both of whose names had been furnished by the hospital. The surgeon had had nothing to add to the medical report. The GP, on the other hand, had been informative.

"The GP's Elizabeth Peters. Been practising for over thirty years."

Elizabeth Peters, thought Edward. He knew that name. Then he remembered. She was married to Gillian's old supervisor, Basil Peters. They had all had dinner together a number of years ago. A person in exactly the right job, he'd thought then. She was practical, energetic, humane and shrewd. What had she made of her young patient?

"Cynthia Perdreau went to see Dr Peters on April 10th. She was very nervous but discussed the situation freely once she knew Dr Peters could not be made to give information to her parents. Peters gave me the gist of her conversation from notes in the file and her own recollection of the patient. Perdreau was sad about terminating her pregnancy but had made up her mind. She was too young to have a child, she said; she hadn't even finished her studies yet. And she had only realized she was pregnant after she and her boyfriend—Tod French—had broken up. Their relationship had ended in February. She'd missed a period in early March and had waited several weeks, hoping it would come, so she didn't know for certain that she was pregnant until April. She didn't have any other boyfriends. It was her first sexual relationship. She was going to tell French about the pregnancy and her decision to have an abortion, she said, because she thought he ought to know, but she didn't think he would be helpful. Peters said she told Perdreau that if he wasn't, and she still didn't want to inform her family, she should find a friend to drive her home after the procedure—that she couldn't leave on her own."

Edward was thinking hard. Tod French had told DC Paris that he hadn't seen Perdreau for a couple of months. So he was lying, or else she'd changed her mind about going to see him. Maybe he *had* collected her from Addenbrooke's. After all, what friend would have done so and be keeping quiet about it now? He still had the old banger he'd bought when he was employed, Paris said. It didn't run well, but it had plates.

Hardy was still talking. "Peters said she thought Cynthia Perdreau was lonely and in a state of great anxiety—that she was carrying a heavy emotional load with no one to confide in. Peters urged her to take her parents into her confidence but didn't believe she had made any headway. Perdreau was determined to handle the problem on her own. Peters told her to come back if she needed to talk or ask any further questions. She went ahead with arrangements, however, since Perdreau appeared certain about what she wanted and the procedure is best performed as early as possible."

The next interesting piece of information to emerge came from DC Paris. Edward had been expecting something, having noticed that Paris was sitting forward, looking eager to speak. He had asked Cynthia's parents whether they knew Roger Hill, who lived near the church. Alarmed and bewildered, they had told him that indeed they did. He was an old acquaintance, a member of the local bridge-playing set. But what was more important, he gave Cynthia a lift into Cambridge once a week, when her part-time hours coincided with his usual commute to the chemistry labs.

This bit of evidence made everyone sit up as straight as DC Paris. It was the first link between the two deaths.

TWENTY

For a while after Edward left, Gillian accomplished very little. She shuffled her cards inattentively, her mind elsewhere. It was not on the PIS and the murders, or on her work, but on her own divided self. People talked about the global village, about how all the different parts of the world were linking up, coming closer together as jets and E-mail and cellular telephones connected everyone everywhere always. Families were stitched together with frequent-flyer bonuses, and friendships kept their health with regular exercise of the fax and the answering machine. On the other hand, the points of attachment that fastened each life to others were moving further and further apart, like the universe after the big bang. Her mother's life had been triangulated by New York, Toronto and the farm—manageable distances in her era. Until Gillian had moved west, husband, children, friends, beloved landscapes had all remained within reach. Now mother and daughter lived thousands of miles apart, and Gillian's own points of attachment were stretched across oceans and continents. My generation has grown wings, she thought. We are people of the air, always flitting, always just arrived or about to go, always conscious of other places, of absent friends.

She collected her file cards from behind the cushions and carried her books upstairs to the bedroom. Edward's leather slippers poked worn toes from beneath the counterpane. His shaving kit stood on the little table under the window, there being hardly room for three towels in the bathroom, and no shelves. Two books—a dog-eared copy of *Gulliver's Travels* and a review of the British criminal justice system by a former Labour MP—neither of which he had opened since he arrived, lay on the chair beside the bed. The cupboard door hung slightly ajar, offering a glimpse of white sleeve. Domesticity.

She went downstairs again and called Bee. She explained about the photograph of Cynthia Perdreau and asked for the telephone numbers of the rest of the PIS.

"I don't remember anyone named Cynthia," Bee said, "and of course we don't have the bloody book, so we can't look her up, but if she did come in, it shouldn't be too difficult to find out when. How far along was her pregnancy when she had the abortion? Do we know?"

"A bit over nine weeks."

"She must have missed a period before she came in, and it takes a bit of time to schedule an abortion once you've tested positive—not many Saturdays in there. Why don't you ring the others and see if anyone remembers a Cynthia or a 'C' having a test about a month ago? I'll pop round in twenty minutes and take a look at the photograph, just in case. She might have used a different initial."

There was no answer at Margaret's home number. Gillian hesitated and then elected not to ring the language school. Margaret was probably teaching. It would be better to ring her at home that evening, if she had drawn a blank with everyone else. She tried Vicky and got an answering machine: She left a brief but explicit message and tried Pat.

Pat was in. She was relaxing between clients, poking about her kitchen.

"I'm making soup," she said. "A gigantic pot of lentil soup. It's a soothing activity, and I don't get anxious about feeding the hordes if I know there's soup to fall back on. My husband does cook, quite well, actually, but he doesn't think. You know the real difference between women and men? The knowledge that three days from now, people will have to eat.

Somehow, men have never figured that out. They know they have to eat today, but no matter how many times it's happened, they still don't know that they'll have to eat again tomorrow. I'm convinced that women invented civilization because they realized this basic truth about human existence."

"I'm not a ruminative cook," Gillian replied. "I tend to slap things together, and if I fix something elaborate I'm too busy fussing to meditate on civilization. But I do think about trade routes and empire sometimes, Venice growing rich on the spice trade, Gandhi breaking the government salt monopoly in India, and so on. We've been eating lentils for about 10,000 years, haven't we? They must be good for us. But I'm sorry to say I didn't call to discuss the merits of legumes." Gillian explained about Cynthia.

"No," said Pat. "I saw her picture in the Cambridge paper. I'm sure I don't remember her. I was at Grafton Street one Saturday in April, hang on, I'll just look at my calendar. Yes, Saturday April 20th. I know who came in, and there was no one like her. The time before that was in late March—the 25th. I'm not as clear about who came that day, but I'm sure I would have recognized the photograph if she'd been in. One doesn't forget very quickly, since people are fearfully wrought up about the tests. Most of the time, at least. Have you tried anyone else?"

"Not yet. Bee's on her way over to look at a photograph I've got."

"The police want to know whether she had a test from us, do they?"

"Yes, in case she told anyone in the PIS about her situation."

"I see." Pat was silent for a moment. "Anything the customers tell us is confidential, but since she's dead, it's different."

"Irene rang up, right after you did," Bee said as soon as she sat down. "I told her about the photograph. She said she's at home this afternoon, not working, so you should drop by whenever it suits you. Where is it?"

"Here," said Gillian, handing Bee the photograph, a glossy colour print.

Bee stared at it for a moment. "No." She shook her head. "I haven't seen her. At least not recently. Poor thing. She looks like a perfectly nice middle-class young woman with a pleasant, perfectly normal future in front of her. I wonder what happened."

"So does Edward. Nothing obvious has turned up."

"If it's the same man who killed Wendy, they'd better catch him soon. Two murders!"

"Would that be worse than two murderers?"

"I can't believe in two murderers."

"I rather wish I could," Gillian said. "One is more frightening. To us, I mean. Especially if Cynthia Perdreau did go to the PIS for a pregnancy test. I hope Irene has never seen that girl in her life. If she did see her, then what's the link between the two murders? The PIS."

"Aren't you jumping to conclusions? Why shouldn't they find a connection between Cynthia and the chemistry labs?"

Irene lived on the other side of Midsummer Common, in a cul-de-sac behind the university boathouses. Gillian crossed Maids' Causeway and strolled along Brunswick Walk and through the common. The broad swath of green wound along the riverbank. Overhead, a few clouds sailed across the sky. The trees were heavy with leaf, the tender, sappy, shining leaves of spring, untouched by summer dust. What she loved about Cambridge, Gillian thought, in the middle of the common, was the way space expanded and contracted. The tiny streets in the Kite, with their narrow pavements and squat terraced houses, the colleges with their sheltering walls and compact cloisters, the tightly squeezed shops in the passages near the market square, these complex densities that pressed against the senses suddenly opened into soaring spaces like the common or Parker's Piece or the Backs behind King's, spaces where the wide sky and the flat green plain dwarfed the buildings and released their intimate pressure with a delicious exhalation. It was as if a whole countryside, with its concentrated towns and open lands lying between, had been repeated within a circle that might be traversed in half an hour's brisk walk.

The daily drive from the house to her office at the southern edge of Vancouver, which covered more than twice the distance, offered no such contrasts. The streets were wide and regular, the large houses rhythmically spaced, set back at a uniform distance on their rectangular lots behind a palisade of boulevard trees. It was a padded grid, a perfection of suburban privacy, retreating from the compression of older cities and spreading itself over the adjacent open spaces. It had its own beauty, but no thrills. It was contrast that made the pulse race, in landscape as in romance.

Once out of the heart of Cambridge, Gillian knew, one found the same phenomenon, though the houses were smaller. Canadians, she had read in her Vancouver newspaper, had on average the largest houses in the world. This, she was certain, followed from the illusion of limitless space produced by the enormous northern landscape. The fact that nearly everybody in Canada lived in crowded centres close to the southern border apparently had no effect on the illusion. Everyone wanted a house, the bigger the better. She was no exception; her house was absurdly large for one person. If she sold it, she thought, she would have plenty of money to live on while she looked for a job; she could manage for a few years, quite comfortably. But suppose no job turned up? What would she do then? And after the first year of freedom, anxiety would set in. She could picture herself still hanging about at conferences after three years, perhaps after having refused to apply for positions in Durham or Aberdeen (if there were any), because she wanted London, facing her fiftieth birthday as an unemployed woman with a dwindling bank account. No. She did not want that. She would be stupid to move to London without a job offer.

She crossed the river. A rowing crew was practising upstream from the footbridge; she stopped to watch the pearly flash of arms and shoulders against the dull water. Wendy's muscular student lover, she remembered, had belonged to one of these crews. The oars dipped and rose, trailing sun-spangled droplets. Then the cox shouted something unintelligible and the rhythm broke. Gillian moved on across the bridge.

Irene's house was small, tucked away behind huge rose-bushes—airy globes strewn with flat ivory-coloured blooms. She led Gillian through the kitchen to a shaded terrace at the rear.

"That's my office," she said, nodding at another doorway. "It means that my clients have to traipse through the sitting-room, but we couldn't afford to do it any other way. At least I do have a room for the purpose now, and when I'm finished, I can close the door. I used to see people in the sitting-room, and after they left, when I was simply trying to live my own life in my own house, I couldn't. The clients would still be there. The room wasn't ours."

"What kind of therapy do you do?"

"Family therapy, mostly. I see young people, but the

problems they have are so often part of larger family problems that I like to work with the family unit as frequently as possible, rather than the individual."

"Do they all come in together?"

"Not always, but they often do. I find it much more interesting. Families are just extraordinary. What's yours like?"

"Small. One mother, one older brother. He's married and has a son. He lives in New York. My father's dead. There's a whole pack of his relations in Toronto, but I've never been close to them, except for one of my cousins."

"Do you and your mother get on?"

"Very well."

"How old is she?"

"Seventy-seven. She was born in 1914."

"How astonishing," Irene said. "I mean, I know it isn't; my parents were born in 1920, but it seems so long ago now. When you say 1914 it sounds as far away as 1814. Is she in good health?"

"She's doing fine. She still lives on her own, with help coming in, and she still marches out to the garden and beats the stuffing out of the dandelions every spring. I hope I'm like her in thirty years. How about your family?"

"Big," said Irene. "That is, as soon as one looks beyond the nucleus in this house. Here there's just me and Patrick, my son from my first marriage, and John, who would be my husband except that I don't want to be anybody's wife again. He's away this week. But then I have three sisters, with children, two parents still alive and heaps of aunts and uncles and cousins. We have immense family gatherings in Dorset every summer." She laughed. "Even Patrick's father comes, with his second wife and their children. We get on very well, now that we don't live together, and his wife's a treat." She turned and darted back into the house. "Tea," she said over her shoulder. "I'll bring it out here." She wore a long dress of loosely-woven Indian cotton, and sandals. Her hands and feet were thin and elegant, her hair wild. She reminded Gillian of Vanessa Redgrave as Isadora.

She returned with a tray. The plump china teapot was whimsically painted to resemble a melon, its belly smooth and striped, the ridged handle and spout a deep vine-stem green.

"One of my sisters is a potter," Irene said. "This is from her gourd period. I also have a tureen that commemorates a prize marrow Patrick grew when he was nine. She poured their tea. "You've brought a photograph?"

Gillian handed it to her.

"But I know her," Irene said, startled. "She came in last month for a test. I remember her very well. I don't think she gave her name; she was just 'C.' Not that she looked much like this photo then, poor duck. She looks happy and free here; when I saw her, she was a nervous wreck. She'd already missed one period and the second one was late. I've looked up which Saturday I was on; it was April 6th. So that must be the day she had her test. The test was positive. It was a nasty shock for her, even though she'd suspected it. You know, we ask as tactfully as we can how they feel about being pregnant, so that when we give them their results we don't hit the wrong note. It's such a sensitive moment for women—one doesn't want to be forbiddingly neutral, but then one has to know a little of what they're feeling or one could end up congratulating a rape victim." She smiled briefly. "And it's lovely when you know a woman wants to be pregnant and you can tell her she is." Then she looked thoughtful. "It wasn't like that with 'C,' of course. Cynthia. I remember I said, 'I'm sorry, it's positive,' and she went quite silent and stared blindly out of the window for a minute. Then she asked about having an abortion, and we gave her the information. She didn't want her parents to know, and she didn't want to go to her family doctor, so we wrote down the names of some sympathetic doctors in Cambridge. A good job we did—she'd heard of Dr Stoner and was going to try him. We warned her about his views."

"You said 'we.' Who else was there?"

"Wendy was testing with me that day." Irene sat down the photograph, which she had continued to examine. "Do you think that's significant?"

"What else do you remember? Anything might help."

283

"I wish we had the book. I don't remember things like what Cynthia said about using contraception or when the first day of her last period was. She found us through the advertisement in the yellow pages, I know she said that. She hadn't liked to ask anyone, because she didn't want anyone to know she was worried about being pregnant. She was very sure she couldn't have the child. She couldn't support it, and she wouldn't ask her parents to."

"Did she have anyone to talk to? A sister? A friend?"

"No one in her family. She thought they'd be disappointed in her. Apparently they were straining the family budget to support her while she studied part-time, and she was afraid they'd say she hadn't behaved responsibly and cut off her funds. I tried to suggest that it was unlikely, because they'd be cutting off their own noses to spite their faces, but she started to cry, just thinking about telling them. So we asked her whether she had anyone to confide in, and she said she had a friend but didn't know whether she should tell her. She was going to tell the father, but she wasn't thinking of marrying him— she'd realized she'd made a mistake and he wasn't at all right for her. She seemed quite isolated, so we gave her our telephone numbers in case she needed someone to talk to."

"Did she come back? Or did she ever call you?"

"She didn't come back to the centre, at least I don't think she did. No one's mentioned it, and we do discuss the sessions at our meetings. I didn't speak to her again, but she may have rung me when I was out, or while I was working. I switch on the answering machine when I'm with a client; she could have called and then decided not to leave a message."

"She might have called Wendy."

"It's possible."

"The man she was seeing—did she say anything else about him? What he's like, or why they broke up?"

"Nothing that I know of. It's not the sort of question we ask, obviously."

"Not even Wendy?"

"No. She was a bit nannyish, but she wasn't a fool."

"I don't understand why the group found it so hard to tell her what she was doing wrong."

"In my opinion it's female training. Women—most women—don't like direct confrontation. They'll do almost anything to avoid it. It threatens their relationships, which girls learn are their key to survival. Whereas boys, you know, often bond through confrontation. Status is their key. You can see the difference even in small children. A boy will say, 'Give me that stick or I'll punch you,' where a girl will say, 'We need to use that stick. Let's put it here.' Also, women generally don't like to criticize directly, because it's too much like boasting. It's saying, 'I know, or I am, better than you.' Boys can boast, but not girls. Girls who show off are punished—ridiculed or ostracized.

These patterns aren't unique to our culture, either. They pop up everywhere. Women who operate more directly—like Wendy—are unusual in any society and tend to raise hackles in both sexes. That was partly why I was so reluctant to criticize her; I thought she might be quite a lonely person, who found it difficult to make friends, and I didn't want to drive her away."

"Do you think Wendy would have told you if Cynthia had talked to her?"

Irene looked thoughtful. "I'm not sure. Anyone else in the group would have, but Wendy didn't chat. You might ask Vicky."

TWENTY-ONE

Edward and Hardy were on the riverbank. The diver, his goggles glistening wetly in the sunshine, was explaining how he had found the spade on the bottom of the river, lodged among the sunken branches of a willow tree.

"It's a good spade," Hardy said. "Decent quality. Not one of your flimsy bits of rubbish that buckle when they hit a pebble. And it's been well cared for."

"If you say so," said Edward.

"Not chummy's, unless he's a gardener. Hill has a garden in Grantchester; Bottomley lives in college, so he has none. Kennedy has a garden, but if he knows a dandelion from a dahlia I'll eat my boots."

"It's more likely to belong to one of the houses along the road, isn't it?" Edward asked mildly.

"Yes. We'll see if anyone's missed it."

Murray went home after tea, unable to concentrate after his theft of Bottomley's cup. He found Gillian sitting at the little desk with her manuscript. She was scowling while drawing circles around paragraphs and peppering the margins with question marks. A hail of arrows jabbed at the text.

"I've just been to see Basil Peters," she said. "He had some terrific suggestions for the chapter on the Duchess of Devonshire, but oh Lord! it means reorganizing it from scratch."

"Look what I've got," Murray said, dangling his plastic bag.

"What is it?"

"A rare specimen. The teacup of Ronald Bottomley!" He opened the bag so she could look in.

"How did you get it?"

He chortled. "It was easy. It's covered with fingerprints, too. I'm sure it is."

"'Oh frabjous day!'"

"Do you think Edward will be coming back soon?"

"That depends on the elasticity of the concept."

"Couldn't we phone him? I'm going out later, and I want to give this cup to him before the fingerprints dry up or something."

Gillian grinned. "Why not?" She went to the

telephone and was put through after several minutes.

"I was just going to ring you," Edward said.

"Could you stop in at your Earl Street HQ? The local Sherlocks have dug up some evidence that could be important."

"Sherlocks, plural?"

"Murray's been sleuthing too."

"Which case?"

"Both."

"What is it? Never mind. We've just finished chatting here; I'll be along in a couple of ticks."

Gillian smiled at Murray, who was looking better than he had since Sunday. "He's on his way."

"Now then, wot's all this?" Edward said cheerfully when he came in.

Murray was suddenly struck dumb.

Gillian glanced at him and launched into an account of Cynthia Perdreau's visit to the PIS. "She didn't tell them anything about the father," she finished up, "but the interesting thing is that Wendy was there."

Edward, who had been sitting in a relaxed attitude, taking the occasional note, came to attention. "That's certain?" He looked at his notes. "April 6th. And she went to see the GP April 10th. It was Elizabeth Peters, by the way."

"Elizabeth! Have you seen her?"

"No. I was interviewing the exquisite Samantha."

"And did you ask her whether she injects her lips?"

"I couldn't think how to put the question."

"I see. Your brain just turned to jelly. Murray, my dear, your Turandot idea seems to have something to it. Edward, Murray has a present for you."

Murray handed Edward the plastic bag, and Edward looked inside.

"A teacup?"

"A cup and saucer that Ron Bottomley used this afternoon. I've touched the saucer," Murray said gruffly, "but only through a tissue, so my prints aren't on it. I hope I didn't smear anything important."

"I see. You took me at my word." Edward contemplated his booty for a moment. Then he clapped Murray lightly on the shoulder. "As it happens, this may come in very handy right now. Tell me all about the purloined teacup."

Murray explained. Edward was amused. "Wouldn't it have been easier to ask him to write something—a diagram, for example—and keep the piece of paper?"

Murray looked crestfallen. "I didn't think of that." Then he laughed. "Besides, the tea-ladies would have been giving me the evil eye the whole time. I was jumpy enough, without that."

"Never mind. With any luck, the crockery will do the trick neatly. I'll even return it so you can insinuate it into the tea-room again." He looked at his watch. "I'd like to ask Irene a couple of questions, but I'd better ring the nick first. We've a lot to do tonight."

"Dinner?" asked Gillian.

"No time."

She left it at that. If he starved, it was his lookout.

When he came back he said, "I should just have time to see Irene after I run this cup over to the station. Want to come along?"

"Definitely."

"Let's go, then. The car's outside."

"You drove here from the station?" Murray asked, looking faintly scandalized. "But we're just around the corner."

"It's a bad habit," Edward replied. But he was unrepentant.

Gillian waited in the little car while Edward darted into the station.

"Where do I go?" he asked, sliding behind the wheel again.

"Emmanuel Road and straight across the roundabout. Over the river and turn right on Chesterton Road."

The car scooted past Midsummer Common. It was nearing six, and the children had gone in for dinner, but the dog-walkers were out, and the cyclists. The river came and went in a moment, and they were into the scuffle of Chesterton Road and then turning into the quiet streets behind the boathouses. Edward pulled up in front of Irene's house. No one was in sight. He slid his hand up Gillian's thigh, under her skirt, and whispered in her ear. "She *does* have collagen injections. The au pair told me." Then he jumped out of the car.

Gillian was still laughing when they rang the bell. A tall youth of sixteen, with bushy brown hair, freckles on his snub nose and a wide good-humoured mouth, opened the door.

"You must be Patrick. Is your mother here? She said she'd be home this evening."

He invited them in. "Mum!"

Irene called from the kitchen. "You're early," she cried. "It's not fair." Then she saw them. "Oh! I thought it was Bee and Pamela. They're coming for dinner."

"This won't take long," Edward said.

"You're Edward," said Irene, the light dawning. She looked quickly at Gillian. "Is anything wrong? Anything new, I mean?"

Gillian shook her head. "But we're not just dropping in," she said.

Edward introduced himself officially. "Detective Chief Inspector Gisborne. Gillian's just told me what you talked about this afternoon. Could you spare a few minutes to answer some questions? It might help."

"DCI Gisborne?" Patrick interjected. "I saw your name in the papers last week. Your chaps caught Villiers, right?"

"That's right."

Patrick looked satisfied. "I thought so. See," he said to Irene. "He *is* the same one."

Irene reached up and ruffled his hair. "When was the last time you were wrong? It must have been when you were ten. Or was it nine?"

"It was when you were bigger than me," Patrick shot back. "Can I hang about?" he asked Edward, "or is this confidential?"

Villiers, thought Gillian. The child-murderer. A pity that it was his name that people remembered, and not Lena Ulrych's. They followed Irene to the kitchen. Gillian accepted a glass of wine and they all sat round the table.

Edward went over what Irene had told Gillian about April 6th.

"Did you think Cynthia Perdreau would come back, or telephone? Did you have any feeling about it?"

"Well, I did, actually, at the time. But when I didn't hear from her, I didn't think about it. We'd given her the names of some very good GPs, and I supposed she'd found what help she needed."

"Tell me more about the PIS. Who are you? And why are you, if I may ask? Don't most women go to their doctors if they think they're pregnant? And aren't there kits you can buy?"

"Do-it-yourself kits cost rather a lot, and they aren't quite as reliable as our test. Our test is free. The doctors, um, that's more complicated. It's of course possible for GPs to do the same pregnancy tests right in the surgery. But they often don't. Won't. They say it's not their job, and they send the urine samples off to the hospital labs. What this means in practical terms is that women have to wait days for the results instead of minutes. It's ridiculous, especially when people are often so anxious. Also, it's not always possible to arrange an abortion right away, so a week can make a difference, especially for teenagers who have put off taking a test and might come up against the time limit for early abortions."

"How long has your group been doing this?" Edward wanted to know.

"We started in the early seventies. Groups like ours popped up all over the place; the idea spread through the national women's conferences." Irene heaved a nostalgic sigh. "That was in the good old days, before the splits in the movement, when women were bursting with energy and optimism."

Gillian was amusing herself watching Patrick try to read Edward's responses. He, obviously, would have heard the PIS story many times. How many sixteen-year-old boys even knew it existed, much less why?

"We were going to rescue our bodies from male doctors," Irene went on. "The PIS had a lot of customers then. The DIY kits, when they became available, were—relative to income—far more expensive, and lots of women didn't know about them. And it took even longer to get your test results if you went to a GP. Up to two weeks, if you can imagine. Masses of students came to us for tests, and a lot of women from the housing estates."

"Things have changed since then, surely?"

"They have. And we don't test as much as we used to. More GPs will do the test themselves now, the

BAD CHEMISTRY

results are quicker, and the DIY kits are advertised everywhere. Besides, the garden-variety GP is less Victorian about sexual matters these days. On some Saturdays, particularly in the summers, nobody comes. But we still average three or four women a session. And there are still lots of telephone calls—usually women wanting to know where they can go to get an abortion. We're a kind of information bank. Suppose a single young woman is wondering whether to have the baby or not and wants to know what financial help is available. We can tell her just how little she'll get, and what to do to get it. We can explain how the different forms of contraception work and which ones you need a prescription for, where you can get the morning-after pill, what doctors to go to if you need an abortion and which ones to avoid, where to go for counselling—all that sort of thing. And the fact is, there are still young women like Cynthia Perdreau, who don't want to reveal their problem to their GPs, and who come to us because it's free or because it's more reassuring than a little box from the chemist's."

"The early seventies. Almost twenty years," Edward commented. "That's a long time to keep a voluntary organization going, and it sounds like a fair amount of responsibility. How many of you are there?"

"Six. We've shrunk. We used to have twice as many. Loads of students used to join, but we haven't had any undergraduates for years now." Irene reached for the wine bottle. "We're not exactly the cutting edge any more. Student feminists have other fish to fry and the rest don't care. There are too few of us now to have two testers on every Saturday. We like to have two, one to test the specimen, and one to ask the questions." She filled her glass and pushed the bottle towards Gillian. "So that's why we were glad when Wendy wanted to join."

"If one of you asked the questions and the other did the test, which did Wendy do when Cynthia came to see you?"

"Wendy asked the questions."

"In her usual style?"

"She wasn't too bad that day, actually. I thought she was starting to catch on. There was nothing to bother about. I was feeling relieved afterwards, thinking it was all going to work out. Then the next time, with Margaret, I think, she tore a strip off a student who'd missed three periods before coming in for a test, just closing her eyes and hoping for a miracle. That's not what we're there for."

"No. One other thing. What's in the book that's missing? And what does it look like?"

"It's a big black diary. A log of all the people we see. We record the date, who was testing, the customer's first name or initial, data about her menstrual cycle, and so on. We write down what contraception they were using, if any, and whether it's a wanted pregnancy or not, and the test results, of course. And

often we write comments about the situation the person is in—trouble at home, passed out and didn't
know what had happened until afterwards—that sort
of thing. But no surnames are ever recorded."

"Why do you keep all this information?"

Irene laughed a little. "Well, we all went to university, didn't we? We have the scholar's reflex when
it comes to documentation. Who knows what golden
nuggets of knowledge could be panned from twenty
years of our data? That's not it, though. There are lots
of reasons. The questions occupy the time while the
test's being done. They give us a way to connect with
the woman—to be friendly and at the same time find
out how she feels and how we might be useful.
There's also the fact that people come back and
there's usually a different tester the second time.
Then it can be helpful to have some notes to go on."

"What would Cynthia Perdreau's comments have
said?"

"That she was very anxious, and only seventeen,
and wouldn't tell her parents, and might call for more
advice. Not more than that, I think."

"Thank you," said Edward. "You've been most
helpful. I hope I didn't intrude too disastrously on
your dinner preparations."

"Not at all. Why don't you stay?" Irene said, looking naughty.

"That's very kind of you, but I'm due back at the
station in a few minutes," he said gravely. Then, with

a comradely grin at Patrick, he added, "Besides, with two of us, the testosterone index might run a little high for one of your other guests."

Gillian, who decided to remain at Irene's, saw Edward to the door.

"Testosterone index?" she heard Patrick asking Irene as she went back to work.

"I'll see you later," Edward said. "Probably much later."

"Good hunting."

When she returned to the kitchen, Patrick had departed.

"I've sent him to do his homework," Irene said. She chuckled. "Thank God Edward was busy. Pamela would not have been amused. I don't know what devil possessed me to ask him."

The bell sounded.

"They're already here."

Gillian hooted. "He probably opened the front gate for them."

TWENTY-TWO

Back at the station, Edward conferred with Hardy. The cup and saucer had been dusted for prints, and although they were a bit of a dog's breakfast, according to Reagan, with a lot of smears and overlaid prints—two people's, one of them probably a tea-lady—he had found enough to match Bottomley's prints to the set on Wendy Fowler's flask.

"Let's pull him in," said Edward. "It's time he coughed up an answer or two."

"As soon as we've questioned Kennedy. DS Temple's here; she'll go along in case Mrs Kennedy requires handling."

"Anything on his clothing?"

"No. If he killed Fowler, he kept his shirt clean when he did it."

After days of unbroken sunshine, a tattered fringe of clouds was moving in from the east, but the sky was still clear in the west, and the grass and trees glowed green-gold in the evening light. According to DC Paris, Kennedy had left Lensfield Road early and had gone home. His car was still there.

The traffic was thick on Parkside.

"It'll be worse in a month's time," Hardy said. "The town will be crawling with tourists."

Beyond the centre they made good time, and within fifteen minutes were pulling into the Kennedys' driveway behind Alan's BMW.

"The Audi's not here," Edward said. The garage door was open, displaying empty space. "Sam Kennedy must be out."

"Pity," Hardy said. "I was hoping for a look at those lips."

"The front door's open," Temple said, inspecting the house.

They hurried up the walk. As they neared the house, Flora appeared in the hall, carrying a suitcase. She looked at them, startled.

"What's going on here?" Edward asked sharply. "Where's Kennedy?"

She jerked her head. "Upstairs."

"And Mrs Kennedy?"

"Gone."

"Gone where?"

Flora set down the suitcase. "Back to America," she said. "After you came here today, she was very, very angry. She called him—at the laboratory where he works. She told him you had been here and she knew he was the lover of the dead girl. He said he was not—she told me that. But I knew it before, because she was shouting into the telephone that he was a liar. He said he was coming home very soon to talk to her. But she told me she was not going to wait for him. She called him a f-fucking pig."

"Where's the baby?"

"She took him." Flora looked indignant. "Do you think she would leave him here? She has gone to Heathrow."

"What about you?" Edward asked, looking at the bulging suitcase on the floor. "This must be rather a shock."

"A friend is here. I can stay with her. Sam—Mrs Kennedy—said I could stay here, but I don't want to be here alone with *him*. She gave me money— my salary for two months, because my job is finished before the contract. And money for my flight home."

"That was decent of her," Edward said.

"She is very generous," Flora said. For the first time, her voice trembled. "I am sorry. I must pack. My friend is waiting in my room."

"Just one or two questions. How long had Mrs Kennedy been gone when Kennedy got home?"

"Two hours. I think he is arranging now to leave his work next week, to go to America."

"How did he react when he came home?"

"He was very angry. Very upset. He says it is the police's fault."

"All right," said Edward. "Where does your friend live?"

"In Cambridge. She works for a family. The Schofields."

"Does she have a car?"

"No. But Mrs Schofield said she will come in her car when we are ready."

"Good. But Detective-Sergeant Temple will drive you if necessary."

At that moment, Kennedy strode into the hall. Flora slipped past him towards the rear of the house.

"What are you doing here?" he said belligerently. "And what the hell were you telling my wife today? She's left me. Flown home to the States and taken my son. I'm holding you responsible, you know. You march in here and tell her a lot of crap about me and Wendy—what do you think you're doing? You think you can get away with this?"

He was a big man, Edward thought, and very strong. He hoped Kennedy wouldn't do anything stupid. He was certainly enraged. And frightened, too.

"I didn't tell Mrs Kennedy anything," Edward said calmly. "I asked her questions."

"What questions?"

"About your whereabouts on Friday night."

"You told her Wendy Fowler was my—my mistress."

"I most definitely did not."

Kennedy was scarlet. "I'll sue your ass."

"Nonsense," Hardy said, looming beside Edward. "If your wife thought you were unfaithful she put two and two together herself. And she got her sums right. We know you've been in Fowler's flat—in her bedroom. We have a witness who saw you there. We know you had dinner with her—bought at the Chengdu—on Friday night, the same night she was killed. We know you've lied to us."

"A witness in her bedroom? You're telling me she had somebody hiding in the closet? You don't think I'm going to buy that load of crap, do you?"

"You should have realized that her flat wasn't very private," Edward said. "Windows don't only look out."

"I don't believe you," Kennedy snarled. But he was pale now.

"You'd better. The witness is quite prepared to swear to it in court. A very credible witness too, I may tell you."

Kennedy suddenly sat down, crumpling on to a low bench along the wall. "I didn't kill her."

"In that case, why don't you tell us the truth?" Hardy said reasonably, as if explaining the problem to a child. "Then we can get on with finding out who did."

Kennedy passed his hand nervously over his

mouth. He was sweating. "We did have dinner, but that's all. I went home after that. She went back to the lab. That was it, I swear."

Edward was harsh. "You were having an affair with her. She told you she was pregnant, didn't she? She threatened to tell your wife."

"No! She wouldn't have done that."

"You were afraid she would."

"No. I—"

"You what?" Edward said, the question like a stab.

Kennedy's voice shook. "She thought she might have the baby. She hadn't made up her mind. We argued. I thought it was totally unfair." He looked up resentfully. "How could she have it without everyone finding out who the father was? I insisted that she get rid of it. Then she said if she did have an abortion, *I* should go with her to the hospital."

"And you didn't want to?"

"Damn right I didn't. I thought Sam might find out."

"Go on."

"Wendy insisted. She said I owed her that much. If I wouldn't go she didn't want to see me again. I—I lost my temper." His face twisted away from them. "I hit her. It was just a slap. She told me to get out. I collected my things and left." He looked at them wearily. "I lied because I was afraid you'd start asking questions and Sam would find out about Wendy. As she has."

"Did you go back to the lab again on Friday night? After nine o'clock?"

"No. I was here all evening. I couldn't face the party—I was all riled up. Sam came back at midnight. Flora was here," he added. "She can vouch for me."

"But she was in her room. You could have gone out and come back and she would have known nothing about it."

"I was here. That's all I have to say."

Edward leaned harder. "You knew she was going to tell your wife. You went back to the lab. You found Wendy alone."

"No."

"What could be easier for a man like you? A strong man like you, a weight-lifter, a man she trusted? She wouldn't have had a chance."

"I never went near the lab that night!"

"We'd like you to come to the station," Hardy said in a friendly tone, good cop to Edward's bad. "Just to make a statement."

Kennedy looked from one to the other and then at Hilary Temple standing quietly in the background, taking notes. "I want a lawyer," he said.

In Irene's kitchen, the plates had been cleared away, and the second bottle of wine was nearly empty. Patrick was dividing the tart, awarding himself the largest slice. Irene leaned into the open doorway to the garden, smoking an after-dinner cigarette.

"So Edward asked you all about the PIS?" Bee said to Irene.

"'Yes, I told him what we do, and why, and even gave him a bit of history. I waxed nostalgic about the old days, before factions split the movement. The good old days when we thought we could change the world in a decade."

"Who says we haven't?" Gillian said.

"How can you say that?" Pamela cried.

"Patrick!" Irene said, noticing his slice.

"I need it. I'm growing," he said.

"It's not polite."

"Neither is smoking," he retorted. "Besides, smoking is bad for you, and your tart is good for me." He waved away the smoke, dropped a kiss on her cheek and vanished with his plate.

"Everywhere you look there's discrimination," Pamela said. "Men still run the world, single mothers are desperately poor, abortion's still a crime in most countries, men batter their wives—"

"I know," said Gillian. "But all that used to be taken for granted. None of it is, now. Women *are* taking control of their destiny, bit by bit. It's just a lot slower and harder to do than we thought it would be."

"That's putting it mildly. They're being murdered, right here in Cambridge. Doesn't that tell you something?"

"Certainly. But not that there's been no progress at all."

"There hasn't been much progress so far as violence against women goes. The police still don't take it seriously. It's a joke to them. But then, they beat their wives themselves."

"No doubt some of them do," Gillian said evenly. "But I wish you'd stop flaunting your bigotry. You talk about the police the way the Klan talks about black people."

There was a shocked silence. Bee looked as if she'd been slapped, although Gillian hadn't been speaking to her. The thready whine of a radio station came faintly from behind Patrick's closed door.

Irene threw her cigarette into the garden and came back into the room.

"This has been brewing, hasn't it?"

"I'm sorry," Gillian said. "But they're human beings too, you know. Individuals. Just like the rest of us."

Pamela's mouth was pinched into a thin angry line. "It's getting late. Bee, I think we should go home," she said, standing up.

"Oh no," Irene said.

Bee started to rise, then sank back in her chair. "Pamela, don't. Don't test me by making me leave. I know what Gillian said was unfair, but you provoked her. You know you did."

Gillian was amazed. It was the first time she'd seen Bee take a stand when Pamela was angry. Pamela seemed rather surprised herself. She stood still.

"I suppose I was tactless," she said in a chilly voice.

"I could have made my point more delicately myself," Gillian answered.

Pamela looked at her. "All right." She sat down again. She turned to Bee. "You can breathe. I'm not going to eat your friend."

"Have some tart instead," Irene said. "What's left of it."

The police didn't find Bottomley until nine-thirty p.m., when he returned to his rooms. He hadn't been anywhere in particular, just reading *The Times* after dinner, he told them. They had decided to ask him to come in to the station. "Better to shift him off his home ground," Hardy had said. "He'll feel like a fox in his own earth as long as he's in his college."

In the glaring light of the interrogation room, a bare box smelling of disinfectant, he looked at once pathetic and sly. His protuberant eyes darted about the confined space; he blinked and moved restlessly in his chair, his bony shoulders hunched unevenly.

Scoliosis, Edward saw. It was pronounced—a deformity. Edward wondered how long Bottomley had suffered from this condition and what it had done to him. Hardy was asking the questions this time. Questions about Bottomley's career at the university, his relations with Wendy Fowler, his reaction when she successfully applied for financing for her research project.

It was still a sore point, and Bottomley didn't bother to conceal his sense of injury.

"She had no right," he said. "Moving in on an area that I had been researching, using ideas I had been

working on for years—without so much as a by-your-
leave. She used my ideas, and because she was young,
and a woman—women are all the go nowadays, men
don't stand a chance—they gave her the money. It
should have been mine. *I* was doing the chiral recognition work in this department. If there were proper
laws, I'd have bundled her into court. I was quite
incensed, I don't mind telling you."

"You didn't like Wendy Fowler, then?" Hardy said.

"She had no scruples. She was a slut, too."

What do you mean?"

"Sleeping with married men in the department."

"Who?"

"Alan Kennedy, for one. Others, for all I know.
The ones who could help her career along, no doubt."

"You believe she was sleeping with Kennedy?"

"I know she was. I saw their little tête-à-têtes—they
were careful, but that sort of thing is always found out."

"Did you tell anyone else?"

"I might have. Why?" Bottomley said truculently.

"How many people do you think knew or believed
she was seeing Kennedy?"

"I've no idea. Roger knew—Roger Hill. We talked
about it. He said Kennedy was a regular Don Juan—
always had one or two of these little affairs going,
even when he was first married. None of them was
supposed to know about each other, of course, especially not the beautiful wife. But she knew."

"What makes you say that?"

"She watched him like a hawk. I saw her, at parties."

"You don't seem to like Kennedy much, either."

"A self-important muscle-bound American."

"He's a good chemist, I understand."

Bottomley sniffed. "Overrated."

Edward had said nothing so far. Bottomley was possessed of an apparently limitless fund of resentment, which Hardy was drawing on with great success.

"About Wendy Fowler," Hardy said. "You couldn't take her to court. So what did you do?"

"I didn't kill her, if that's what you mean," Bottomley answered scornfully.

"What did you do?"

"Nothing. I told you there was nothing I could do."

"Really? What about the floods that came from her bench? What about the strange things that went wrong with her experiments?"

"She was accident-prone," Bottomley answered. "She had a nickname, didn't anyone tell you? The Sorcerer's Apprentice."

"You say those were all accidents? She didn't think so."

"Naturally not. Someone that sloppy is bound to look for excuses. The idea that anyone tampered with her experiments is simply fatuous. Everyone in the department would tell you that."

"We don't think so," Edward said, stepping in at the agreed moment. "We know you tampered with her apparatus."

"Rubbish."

"Your fingerprints are all over the flask she was using the night she was murdered."

Bottomley, who was sitting with his arms folded, looked involuntarily down at his hands. The nails on his left hand whitened as the fingers clenched on his upper right arm. "That's not possible."

"We have the prints. Very clear ones. And they're on the plastic bag that caused the second flood. What happened? Did the first flood give you the idea of discrediting her with the other two? Or did you flood her lab first and then decide it was better to flood Hill and Scudder so she would get the blame?"

"You must be mad," Bottomley said. "And you've never taken my fingerprints."

"Where were you Friday evening? You lied about being in your room all evening. You went out before nine. You could have gone to the lab and killed her then."

"I didn't." Bottomley's voice squeaked.

"We know you went out. You were seen leaving your staircase."

"I just went to the Fellows' garden. I like to walk there in the evening now and then."

"Did you see anyone?"

"No, but I was there. I didn't leave the college."

"Why did you lie about going out?"

Bottomley drew himself up a little. "I didn't want to be involved in this—this sordid little inquiry."

"If that's the reason, you may as well tell us the truth," Hardy replied. "As you're in it up to your neck."

Bottomley shrank a little, but he stubbornly maintained that he hadn't left the garden Friday night. He insisted that he had neither killed Wendy nor had anything to do with the floods and failed experiments. If his prints were on the flask, which he doubted, then she must have borrowed a flask from his lab. He had gone up after Scudder told him about the flood and had handled the plastic bag. And so on. By eleven o'clock Edward was worried. Bottomley was made of tougher material than they had thought, and they couldn't keep interrogating him all night.

"Do you realize," he said suddenly, "that we could charge you with attempted murder on the evidence of the flask alone? If she had gone on to distil the contents, it might have exploded and could even have killed her." The prosecution would have his hide if he hadn't a better case to give them, but Bottomley was not to know that.

Bottomley jumped as if prodded from behind. "Killed her! It couldn't have!"

"How do you know, if you didn't tamper with it?"

Bottomley turned sullen. "I refuse to answer more questions."

They couldn't squeeze another word out of him.

TWENTY-THREE

The next day was Friday. Gillian went to see Vicky after breakfast. Edward had come back at about midnight, had slept like a stone until seven and then rushed off, having bathed, dressed and consumed two cups of coffee while Gillian was still blinking and tottering about in her dressing-gown.

"What happened last night?" she'd asked Edward sleepily.

"We cleared away a lot of undergrowth."

"That's good."

"Samantha Kennedy's flown the coop."

"Left England? Gone back to Santa Fe?"

"Presumably. She boarded a flight to Los Angeles yesterday."

"Does that worry you?"

"Not unduly. It certainly confirms her husband's motive for wanting to keep Wendy Fowler quiet."

"He's the one you suspect, then?"

"He could have done it. He's extremely strong; it would have been easy for him to carry Wendy and crack her head against the shelf. As easy as cracking an egg on the edge of a table. He has a weak alibi. We could rubbish it in court. He was having an affair with Wendy that he didn't want his wife to know about; Wendy was pregnant; what he's told us is that they had a fight about her right to choose to have the child. He insisted on an abortion, but then when she wanted him to help, to accompany her to hospital, he wouldn't. After that she threw him out, he says. What if she threatened to tell his wife?"

"Would she do that?"

"It was the only power she had. The only power, whether to hold or to punish. She might have used it." He looked at his watch. "I'm off. We have to decide what to tell the press this morning. They're baying at our heels."

Vicky's studio was in her flat, downstairs in a squat little brick house with a bay window, a shiny buttercup-yellow door and white trim. She lived not very far from Irene, but north of Chesterton Road. It was a chilly, clouded morning, and Gillian could smell coal-smoke in the air. When she had first come to Cambridge, these little streets, like some in the Kite, had been down-at-the-heel: the houses shabby, with sunken steps and peeling paint, and the occasional derelict standing empty. Now, she noticed, many of them had been smarted up with new paint and brass knockers and perennials from garden shops.

Vicky opened the door as soon as she knocked.

"I saw you coming down the street. It's cold today, isn't it?"

She was wearing the same wide black trousers that Gillian had seen on Tuesday, and a thin grey knitted jersey with the sleeves rolled up. They stepped through a narrow hall made even narrower by a storage heater and into the room with the bay window. A long white table took up most of what had been a sitting-room. It was set near the middle of the room, and Vicky's chair stood between it and the east-facing bay window, so that the light, when she sat, would come from behind and flood the white surface of her table. Pots of glue, jars of brushes and pencils, various erasers, inks and paints stood on the table and on shelves adjacent to it. An easel and a stack of wire-mesh drying racks filled two corners of the room, and an old sofa occupied the remaining space.

"This is my studio," Vicky said. "There isn't much else—just the kitchen and a little bedroom. We'll sit in here."

Gillian followed her to the kitchen while she made tea. The kitchen was dark and so tiny that

Vicky, a small woman of neat movements, quite filled it up. Gillian stood in the doorway, feeling large and untidy, like a rose that wanted pruning. A framed photograph hung on the wall where it caught the light from the tiny kitchen window. It was a portrait of an old, worn face, cross-hatched with fine wrinkles, the thin flesh lying hollow on the bones.

"That's my grandmother," Vicky said. "I'm half Chinese. She's very old now, something like ninety-three, although we're not sure exactly. I took that picture of her last year."

Vicky carried the tea into her studio and set it on the floor in front of the sofa, which was long and deep and covered in mangy dark green velvet.

Gillian edged past the long table and saw a map of Lincolnshire, an ordinary nineteenth-century map, sparsely decorated.

"What are you doing with the map?"

Vicky waved a dismissive hand. "Only colouring it. It's boring work, but it fills in when I'm not doing anything more interesting. Hand-colouring bumps the price up." She pointed to a large, muddy brown canvas, unframed, that stood against the wall. "That's more interesting. I'm cleaning it, and God knows what I'll find underneath all that varnish. It's been laid on with a trowel. I picked it up in a junk shop; a brass bedpost had near as anything pushed a hole through it. Perhaps it will make my fortune," she said lightly. "See that corner there where I've got down to the paint? It's a very promising blue, don't you think?"

Gillian peered at the patch of blue. It had a celestial gleam, like a high window in a prison cell.

"You wanted to talk about Wendy and the PIS?" Vicky, asked.

"In a way. What I really wanted to know was whether she ever talked to you about any of the women she saw on Saturdays when she was testing with other members of the group. According to Irene, most of you were in the habit of reviewing the sessions and comparing notes, but Wendy didn't. She thought maybe Wendy talked to you, since you were closer to her."

"The subject came up sometimes, but Wendy didn't have a lot to say. She wasn't awfully interested in stories, or in what people were feeling; she was a practical person."

"What about practical matters, then? Did she ever talk to you about any of the women calling her, something like that? You see, Cynthia Perdreau, the young woman who was murdered in the woods behind Pamela and Bee's house, went to the PIS for a test. And Wendy—"

Vicky interrupted. "She did? I didn't realize that. When did you find that out?"

"Last night. I went to see Irene, and she recognized Cynthia's picture. She came in on April 6th, when Irene and Wendy were testing. I'm wondering whether she saw Wendy again. What concerns me is whether there was a link between them that has something to do with their deaths. And if that link is the PIS, then is anyone else in danger? It worries me. You're my friends. And the police—the police have a lot on their plate right now."

"Wendy never mentioned a Cynthia to me." Vicky meditated, her tea forgotten at her feet. "But I remember that a few weeks ago she said something about a young woman who rang her up. She didn't mention any names—she was nothing if not discreet—but she said that this girl had come in for a test and didn't want to tell her parents that she was pregnant. She had Wendy's telephone number in case she needed more advice. Wendy said she called about a week later, after she'd seen the GP, because she needed someone to collect her from hospital after her abortion. She'd asked her boyfriend, and he wouldn't help her at all. In fact, he got angry and told her it was a sin against nature, or some rubbish. Apparently, the girl said something like 'Well, you don't want to look after it, do you?' And he said, 'That's the woman's job.' But he was so insistent she got scared and told him she'd changed her mind about the abortion. Then as soon as she was alone, she telephoned Wendy. And Wendy said she would help her. She said the girl needed support and had no one else to ask."

"When did she tell you that?"

"I'm not sure of the day, but it was three or four weeks go."

Gillian counted backwards. "This is the 10th. So that would have been about April 12th to 19th. The right time. Cynthia Perdreau had her abortion on the 19th. What else did she tell you?"

"Not much, I think. She said the girl told her she couldn't understand his attitude. When she'd broken off the relationship two months earlier, he'd called her a little whore and acted as though he didn't care. He hadn't tried to ring her up or anything. I don't think Wendy told me anything else about her."

There was a pencil on the floor near the sofa, and Vicky absent-mindedly picked it up and stuck it behind her ear. "It's funny, though, Wendy told me later, after she found out she was in the same boat, that she'd felt an extraordinary sympathy with the girl at the time, a conviction that she must help her. She wondered whether it was because she subconsciously knew she was pregnant herself. It was a most un-Wendyish idea, but she knew that, too. She said 'This isn't like me. I don't think this way.' I think the pregnancy really rocked her—she was always so straight-ahead; she'd never questioned the direction of her life before."

"Was it out of character for her to offer help like that?"

"Oh no. Definitely not. Wendy was terrific when it came to real, practical help. If you needed, like, someone to help you move, she was the sort of person who would turn up and carry boxes and clean filthy floors.

She'd show up on time and work like stink. She was a genius at packing the maximum number of objects into the minimum amount of space. And at spatial relations generally. This sofa—" Vicky patted the green velvet—"wouldn't go through that door. It was so big it got stuck when I tried to angle it through the front door and then into this room. We tried everything. I thought I'd have to junk it. But Wendy came along and figured out the one way it could go through. It didn't even scrape the woodwork." Vicky looked bleak. "Maybe we weren't as close as we could have been, but she was a special person to me. And I think I understood her better than most people."

"Tell me, do you think that if she were pregnant by a married man, she would inform his wife?"

"No," said Vicky. "She wasn't the sort that told." She stopped. "Not out of spite. She might tell if the wife asked her. She'd think she had a right to the truth."

Belatedly, they had tea. Gillian thought, I should let Edward know about this. But she didn't want to tell him immediately. She had another idea that she wanted to try first.

"Vicky," she said tentatively, "do you know anyone who lives in Wendy's building, or near it?"

"I know Vrinda. Vrinda Kumar. She lives in the building next to Wendy's."

"What would you think of going to see her with me? I'd like to talk to her, and it would be easier if you came along."

"Now?"

"Right now."

They walked into the centre of Cambridge in a light drizzle, crossing Jesus Green and then making their way past the pretty houses in Portugal Place.

"This is where I'd live if I had the money," Vicky said.

"Then you want to stay here in Cambridge?"

"I'd like to come back eventually. At least I thought so before—before all this. Now I'm not keen. I'll need to move to London soon and work for one of the big museums to broaden my experience. But I don't like big cities. My dream would be to get a job in Venice—no cars, it's even smaller than Cambridge, and almost everything in it needs restoration."

"What about working in China? There must be all sorts of extraordinary things that need restoration there."

Vicky shook her head. "Not while the present government is in power. Not for all the tea in England."

In Trinity Street bicycles squeezed between the cars and the crowded strip of pavement while pedestrians jiggled unevenly over the kerb or scythed sideways through slower clusters of shoppers. Conversation was impossible until they reached the broader space at the foot of Great St Mary's. But there they looked ahead to King's, where Wendy had had her fellowship, and found nothing to say.

They came to Wendy's building, walked under her window. Vicky looked up once and quickly averted her eyes.

"Vrinda lives in the next building."

Vrinda was working but accepted the interruption good-naturedly.

"Vicky! I haven't seen you in weeks. Come and have some tea."

"We've just had some. This isn't quite a social call. It's about Wendy, my friend Wendy Fowler."

"Oh, poor Wendy. You know, I had forgotten that she was such a good friend of yours. I am so sorry about it. It is such a tragedy. And so strange."

"This is Gillian Adams. She thinks it might have something to do with the PIS."

Vrinda looked at Gillian. "Really? Why?"

"Because of the other murder—the young woman who was found in the woods. She came to the PIS last month, when Wendy was testing."

Vrinda's brows contracted in a worried frown. She wound her thick black braid in her fingers. "That's not much of a connection, is it?"

"Maybe it isn't. But Cynthia Perdreau was killed only a couple of days after she had an abortion."

"Are you a police detective?"

"No."

"That's good. The police have been here twice already." Vrinda rolled her dark eyes. "Once two oafs who blundered about my bedroom like bees in a bottle, and once a woman sergeant who interviewed Jenny, my room-mate. I don't think she asked any questions about Wendy and the PIS, though."

They went through to the sitting-room, which was furnished with the usual student hodge-podge of abused furniture. Another woman, long and lanky, with her hair in a ponytail, was lying on her back on the sofa, her large feet hanging over the arm. A mound of books on the floor beside her attested to good intentions, but she appeared to have been dozing. She sat up when they came in and gave them a sleepy nod.

"Wake up, Jenny," Vrinda said briskly. "I'll make tea."

"Ungh," said Jenny. "I'm never going to drink brandy again. I had no idea what it could do to you."

"You must have had an inkling," Vrinda said.

"I thought it was liqueurs that were bad," Jenny said without heat. "Anyway, from now on I stick to gin. I'm a true Brit, I am; so it's gin and roast beef from now on."

"And when are you moving out?" Vrinda asked, going towards the kitchen.

Jenny laughed. "She's vegetarian. And she doesn't drink." She sat up, her long legs seeming to stretch halfway across the room. "How can we be such good friends?" she yelled over the sound of running water in the kitchen. "We have nothing in common."

"So what is it that you want to know?" Vrinda asked, when they were all settled with tea.

Gillian opened her shoulder-bag and extracted Cynthia's photograph from its envelope. "Have you ever seen her before?"

"No. I don't know her," Vrinda said after looking at it carefully. She passed the photograph to Jenny.

"I've seen her somewhere," Jenny said slowly, "but I don't know where. I don't know her, just the face."

"Try to remember where, if you can. It could be important," Gillian said.

They went on talking, about Wendy and her death, and the other murder, and whether they were linked and how quickly the police might find the killer or killers. Jenny held the photograph in one hand and sipped her tea. She said little, but wrinkled up her brow.

"Did Wendy have a car?" Gillian asked.

Suddenly Jenny started, slopping tea on her jeans.

"I know. That's where I saw her! It was in Wendy's car. I was coming up King's Parade. Wendy had an old red Mini that she babied along. But of course she didn't keep it here; I think she might have left it in the chem-lab car park most of the time. So I hardly ever saw it. That's why I noticed it that day when she parked in front of her building. She came round to the passenger side and helped someone get out. It was this girl, the one in the photo. She wasn't well, I could see that. She was very pale. Wendy took her inside, and upstairs, I presume. We didn't speak; she was busy and I was probably in a hurry. I usually am.

Then she must have moved the car, she'd have had to. Anyway, when I came out again it was gone."

"Can you think when you saw them?" Gillian asked, excited.

"Weeks ago. Let me see. It was after the Easter vacation, and it wasn't just before Wendy was killed. That was at the weekend, and I know it was well before that. It must have been about the middle of April. I can't pin it down to the day. But I'll think about it. Maybe something will remind me."

"What were you doing?" Vrinda asked her. "Can you remember why you came home and went out again?"

Jenny's eyes widened. She looked mischievously at Vrinda. "Yes, I was bleeding," she said. She turned to Gillian and Vicky. "I have the most filthy rotten periods. Ferocious pains, and I bleed like a pig. So even when I'm careful, I sometimes leak. Then I have to go home and change, because I hardly ever remember to bring a spare pair of pants with me, and anyway, the others need to be put to soak . . . Vrinda thinks I should use those super-absorbent tampons, but I'm afraid of toxic shock syndrome."

"Well," said Vrinda drily, "at least that should tell us the date."

Jenny got out her calendar. "Pig days," she said. "April 18th to 25th. So it was that week. And the heavy days are always near the beginning, so it must have been the 18th, 19th or 20th. And it wasn't early in the day; I don't usually go out before ten, unless I'm swimming, and I don't swim on those days."

Gillian said, "Cynthia Perdreau didn't go home on the 19th, the day she had her abortion. She told her parents she was staying with a friend. Probably she was afraid they'd find out if she went home the same day. So Wendy must have picked her up from Addenbrooke's and brought her here to spend the night. Then Cynthia went home for three days. The second day she went out, she disappeared. She was murdered that day, I'll bet my bottom dollar."

TWENTY-FOUR

DC Paris tapped on Edward's office door.

"McClure asked me to show you what he's dug up on Roger Hill," he said, proffering a file.

"What is it?"

"He's a pervert."

Edward glanced up at him and flipped open the file. "Any previous?"

"Indecent exposure. Not here, Manchester. And the parents of a fifteen-year-old girl brought a complaint which was later dropped when the girl didn't want to go to court."

"He's not exactly Mr Clean, is he? I wonder if the university is aware of this," Edward said, looking over the sheet. "Sit down," he added.

"He wouldn't have told them, would he?"

"The charges are old. They go back twenty years."

"Doesn't mean he hasn't been up to the same tricks. It might be he just hasn't been caught again."

"Very likely."

DC Paris was excited. "What if Cynthia Perdreau was too great a temptation? Say he molests her. Maybe he rapes her. He frightens her into keeping quiet—maybe he convinces her that no one will believe her. But then he thinks, what if she tells on him? All the old dirt will be dug up again. There goes his job and reputation."

"But she went on accepting lifts into town. She would hardly have done that, even if she kept quiet about what he'd done. You're not suggesting that she was willing?"

Paris looked rather appalled. "No, sir. He's not very good looking, is he, and he's much too old."

Six years older than I am, Edward thought. DC Paris was all of twenty-three.

Paris returned to the attack. "It might have happened all at once—when she went back to work. We know he didn't drive her to town on the 24th, because she only worked in the afternoon, but he might have offered her a lift home and molested her then. And then he decided to kill her."

"After he molested her he suggested they stop for a nice little stroll in the wood?"

"He might have followed her there. Look—"

Edward raised his palm, stopping the flow. "Listen, Paris," he said, not unkindly, "she wasn't raped; the autopsy would have told us if she had been. There was no violent struggle in the wood. Do you really think Hill could have followed her there and managed first to assault her and then to kill her without any row? I don't think it's possible. You're a bit carried away by these old reports, I think. I grant you, he's a dodgy fellow, but I don't think he can be our man."

"But I don't see how we connect Kennedy or Bottomley to the Perdreau girl," Paris said glumly.

"Nor do I. What are the possibilities? Number one: we've missed something essential about either Kennedy or Bottomley, which would explain the connection. Number two: the murderer is not one of them, but someone else. Number three: there are two murderers."

"But Roger Hill knew both victims!"

Edward sighed. "So he did. But this is a very small town." He took pity on Paris. "Tell you what. Go back to Grantchester and find out why the neighbours were so keen to talk about Hill. What have they got against him?"

He went back to his typewriter. It put him in a bad humour. He missed the Yard. His own desk, and especially his computer. There were few things in life more irritating than being forced to use a typewriter after one was used to a computer. He made another error, swore, and gave it up. Hardy came in carrying a mug of tea and a sticky bun. He sat down and bit into the bun. Little white flakes of melted sugar showered his desk.

"We've found the owner of the spade. Not a neighbour after all."

"Don't tell me it's Hill!"

"No. College gardener. King's owns some houses down there, and there's an old fellow keeps the gardens in order now and then. He left his spade leaning against the fence at the back while he went to rake up a load of weeds and trimmings at the front, and when he went to fetch it, it was gone. He was quite narked about it. His favourite spade, he said it was."

"When did he lose it?"

"April 22nd. Late afternoon—near four o'clock."

"Two days before Perdreau disappeared. Then the bastard planned it."

"It seems to me," Hardy said when he had finished his bun, "that we're getting nowhere with connecting the two deaths. We've gone through Kennedy's life with a fine-tooth comb; all we've got is the au pair's suspicion that he was seeing more than one woman. We haven't found a trace of the second woman; we're not even sure she exists, let alone that she was Perdreau. We've poked about in Bottomley's affairs and shaken him till he rattled; there's no indication that he knew Perdreau or has any sexual interest in women, young or otherwise. As far as we can determine, he did nothing out of the ordinary on April 19th or April 24th. He ate his meals in college; he went to work. He went out the night Fowler was killed, and he lied about it, but we've no proof he was in Lensfield Road. So we can't even tie him to the Fowler murder. Hill knew both victims, but we haven't made much out of that. Not yet, at least. There was a nice kerfuffle in the murder room when his previous came in, but unless we can put him in the wood with Perdreau, I don't give a monkey's what he did twenty years ago. There's no indication he was at the lab Friday night. He says he went home, and we've got nothing to contradict it. Pity his dog can't talk."

"We've kept trying to link the chemists to Perdreau. What about the other way round? Perdreau's boyfriend. Can we connect him to Wendy?"

"Through the PIS, you mean?"

"Or in any way. He's not faculty, he's not a former student, but could he have been connected to the lab in some other way? He's unemployed now, and before that he worked at a pharmaceutical company for a couple of years; what was he doing before that?"

"I don't know. I don't think anyone's asked." Hardy flicked the crumbs from his shirt. Then he pulled the file from the heap on his desk and leafed through it. "Nothing here. I'll call Scudder. He's been in the department ever since he was a student in the fifties."

"That's before Tod French was born," Edward said drily.

Hardy laughed and picked up the receiver.

Edward stretched and went to the window. He frowned abstractedly down at the car park while Hardy telephoned.

"Do you know whether a Tod French was ever connected with the chemistry department?" he heard Hardy ask. He turned round to observe Hardy's expression and saw that he had already tucked the receiver between his ear and his shoulder and was reaching for a pencil and paper. Edward came back to the desk and bent over it, trying vainly to decipher Hardy's shorthand.

"Well?" he said instantly, when Hardy put down the receiver.

Hardy's face was jubilant. "He was once a lab technician there. They fired him."

"When?"

"Five years ago. His behaviour was erratic, Scudder said. They didn't think he was safe."

They went first to Tod French's little flat in Histon. There was no one at home. From there, they proceeded to Lensfield Road. They found Scudder in his office.

"Would he have known Wendy Fowler?" Edward asked, standing again in his chosen position by the window.

"He might have done," Scudder replied, frowning because he could give no solid information. "He was here when she was an undergraduate and when she began her graduate work. But there's no particular reason why he should. People do meet one another, however. In the tea-room, waiting for results at the NMR machines, and so on. People are *intended* to meet one another—it's useful."

"Was there trouble when he was fired?"

"A minor amount of unpleasantness. But he went without too much fuss. There wasn't anything he could do, after all."

"What was the problem?"

"He was irresponsible—to a damaging degree. A technician has to be careful," Scudder said emphatically. "Ensuring safety is the essence of the job. French had the odd fit of temper. Didn't like being told when things hadn't been done properly. On one of those occasions he smashed some apparatus and dumped the whole lot—swimming in mercury—in the waste bin. I'm afraid that sort of behaviour is simply not on. We decided he was temperamentally unsuited to the job."

"Have you seen him since?"

"Never. I did hear that he found another job, in industry. A less responsible position, I believe."

"Had you heard he was fired there, too?"

"No. I haven't heard anything about him in several years. But I'm not surprised. He was an awfully moody chap. One or two people floated the suggestion that his moods were perhaps on occasion chemically induced."

"Drugs?"

"It was the purest speculation."

Hardy set loose a small swarm of DCs, who buzzed about the labs, looking for people who had known French, and re-interviewing everyone who had been in the labs on the weekend Wendy was killed.

Meanwhile, Edward paid a visit to the biological suite to ask Tennison about the oily compound on the floor of the cold room. He thought it might belong to Tennison, because it was Tennison who had made such a fuss about his compounds the day Wendy's body was found.

"(E)-2,4-Dimethylpent-3-yl but-2-enoate?" Tennison said, looking at the forensic laboratory report Edward handed him. "Nothing to do with me, I'm afraid. It could belong to any of the organic chemists. Geoff Wrigley's office is just round the corner, why don't we ask him?" Tennison was brusque, but more forthcoming than he had been at their previous interview. "It's certainly not a common compound. What do you need to know about it?"

"We found it on the floor of the cold room, and of course we wondered whether it was from your samples, or whether it belonged to Wendy Fowler or was something the murderer brought with him."

"It's not from *my* samples, but I have no idea what Wendy Fowler was doing. Not my field. Here's Wrigley's office."

The door was open. "Geoff," Tennison shouted, before Edward had a chance to speak. "Do you know anything about this?" He showed Wrigley the paper.

Wrigley was white-haired, with an untidy beard. His bony wrist protruded from his frayed cuff as he reached for the paper.

"That's diisopropylmethyl crotonate," he said loudly, leaving Edward no wiser. "Who are you?" he said, looking at Edward.

"Police!" bellowed Tennison.

"Detective Chief Inspector Gisborne," Edward said.

"Inspector," Wrigley said, shaking hands. Edward waited while Wrigley studied the piece of paper for a moment.

"This was something one of my students made a few years ago. What about it?"

Tennison said, slowly and distinctly, "They found some in the cold room."

"The cold room. Yes, of course. This would be one of Robin Beard's samples. He left them there in case anyone else wanted them. Oh dear. They should have been cleared out years ago. This stuff," he added, waving the piece of paper, "was one of the compounds he made."

"What was it for?" asked Edward in a loud voice.

"For? We were looking at the gamma alkylation of silyl dienyl ethers. And diisopropylmethyl was a conveniently large group." He regarded Edward for a moment. "What else can I say? It was an experiment."

"So the murderer wouldn't have wanted this chemical in particular for any purpose."

"I can't imagine it would have been of the least use. It's hardly likely he would have known what it was."

"Is it unusual, then?"

"Unusual?" yelled Wrigley. "Of course it's unusual. It's not only unusual, it's unique. Just like millions of others made by chemists in the course of their work. It was certainly a new compound when Robin made it. I doubt if anyone's made it since. Certainly no one's made it here."

"Unique!" Edward stared at the paper for a moment and then began to laugh. A unique substance. A detective's dream—if it turned out to be of any use. He thanked Wrigley, who boomed, "Not at all. Glad to be of help, Inspector Bigthorne."

"Sorry," Tennison said in the corridor. "I should have warned you. He's a brilliant chemist but terribly deaf. Won't admit it, either."

"Do you know Tod French?" Edward asked.

"Never heard of him."

"He was a lab technician here once. He was fired five years ago. We'd like to know whether anyone saw him here last Friday night."

"I wouldn't know him," Tennison replied. "I've only been here for four years. Four and a half, to be precise. But you might ask Scudder. You have? Then try Bottomley. He's been in the department far longer than I have. And he was here Friday evening."

Edward was startled. "Was he? You didn't mention that the last time."

"Didn't I? I didn't know it was important. You asked who I'd seen in the labs. I don't know he was in the building; I saw him in the car park at about nine o'clock. I noticed because he's never about on Friday nights."

Edward sped off down the corridor. Where was Bottomley now? He'd wring his scrawny neck when he found him. The Fellows' garden, indeed. He nearly cannoned into Hardy, who was coming to look for him.

"We've got to find Bottomley. He was here Friday evening at nine o'clock!" Edward said. "Tennison saw him in the car park."

Bottomley was not in his office. Nor was he teaching a class, according to the secretary. Edward gazed in exasperation down the endless corridor, the air supply roaring dully in his ears. "He could be anywhere."

"Let's not ride off in all directions," Hardy said. "We'll find him easy enough. None of these fellows ever misses a meal, it seems."

Edward glanced at his watch. Lunch-time was not far away. "All right. Let me tell you about this oily stuff Santini found." He recounted his interview with Wrigley. "It's nothing the murderer would have wanted specifically, so he must have knocked it over without noticing or chosen it at random to lend verisimilitude to Wendy Fowler's fall."

"So it's not something she would have been using?"

"Nothing to do with her work at all."

One by one the constables reported in. Of the

chemists present in the building Friday evening few knew Tod French by sight. The few who remembered him hadn't seen him. Edward and Hardy left the labs. At noon they cornered Bottomley in his college, at the entrance to the dining hall.

"Let's take our sweet time about this," Edward said as they saw him crossing the court from the porter's lodge, tucking his letters into a pocket. "At the very least, he'll miss lunch."

He didn't notice them until they were right in front of him. He paled, then turned dull red, as the Fellows and students trooping in for lunch glanced curiously at the two men blocking his way.

"I've nothing to say to you," he muttered.

"We think differently," said Edward. "What were you doing at the chemistry labs in Lensfield Road Friday night?"

"I've told you, I wasn't there."

"That won't do," Hardy said grimly. "You were seen."

"By one of your own colleagues," Edward added. "Tennison saw you when he was leaving."

"Tennison!" squeaked Bottomley. He was suddenly frightened. His hands trembled; his Adam's apple bobbed up and down. They edged him away from the entrance to a quiet corner of the court.

"I never touched her," Bottomley whispered.

"What time did you go to the labs?"

"Just before nine. You must know that. I saw Tennison in the car park. He was leaving on his bicycle. I waited in the shadows at the far end until he left; I didn't think he'd seen me."

"What were you doing there?"

"I thought I'd have a look at Wendy's experiment. See what had happened to it," Bottomley said dully.

"And did you?"

"No. She was there. She was sitting at her bench."

"Did she speak to you?"

"No. She didn't see me. I walked away."

"Why didn't you tell us this before?"

"I thought you'd think I . . . Everyone knew how I felt about her. But I didn't kill her. I didn't do anything."

"Did you see anyone else while you were there?" Edward asked.

Bottomley hesitated, his expression wavering between fear and hope. "Just one person. Only for a second. After I climbed the stairs to the third floor and came round the corner into the corridor, I saw a man at the far end. He didn't see me; he just went into a room and closed the door. All I thought about it at the time was that I was glad he wasn't looking in my direction."

"Did you recognize him?"

Bottomley sounded genuinely puzzled. "I thought he looked like a lab technician who used to work for us. His name was Tod French. But I supposed it must have been my imagination. I was rather nervous at the time. He hasn't been in the labs for years."

Edward stared at Bottomley, disgusted. "And after Wendy Fowler was murdered, you didn't tell us this. You kept quiet to save yourself a spot of bother."

On the way back to the station, Hardy called in. There was an urgent message from Gillian waiting for Edward. He had Hardy drop him at Earl Street.

"Thank goodness," Gillian said when she opened the door. "It's been all I could do not to call the station every two minutes to see if you'd come back. There really was a link between Wendy and Cynthia." Before she had finished Edward was on the telephone to Hardy.

"If it was Cynthia's boyfriend who killed her," Gillian said when he came back, "you could connect the two cases. Cynthia told Wendy, who told Vicky—who just told me—that he was totally opposed to her having an abortion. He scared her—enough that she told him she'd changed her mind."

"That's very interesting. He told us he didn't know anything about it. She didn't really intend to reconsider, I take it."

"No. She called Wendy right afterwards and asked for her help. She hadn't expected him to give her any support, but she was shocked by his reaction. She told Wendy that when she broke up with him, he didn't seem to care much. He called her a little whore."

"She said *she* left him?" Edward said.

"That's not what *he* said, is it?"

Edward was thinking. "It must have rankled when she dumped him. She was just a kid. He had nothing better to do than sit and brood—having already lost his job. Then she comes and tells him she's pregnant. She wants an abortion. He says, 'Over my dead body.'"

"Over her dead body, you mean. When he finds out she's gone and done it, he kills her."

"He must have thought she might do it. The spade that was used to dig her grave was stolen two days ahead of time. I wonder if he wasn't watching her. But that wood was a risky place to choose."

"I expect she had enough nous not to get into his car." Gillian said. "So they went for a walk."

Edward paced to the window and back. "He must have planned to keep her talking long enough to find out who helped her. But would she have told him Wendy Fowler's name?"

"If he went to the PIS office, he would have found it in the book."

"If he knew Cynthia had confided in Wendy . . . Let's connect the dots," Edward said. "We need somebody at Addenbrooke's who remembers Wendy, and we've got to find the evidence that will tie French to the Perdreau killing, or there's no reason for him to go after Wendy. He has no alibi for the evening Cynthia disappeared, but we haven't found anyone who saw them. He didn't pick her up at work. She walked through the door into the street and vanished."

"But she usually walked home along the river.

She'd been seen in the little wood before. You said he might have intercepted her there. He would have known her hours at the shop."

"Yes, but no one saw him hanging about in Owlstone Road. Anyone just walking by might well not be noticed, but a man standing in those little streets in Newnham would be conspicuous."

"Why would he have to wait right there? She had a natural route home; he might have watched for her somewhere else, where he wouldn't be conspicuous, and then followed her, pretending to meet her by accident."

"That would work. But Lord knows if we can prove it. And I must say, it wasn't very bright of her to go into the wood with him and then tell him what she'd done." Edward sounded impatient.

"She was seventeen, for God's sake. Besides, how could she imagine he would do that? We don't think our lovers are murderers."

He looked at his watch. "I must get to the station. We've a lot to do. Find French, for starters." He gave her a quick, hard hug. "The connection between Perdreau and Fowler has got to be the key to the case."

TWENTY-FIVE

Hilary Temple's feet were tired. She had criss-crossed Cambridge, been round and round the maze of streets. Cynthia Perdreau and her young man, or her older man, hadn't been seen together in any pub near the centre of the town. Nor had they made an appearance in Grantchester, so far as she could tell. No one remembered the couple. They might have been fighting, or morose; the girl might have been frightened or sad. No one remembered. The police had learned nothing in Newnham either. That wasn't surprising. The shops shut at half past five, and there weren't many people in the street after that. The children went in to have dinner. Why would anyone who chanced to be out remember—two weeks later—

a car with a man and a young woman in it, or a couple walking down the road? Why would anyone remember an ordinary girl walking alone down Grantchester Street? Suppose she and her boyfriend had been there before? Would it seem normal and safe to return? Suppose he had said he'd meet her—where? Suppose, suppose.

At the end of the day, DS Temple might have gone back to the station and put her feet under a desk, if not somewhere more comfortable. It had been her own idea to draw a line between Bridge Street and the wood, to think about where Perdreau might have gone on her way home from work if she was depressed, or if she had arranged to meet French and wanted a little fortification first. The line she drew passed right through the Granta pub.

She trudged back across the Fen. This was her first murder case, and she wanted to make an impression. Not to solve the case herself; she was not given to fantasy, and she knew that experience was what counted. She wanted to show that she was as steady on a murder case as on any other, that she was a hard worker who got results: the sort of officer—this was as far as fantasy took her—that Hardy would request the next time he had to gee up for a difficult case. Cutter had given her a chance, sending her along, and she would make the most of it. Murder was the sharp end of policing, and a chance to work a murder case didn't come along often. If she made a good impression on

DCI Gisborne, so much the better. While she didn't want the Met, a contact at the Yard was bound to be useful sooner or later.

At the Granta, she spoke to the bartender. She explained that when she had been in earlier, she hadn't inquired whether anyone remembered a young woman alone, possibly nervous or unhappy. She got out the photograph again.

"Probably about half five on the Wednesday, two weeks ago."

The bartender set down the glass he'd been polishing. He leaned on the counter and looked hard at the photograph. "Still doesn't ring a bell," he said. "Alone, you say? Not with a bloke?" The pub was beginning to fill up, and he moved away to draw a couple of pints. Another man, older and harassed-looking, appeared in the kitchen door.

"Archie," the bartender said. "Got a minute?"

Temple explained again.

"A bird?" Archie said. "Have you any idea how many birds come in here in a week?"

"Not that many come alone, surely?"

"What if they don't? Who's to notice?" He looked at her with irritated sympathy and then stopped short.

"Hang on, there was a girl in here, came in by herself, ordered a Bristol Cream. I do remember her, because she stayed at the bar. There was a table or two outside still empty, and in this weather people always take those tables first. She took a few dainty sips, like a cat, and then—bottoms up. She swallowed the lot. Didn't like it much— I'd say she wasn't a drinker. Then she went outside for a bit and just looked at the water. I didn't notice when she left." He tapped the photograph. "It could have been her."

"Did she say anything?"

"Just her order."

"Can you place which day it was?"

"That's asking, isn't it? Not this week, nor last. Last week was murder. Heh, er, sorry, just in a way of speaking. Trouble with the van and half the kitchen off, I wouldn't have remembered my own name last week if you'd asked me. It must have been the week before. That's the best I can do."

"You've been extremely helpful," DS Temple said, but she left the Granta with a sinking heart. A girl who might perhaps have been Cynthia, on a day that might have been Wednesday the 24th, but might have been some other day that week. Not good enough.

Edward and Hardy had been in ten places that afternoon. At the pharmaceutical company, they learned that Tod French had been fired four months earlier for verbal abuse of his superiors. In Histon, they'd discovered that his flat was one of several in a house owned by an absentee landlord who cared nothing about his tenants so long as they paid the rent. The neighbours had seized the chance to complain about the transient population and periodic drunken parties in one of the flats. They did not mix with the inhabitants. Apparently, French didn't fraternize with the other tenants in the building either. They knew him by sight but found him unsociable. He had lived there for six months. French himself was not to be found. However, the link between the murder victims was confirmed. A nurse at Addenbrooke's, shown a colour photograph of Wendy Fowler, was able to identify her as the person who had collected Cynthia Perdreau on April 19th.

"First nail," Edward said. He went to sleep that night thinking that the pieces were falling into place, but they still had no proof of French's presence at the scene of either crime, nor did they have enough evidence to arrest him or even get a search warrant for the flat. And where was French?

On Saturday morning at eleven, Gillian was drinking coffee and arguing gently with Murray about grocery bills and whether having two people in the house for a week wasn't more than he'd bargained for.

"You can hardly call it two people," Murray said. "Edward's never here."

The telephone rang.

"For you."

"Gillian!" Irene's voice said. "I'm at the PIS office. Can you get through to Edward? I think he should come over here straight away."

"I'll try. What's up?"

"Our book's been returned. And guess who stole it: Cynthia Perdreau's boyfriend!"

From Earl Street to Grafton Street was less than a five-minute walk, and Gillian walked fast. But the police station was even closer to the counselling centre. A car was there that was probably Edward's. She ran lightly up the stairs and entered the front room, where she found Edward already ensconced, together with Irene and a middle-aged woman with iron-grey curls and a large carrier bag. On the desk in front of Edward lay a large book, bound in black.

"Verity Cunningham," the woman said, apparently in response to a question from Edward. "I live in Histon."

Gillian slipped quietly into a chair next to Irene, whose hair had escaped from its pins and had bushed out in all directions like some rock star's from the sixties. She gave Gillian a sidelong glance of suppressed excitement but said nothing. Verity Cunningham looked her over and then turned her attention back to Edward.

He opened his notebook. "Could you just tell us how you came to be in possession of the diary?" He nodded at the black book.

"As I was saying," Verity replied, "I live in Histon. That's why I haven't been here before now."

New Zealand, Gillian thought, hearing the ironed-out A's.

"Saturday's my shopping day, you see. I come on the bus, unless my son's about and he'll bring me in the van. So it wasn't convenient to come before today. If I'd known it was important to the police—"

"That's all right," Edward said. "Go on."

Reassured, Verity Cunningham embarked on her tale with zest. "It was the Wednesday," she said. "The day the murder of that poor girl was in all the papers. I put the rubbish bin out in the lane on the Wednesday night, because the dustmen come very early in the morning. They like to wake folks up, banging the bins about, that's my belief. So I carried it out and left it. Then I watched the TV for a bit and went to bed. But I couldn't sleep. Not at all. So after a while I thought I'd make a cup of tea. It was a hot night and the window was open. It's upstairs, so I don't worry about robbers and such. I thought I heard a noise, out in the lane. The bedroom's in the back, see, and the back gate's in full view. So I tiptoed to the window and looked out. And there's that lad, Tod French, fossicking about in my rubbish bin."

"You knew him?" Edward said.

"I'll say I knew him. He lives in a poxy little flat just down the street. Thinks he's too good for his neighbours, but he can't keep a job. A handsome chap, I'll give him that, but not one to smile unless you paid him a pound."

"And what did you do then?"

"I thought: You're up to no good, my lad. So I

waited. I stood by the window in the dark and waited. He looked up, but he couldn't see me. I could see him well enough; there's a lamp in the street that lights up a bit of the lane. So he went off, and I waited a good long while, and then I crept out and looked up and down the lane. There was nobody about, so I took the lid off the bin to see what he'd been doing. I could see the rubbish had been messed about, so I poked it here and there. My heart wasn't half banging, I can tell you. I thought he might come out again. But he didn't, and I found that book there under my papers." She pointed to the diary. "Now I know that book wasn't in my rubbish bin at nine o'clock when I put it out. So he must have put it there."

Edward nodded. "Did you tell anyone?"

"Not that night. It was late. I didn't even want to put a light on, in case he was watching. I had a torch, though, so I made a cup of tea and had a peek at the book. I saw it belonged to this Pregnancy Information Service with a telephone number and address in Cambridge. Which I looked up and found was a place you could have a test. And I thought he must have stolen their book. But I couldn't think why, unless maybe he was going to blackmail someone. I read a bit in the book, but I couldn't make much out of it. I thought he might have known what he was looking for." She frowned. "He might be one of those that thinks there should be no family planning, and that's an opinion I could never agree with."

"Did you sleep at all, that night?" Edward asked.

"Precious little. I was up again at the crack of dawn, and I rang my son. He's always up early. And I told him Tod French had been where he'd no business to be, and had left this book there. My son thought I should throw it away; he didn't want me getting mixed up in anything. But I said that wasn't right, the book ought to be returned. And maybe the PIS would know why Mr Tod French wanted their book. So he drove me into town this morning, and here I am."

"And a very good thing too," Edward said. "This book could be a very important piece of evidence."

Verity Cunningham looked pleased but puzzled. "Why? What did he want with it?"

"Let's see what we can find out." Edward put down his pen and opened the diary, just touching the edges of the thick binding. Each double set of pages was ruled into more than a dozen columns, the first of which recorded the date. The second was headed "name." Then there were several columns headed by questions pertaining to menstrual cycles and contraception, followed by "wants to be pregnant?" and the result of the test. Finally, there was a broad column for comments and three narrow ones recording information about donations, how the customer had heard of the PIS, and who the day's tester(s) had been. Edward leafed quickly through the pages, stopping to read a comment now and again. The room was so silent Gillian could hear the faint voices from the kitchen below and was aware of each car passing in the street. She was sitting where she could see the pages sideways; Irene and Verity leaned over the desk.

Edward turned the pages until he came to April 6th. There were three entries that day. In the third, "C" was entered in the name column. Noting that the first day of "C's" last period coincided with what they knew of Perdreau, he went on to contraception. "Condom," he read. "Wants to be pregnant?" "No," it said baldly. Result: "+". He read the comments out loud: "Used condom but he didn't like it. So sometimes they didn't. V. worried. Only seventeen and determined not to tell her parents or own GP. Gave names of GPs in Camb. May ring back."

Edward looked up. "The testers' names are Irene and Wendy."

Irene examined the entry. "That's right. That's what Wendy wrote. It hasn't been changed."

The next set of entries was dated April 13th. Edward ran his finger down the name column and moved on. April 20th, April 27th. The rest of the right-hand page had been torn off.

"What's missing?" Edward asked.

Irene shook her head. "The next Saturday was the one when Bee found everything gone. There shouldn't have been anything else written there."

"Unless Wendy wrote something in the book when she borrowed the kit. Something seems to have worried the thief. He took precautions before he used your dustbin," Edward said to Verity.

"I said he was a nasty piece of work," Verity announced.

Gillian looked at Irene, who was white.

"Is there a loose sheet of paper anywhere?" she asked.

Edward turned first to the front and then to the back. "Unless it's tucked in the middle somewhere, it's not here. What is it?"

"The current list of members' names and addresses and telephone numbers. Mine's there, of course."

"What's wrong with her?" Verity asked Edward, bewildered.

"If you would be so kind as to come along to the station, I'll explain."

"Will it take long? I've my shopping to see to."

"Not too long. And we'll send you home in a car. The station's just round the corner." He picked up her empty carrier bag and slipped the book into it.

When they'd gone, Gillian said, "What do you think?"

"I think," said Irene, whose colour was returning, "that he must be a dangerously confused young man. I hope they get him soon." Little beads of sweat stood up on her forehead.

"What was he doing with the book? He stole it after he killed Cynthia. But he could have found out Wendy's name and left the book here."

"Maybe he came because he was worried about what we knew. He must have had a dreadful time waiting for someone to stumble on to the body. Maybe he wanted revenge. I suppose he thought there might be names in it—secrets—something he could get us with. But there aren't."

"And then he found Wendy's entry. So he got rid of her."

"He obviously panicked once Cynthia's body was found. He must have known the police might search his flat, so he dumped the book." Irene pushed her hair back from her sweaty face. "Right after he saw the evening papers, probably."

"But if he was worried about what Wendy knew, how did he know Cynthia hadn't told both of you?"

"He couldn't know that. If he knew what day she came here, then he saw my name as well as Wendy's on that page. That's why I'm scared."

At the station the reports trickled in. Tod French had not been seen in his street since Thursday, the day Hardy had interviewed him. But he had been seen at the chemical laboratories the night Wendy Fowler was killed. Bottomley's doubtful sighting had been confirmed by another chemist, Ivor Fleming.

"As a member of the safety committee," he said, "I try to keep half an eye on who's in the building out of hours. People are unconscionably careless about signing in and out. I've sent memos round, but it does no good. The regulations exist for a reason; maybe now people will see that," he added, a trifle peevishly.

He'd been crossing the corridor on the second floor, when he'd seen someone opening a door further along. He believed it was the door that gave access to one of the ladders used to reach the space between the second and third floors. It had been about six o'clock. The man had looked his way for a moment.

"I have a photographic memory for faces, you know. I recognized French immediately, although I hadn't seen him for five years."

"Did you wonder what he was doing in the labs?" Edward asked.

"I imagined he was doing some contract work for another chemist. He had on some sort of windcheater and was carrying a little bag. As it was the end of the day, I supposed he was on the point of leaving."

"Is that why you didn't mention him when you were interviewed before?"

Ivor Fleming looked offended. "Well, yes. Your man did ask me about Friday *night*. After seven, he said, and when I'd seen French it was just six. I didn't see what he could possibly have to do with Wendy Fowler."

Edward, remembering the crumpled can of Diet Coke he had seen, and thinking that the space between the floors would have made a perfectly safe hiding place until French chose to emerge, had a search made of the space at the top of the metal steps Scudder had shown him. Santini came back covered with dust and bringing the can and some threads that he had found caught on a nail and said might match the threads under Fowler's fingernail. There were several cigarette butts scattered about, he added. "Player's. No filter."

Reviewing the case with Hardy later, Edward snorted, "Chemists! Ask them a question and they answer exactly that question. No more, no less. Friday night, he says."

"The DC didn't phrase his question properly. I'll see who it was and have a word with him."

Early in the afternoon, DS Temple bounded up the stairs and rapped on the door-frame of Hardy's office, where he and Edward were waiting for a warrant to search Tod French's flat for further evidence pertaining to the burglary at the PIS office. She had found a woman in the playground in Lammas Land who had seen Cynthia Perdreau there at six o'clock on Wednesday evening. Perdreau had been alone, on foot, and walking in the direction of Newnham. The woman, a young, pretty mother in a loose cotton dress and sandals, remembered her because she'd stopped to watch the children and had asked how old they were. She'd said she hoped she would have children someday. She'd sounded so wistful the woman had wondered if something was wrong. Boyfriend trouble, she'd guessed.

She'd forgotten the encounter until Temple found her sitting on the same bench she had been occupying that Wednesday evening. She was able to identify the photograph as the girl she had seen.

Hadn't she heard about the murder? Temple had asked. Yes she had, but she'd never thought to connect the two. It was two weeks later when the body was found, wasn't it? Hadn't she seen a picture of Perdreau? She wouldn't have a television; it was bad for the children. And the papers? She read the *Guardian*. She hadn't noticed a picture there, just heard the local gossip.

"Did you notice anyone else about? A man, perhaps?" was Temple's last question.

There had been a man a short time earlier, the woman said. He had watched the children for a little while, but when he saw that she was keeping an eye on him, he went away. "You can't be too careful," she said sharply. She remembered that he was a tallish man, in his twenties, a good-looking dark-haired fellow, and he kept looking at his watch. He was smoking. He'd gone off towards the paddling pool, where there were more children, so she'd kept watching him for a few minutes, but after she'd talked to the girl she'd looked round and he was gone. She thought she would recognize him if she saw him again.

"It's got to be French," Hardy said. "It's got to."

"As soon as we've got him, we'll let her take a look at him."

"Some of the parents at the pool might remember him, too."

DC Paris came back from Grantchester looking discouraged.

"I talked to the neighbours," he said. "It's Hill's dog. It's got out once or twice and ravaged their flowerbeds. And it barks when he's out. They've had words."

"But it didn't bark Friday night after ten o'clock?"

"On Friday they were listening to Scarlatti. They play Wagner when the dog barks."

Irene stepped out of the shower.

"Is that you, Patrick?" she called through the bathroom door. Surely John wasn't back early; she was meeting his train in a few hours. There was no answer. But she was sure she had heard someone.

"Patrick?"

She dried herself, listening. There was nothing to hear. She must have imagined the sound. She put on her dressing gown and tied the belt, humming quietly. She'd missed John. It was nice to miss him, she thought. Sometimes one needed that sort of reminder. Her hair was still wrapped in a towel. She would go sit in the garden and comb it out. Rubbing the mist from the mirror, she peered briefly at her blurred image. With any luck, she'd look pretty much the same for another ten years.

She stood still. If she had another ten years. If she

had indeed imagined that noise. What if someone were outside the door, waiting? It seemed an outlandish idea, but nevertheless she looked for something with which to defend herself. She could try throwing a towel over his head . . . the hair-dryer was too small and light . . . She looked in the cupboard under the sink. Rolls of loo paper, soap, a large plastic bottle of shampoo. Too soft. There was a spray can at the back. She pulled it out. It was that left-over tile cleaner she'd vowed not to use any more because it was bad for the environment but that she hadn't got rid of because it was still nearly full. Throwing it in the dustbin was no better than using it, and she hadn't found out where to recycle it. Probably some special toxic waste dump forty miles away. She'd use so much petrol driving there that she might do better to bury the thing in the back garden. She picked up the can and shook it vigorously. Then, feeling extremely foolish, she placed her index finger on the button, and holding the can ready, opened the door.

The door opened inward. As soon as she opened it and stepped towards the hall, she saw him. He was waiting just beyond the door, but he had expected her to walk into the bedroom, not towards the stairs, so she was facing him. A young man, she thought, not thirty. She was aware of an overpowering smell of ether. He lunged, pinning her against the wall and jamming a thick wad of cloth over her mouth and nose. Desperately, she tilted the can upwards, pressed hard on the button and sprayed him straight in the face.

Hardy had the warrant in his pocket. He and Edward were on their way to the car park.

"Well done, DS Temple," murmured Hardy. "Cutter knew what he was doing when he sent her along."

"She requested it," Edward replied. "Cutter told me. He said it went against the grain, but since she had the brass to ask, he couldn't very well turn her down."

"She bypassed her inspector?"

"No. Her inspector thought the decision was a little on the sensitive side, so he passed it to Cutter."

"Did he? Well, times certainly are changing. Even in the CID."

"Could you work under a woman, do you think?"

"I often think I can't work under anybody."

"A woman CC?"

"I haven't tried it, have I?" Hardy growled, rubbing his nose. "I could, I suppose. But I'd rather not." He held the door for Edward. "What about you?"

"It might be worth it, to watch the commissioners cope."

The call came as they were reversing out of Hardy's parking space. Instead of going straight to Histon, they drove to Irene's house. She was sitting on the sofa shivering and drinking a cup of tea which Patrick had made. He sat on the arm of the sofa, hulking protectively over her. The spray can was lying on the floor near the door.

"I felt like such an idiot, carrying it," she said. "But it was a good thing after all. He actually yelled when I sprayed him, but I think it was the surprise as much as the pain." She giggled a little hysterically. "He didn't expect me to be armed."

She sipped her tea. "He had a scarf or something absolutely reeking of ether. If it had stayed on my face very long I'd have been out like a light. But he was so startled he loosed his hold. I twisted away and ran down the stairs. He came after me, but I got the front door open before he caught up. I was half way through it when he just ran right over me. He hurled himself through the door and down the steps and out of the gate. I had the wind knocked out of me. Then Patrick came home."

"I thought she'd fallen down the steps," Patrick said to Edward. "Then she said to ring you."

"Did you know him?" Edward asked Irene.

"No. He was an utter stranger."

Edward showed her a photograph, a copy of one from Cynthia Perdreau's snapshots.

Irene nodded. "That's him."

It was a mean little flat. The front garden was full of litter and weeds. The sagging curtain at the window was pulled closed, as it had been the last time they'd been there. Silence answered Hardy's knock. He knocked again. Nothing. He put his meaty shoulder to the door and pushed. The dry wood of the doorframe splintered as the screws of the lock rasped loose. Hardy shoved the door back and they went in. A filthy little kitchen to the right. A dark and smelly loo. A few feet of dim hallway. They stepped into the room where the sagging curtain obscured the window.

The room was untidy and smelled of old cigarettes. The bed was unmade; the clothes cupboard door hung open. Some shirts and trousers hung limply above a heap of laundry below. An empty pint of gin stood next to a sticky glass on the scarred table near the window. Beside them was an empty pack of Player's and a metal ashtray heaped with butts.

Hardy sniffed. "Wholesome atmosphere."

Edward noted the cigarettes and the two empty cans of Diet Coke on the floor by the bed. Then he moved to the cupboard and began to go through the pockets of the clothes.

Hardy was in the kitchen. "A deficient sense of smell should be a qualification for this job," he said. Edward could hear him opening doors and moving things. Then he reappeared. "I take it back," he said. He was carrying a glass bottle. It resembled many of those Edward had seen in the labs.

"What have you got?"

"Ether. Have a whiff."

The bottle was nearly empty. Edward sniffed briefly

at it. There was the unmistakable sweet sickly smell. A smell he associated with death. "He used it on Irene," he said, thinking aloud. "So it could explain what happened to Wendy Fowler. The stuff's everywhere in those labs."

"Funny thing to keep in your kitchen," said Hardy. "I wonder if he liked the stuff himself. It might explain some of his weird behaviour."

"It wouldn't leave a trace. Maybe he used it on Perdreau, too, before he cracked her skull." Edward went back to the cupboard. Gingerly, he lifted the clothing heaped at the bottom, piece by piece, checking the pockets. He found nothing of interest there. French had been described as well dressed. Indeed the clothes were trendy, and more expensive than French would have been able to afford once he had lost his job, yet he had stopped taking care of them. Evidence of his recent state of mind. Under the clothes were two pairs of shoes and a pair of cheap brown leather boots, scuffed and cracked. He picked up the shoes, one at a time. The right leather boot was stained with oil: several smears on the toe, and a patch on the sole. A unique compound, Edward thought. Let the lawyers try to get round that one.

When they had finished in the flat, they went out into the yard again. At the back, bordering the lane, was a wooden shed. It was unpainted, and some of the boards were rotting. The door hung crookedly on its hinges, a rusted lock dangling uselessly from the hasp. The grass grew tall among the dandelions and thistles. The door of the shed was shut, but it had recently been opened; the grass in front of it was bent and broken. Without needing to consult, they walked quietly through the rubbish-strewn weeds. Edward gave Hardy a brief glance and pulled on the door. It dragged over the threshold and then dropped heavily towards the ground. Edward could see the rusted teeth of a garden rake pointing up at him, just inside the door. Slivers of light struck inward through cracks between the boards. A mouldy smell stirred in the breeze from the open door. He stepped cautiously forward and looked in. Hardy peered over his shoulder.

"Oh shit," said Edward.

The eyes of Tod French stared sightlessly down at them.

TWENTY-SIX

"Where did you find him?" Gillian asked.

"In the garden shed behind the flat," Edward said. "He'd hanged himself from the cross-beam with a piece of plastic clothesline."

"When?"

"Not very long before we got there."

"How do you know it was suicide?" Murray handed Edward a glass of neat whisky.

"Hangings are almost never murder. And in this case there was a note."

"What did it say?" Gillian said, forgetting her drink.

"Not much. It was a kind of peculiar diagram more than a note. It said 'An Eye for an Eye' across the top.

Underneath was the word 'baby' and a lot of initials: 'CP' for Cynthia Perdreau, 'WF' for Wendy Fowler, and 'TF' for Tod French, all with heavy black underlining and red circles around them, and red arrows connecting them."

"What a warped mind," Murray cried. "Didn't anyone know he was crazy?"

"An eye for an eye? If that was his thinking, he wasn't much of a mathematician," Gillian said bitterly. "He killed two people and tried to kill a third. And that's not even counting Wendy's baby. He would have had to kill himself two or three times to even the score."

"The other interesting point is what the diagram was written on. He kept the page he tore out of the PIS diary and wrote on the back of it. It was folded up in his pocket."

"Then what was on the missing page?"

"Wendy's entry, written on Monday April 29th. I made a copy to show you." He laid it on the table and read it out.

"'C, April 6th, rang me after seeing Elizabeth Peters. Asked me to pick her up at Addenbrooke's. Reluctant to go home in case parents found out. Spent night at KP with me Friday 19th. Seemed OK Sat—went home. Cautioned her about ex-boyfriend, but she said there's nothing he can do about it now. I said she should ring one of us straight away if he gave her any trouble.'" Edward handed the note to Gillian, who read it over again.

"Trouble! God."

"So he found this when he stole the book," Murray said, reading over her shoulder.

"On Tuesday at the earliest," Edward said. "Maybe Wednesday. And Wendy was dead on Friday night. That must have been his first opportunity to catch her when the labs were empty enough. That left Irene. When he failed there, he knew the game was up." He swallowed the last of his whisky and then rubbed his temples. "You know, I think I have to go to bed. I don't know when I've been so tired."

Later, Gillian telephoned Irene. "It's over," she said. "You don't have to be afraid any more. He's dead." She told the story and described the note. "What do you make of it? Was he insane?"

"I don't know. I'm not an expert in criminal psychology," Irene answered. "But is that the most useful question to ask? 'Insane' is a label we want to use in these cases because it sets the person apart from the rest of us. It tells us our culture isn't a problem; he's just an aberration. Well, we both know our culture is a problem, don't we?" She stopped. "Hang on a minute, will you? Being a near-corpse seems to have upped my craving for nicotine. John's home, by the way. Thank God. I wouldn't want to sleep alone tonight."

Gillian heard a lighter click and then a long exhaling breath.

"I can only guess why the abortion set him off,"

Irene went on. "He was full of resentment and he lacked self-control—look at his dismal employment record. He didn't have much going for him, did he? He was probably one of those people who think there's a conspiracy to keep him at the bottom of the pile. Such people feel they have no control over their lives. In some ways they're right, I mean their options are in a real sense pretty drab and curtailed, but their solutions can be worse than the problems. Here we have a chap who's been fired from two jobs in a row. He doesn't seem to have friends or close family ties. Then Cynthia drops him. What's his reaction? He calls her a whore and pretends he doesn't give a damn. But he's probably feeling humiliated. *He's* the one who should be telling her to kiss off. He's the man, and he's ten years older. Then he finds out—because she tells him—that she's pregnant but doesn't plan to have the child. He doesn't like girls doing what they please, does he? I expect the whole drama, in *his* mind, was about who was boss. I don't know whether you've seen any of the extreme anti-choice literature. It's pretty nauseating. The agenda is not really about saving babies. What those people are interested in is controlling women. I would guess that his mind worked in the same way. He killed to gain control. Not to be the pathetic little sod who's fired, who has a grotty little flat and is ditched by his lover, but to be 'a man.' In charge. He ordered her not to have the abortion. But he didn't trust her—he was angry and suspicious. He had fantasies about killing her and even made preparations. It's quite possible that he didn't know whether he would actually do it. But when he found out she'd had the abortion, when she told him to his face . . ."

"He bashed her head in."

"Yes. And what are the odds that his father battered his mother?"

"It's all too likely. And Wendy—I guess she was an afterthought. He checked out the PIS and went after the women who helped Cynthia and who might have been able to link him to the murder. If only she hadn't told him she was pregnant."

"It was a natural thing to do. And she wanted help." Irene sounded faintly indignant.

Gillian shut her eyes. She didn't want to talk any more. "I know. I'm not blaming her, just wishing. She'd still be alive—and so would Wendy."

Bee said, "An eye for an eye? What about all the other people who suffer? What about Wendy's parents? What about her poor old grandfather who doted on her? And Cynthia's parents? And all their friends? For that matter, what about his own family?"

"Edward says he hadn't seen them for eight years."

Pamela said, "Good riddance."

The chemistry department said, "How awful. But thank God it had nothing really to do with the department."

On Sunday, Edward wrote up his report on the case. On Monday morning, he said he had a few final knots to tie and disappeared in the direction of the station. Rather to Gillian's surprise, he was back before noon. They went for a walk on Midsummer Common. The sun shone benignly in a sky washed clean by the previous night's rain. Two girls were flying long-tailed kites. Red and white, quartered like heraldic shields, the kites bounced and dipped in the cool breeze, rising gradually higher and higher above the meadow.

"I have to tell you," Gillian said, "that this afternoon has had an influence on my thoughts about leaving my job. I felt wasted by that year at UPNW, and so disgusted with the place I wasn't sure I could bear to be there any longer. But what good would it do to go somewhere else? The problems are the same everywhere. Did I ever tell you about the man who moved to the Falkland Islands?"

"What man?"

"He was a man who lived in Vancouver. The story was in the newspapers. This man was extremely anxious about the possibility of war, particularly nuclear war. So he read up on all the remote places he could think of, and calculated where he would be safest in the event that war broke out. Then he gave up his job and sold his house, and moved himself and his family bag and baggage to the Falklands—the remotest, safest spot on the planet. Six months later, the Falklands war started."

Edward laughed. "Poor bastard."

"Yes. Everybody in Vancouver thought it was horribly funny. You get my point, though."

"Leaving UPNW would be as much use as moving to the Falklands."

"Yes."

"I know that. You know that. But I'm over here. I thought that was the point."

"It is, but I can't up sticks without a job to come to. I just can't. No more than you can leave London. I can promise to hunt for one, though. I haven't looked really seriously yet."

They walked along the river. Two swans floated on the water's ruffled surface. Their black eyes briefly examined Gillian and Edward, then as one they curved their long necks and swam away. Further along the bank, a child was tossing breadcrumbs into the stream.

"What next?" Gillian asked Edward after a while.

He reached inside his coat and pulled an envelope from the breast pocket. "Open it."

Inside were two airline tickets.

"I have the week off, I tied it up this morning," he said. "Didn't you say something about wanting to go to Rome?"

ABOUT THE AUTHOR

Nora Kelly is the author of two previous Gillian Adams mysteries, *In the Shadow of King's* and *My Sister's Keeper*, that garnered her justly deserved comparisons with P.D. James and Dorothy L. Sayers. A historian who grew up in New York City and New Jersey, Kelly studied at Cambridge and now lives in Vancouver, British Columbia. She spends her summers beside a lake in Ontario where she has no telephone, no electricity, and writes with a pencil.